Sherlock Holmes

The Mystery of the Pamplona Bull

SHERLOCK HOLMES
The Mystery of the
PAMPLONA BULL

Mayhew Prewitt

PAX VOBIS
PRESS

Copyright © 2026 by Mayhew Prewitt

All rights reserved.

No part of this book may be reproduced, stored in a retrieval system, or transmitted in any form or by any means—electronic, mechanical, photocopying, recording, or otherwise—without the prior written permission of the publisher, except for brief quotations in reviews.

This is a work of fiction. Names, characters, businesses, places, events, and incidents are either the products of the author's imagination or are used fictitiously. Any resemblance to actual persons, living or dead, or actual events is coincidental.

Certain historical persons and events appear in this work of fiction. While the author has drawn upon historical sources, their actions, dialogue, and circumstances are imagined or interpreted for dramatic purposes.

This work is not affiliated with the Conan Doyle Estate. Sherlock Holmes is a character in the public domain.

Published by

PAX VOBIS PRESS

ISBN: 979-8-9955441-0-4

Printed in the United States of America
First Edition

For

Saint Francis of Assisi

My grace is sufficient for thee: for my strength is made perfect in weakness.

— 2 Corinthians 12:9

CHAPTER I

The Letter from Paris

A Return to Sussex

It was in the early summer of 1924 that I once again took the road to Sussex Downs to visit my old friend, Mr Sherlock Holmes.

The years had not been idle ones. Europe had torn itself to pieces and stitched itself together again with rough, uneven threads. Young men had gone out laughing and returned silent, if they returned at all. England, too, had altered: motorcars rattled along country lanes that had once known nothing faster than horse-drawn carriages, and aeroplanes traced thin white scars across the sky.

Yet as my hired car turned from the high road into the familiar rutted track that led towards Holmes's little farm, I felt a curious sensation that here, at least, time had consented to move more slowly.

The cottage stood on its low rise above the fields, its stones warmed by the sun and half-veiled by the surrounding rose beds in full bloom. Beyond it, like a living cloud, the bees rose and fell in a steady hum, their traffic as orderly as any great city's, and far more harmonious. I confess that the sound had become to me, over the years, as much a part of Holmes as his violin or his old dressing-gown.

I dismissed the driver at the gate and walked the rest of the way, my medical bag in one hand and my umbrella in the other. There is a particular pleasure in approaching a friend's dwelling on foot: it affords a brief ceremony of anticipation. As I drew nearer, I saw Holmes seated on a rough wooden bench beneath an apple tree whose petals lay scattered, with small green fruit forming among the leaves.

He was thinner than the last time I had seen him, and the silver in his hair had advanced its campaign with renewed vigour, but the aquiline profile was as keen-cut as ever, and there was still that peculiar stillness about him.

He did not rise as I approached; he merely lifted his gaze from the paper in his hand and allowed the faintest glimmer of a smile to disturb his features.

"Watson," said he. "You are ten minutes earlier than I had calculated. The driver must have been reckless, or the London traffic unusually charitable."

"I am delighted to see you too, Holmes," I answered, "and I will not deny that the fellow drove as if motor- mad, heading towards the Brooklands race circuit. You are looking well."

"Appearances, as you know, are notoriously deceptive," he replied. "Sit down. There is a matter here which will interest you far more than my pulse rate."

I took my place beside him on the bench. From this vantage I could see the low hives arranged in their disciplined rows, the gentle drift of bees, and, beyond them, the wide Sussex fields softening into the bluish haze of the Downs. For a moment I allowed myself the luxury of imagining that we might spend the afternoon talking of nothing more pressing than honey yields and the eccentricities of country neighbours.

The Mysterious Letter

Then my eye fell upon the sheet of paper in Holmes's long, nervous fingers.

"A consultation?" I asked. "Surely the world has exhausted its supply of baffling phenomena by now."

Holmes made a slight sound which might have been a chuckle.

"The world, my dear Watson, has shown itself inexhaustible in its capacity for bafflement," said he. "But you will be relieved to hear that the letter in question contains no reference to a corpse in a locked room, nor to footprints on a ceiling, nor to any other of the more theatrical anomalies which have so enlivened your pen. No, this is a different species of request altogether."

He handed me the paper. It bore the letterhead of a hotel in Paris, and the date—June 1924. The handwriting was bold, forceful, and yet curiously unadorned.

I began to read.

George V

Paris

5 June 1924

Mr Sherlock Holmes,

I do not know if you still take cases, or if a man like you ever truly retires.

I was given your name by a friend whose opinion I trust. He told me that if something could be found, truly found, you were the man who would know where to look.

I saw a bull in Spain that I can't forget.

I saw the same bull again, later, as a sculpture in Paris.

I am writing a book titled *The Bull in the Field*. It began as a description. It has become a question. I asked where I could and looked where it seemed reasonable to look. I have found no answers, only further questions. I have found myself in the middle of something I do not yet understand. But I believe you might.

I am not a criminal. There is no murder, no blackmail, no stolen jewels that I know of, tho there is something missing. In fact, two things. One, is a bronze bull. The other is my book.

There may be a third thing missing as well. Perhaps it belongs to the rest of us—the ones they call the lost.

If you have any room in your life now for a different kind of mystery, I would like to talk to you. I am staying in Paris for a time. There is a bar here where the Americans and others drink and talk. You would not like the gin, but you might like the questions.

My name is Albert Remington.

The name struck a faint chord in my memory. I had seen it, I believed, in the literary columns of some paper or other, attached to a short story or a cable from Europe. At the time it had seemed one more among the swarm of new writers whose names appeared and vanished with bewildering rapidity.

"Well, Holmes?" I asked, looking up. "What do you make of it?"

He had produced his pipe while I read and was in the act of filling it with his familiar black, coarse-cut, strong tobacco, his gaze turned not towards me but towards the distant fields.

"There are several points of interest," said he, after a pause. "The first, naturally, being that the writer believes himself to be engaged in a mystery which does not involve the usual apparatus of crime. That is a novelty. The second is that he is almost certainly wrong."

"Wrong?"

"Not in believing there is no murder, perhaps," Holmes conceded, "though one never knows where men and valuable objects are concerned. But wrong in supposing that a stolen bronze, a book, and a missing—what shall we call it?—purpose, identity—wrong in supposing that these things have no connection with the ordinary criminal motives of greed, fear, and desire. Men are distressingly consistent, Watson. Even when they imagine themselves noble, they behave according to the same base impulses. The difference here is that the writer is aware—dimly, but aware—that something larger is at stake."

"You know the name?"

Holmes exhaled a thin stream of smoke.

"Albert Miller Remington. American. Twenty-five or thereabouts. Served as an ambulance driver in the late war—Italy, if my memory serves. Wounded, decorated, returned home restless. Now in Paris among the so-called Lost Generation. According to *The Times Literary Supplement*, he is one of a growing army of young men who have seen too much of death to be content with tea and parlour games."

"You astonish me, Holmes. I had no idea you kept up with modern literature."

"That is because you persist in imagining me as a relic of the gas-lamp era," he said dryly. "I assure you, Watson, that the world has not ceased to be interesting simply because it now insists upon roaring past in internal-combustion engines. As for literature, I read it in self-defence. When the newspapers declare some young man to be the voice of his generation, one does well to investigate whether that generation is worth hearing."

"And do you find that it is?"

Holmes gave a slight shrug.

"I find," said he, "that the war has made many men old before their time. They are searching for a language that is as bare and unforgiving as what they have seen. This Remington appears to be one of them. His letter is notable for its absence of ornament. No appeals to sentiment, no excessive courtesy. He offers me a problem, not flattery."

"And yet," I ventured, "there is a certain humility in that last line. 'I believe you might.'"

Holmes's lips curved.

"Just so. He believes I understand something he does not. That, Watson, is the first condition of an honest inquiry."

A New Kind of Mystery

"But is it truly a case?" I asked. "A man troubled by a bull in Spain and a statue in Paris, surely that is more the business of a clergyman or a philosopher than of a consulting detective."

Holmes's eyes left the horizon and fixed themselves upon me with that old, penetrating brilliance which had once reduced Scotland Yard inspectors to a state of defensive irritation.

"You disappoint me, Watson," said he.

"Have I taught you nothing? The man speaks of three missing things: a bronze sculpture, his manuscript, and an intangible—call it meaning, if you like. He senses a connection between them but cannot name it. He writes from a city that has become a kind of clearing-house for the disillusioned. He offers me, in short, a problem of perception.

"You ask if this is a case? I tell you it is the only kind of case I have any interest in at my age. If there is anything left in the world that can surprise me, it will not be a footprint in the flowerbed, but the shape of a man's soul when it is trying to understand itself."

I was silent for a moment, struck by the seriousness of his tone. There had been, in Holmes's most intense periods, times when he seemed scarcely human in his abstraction from ordinary feeling.

Yet now, in his seventies, there was something gentler, almost wistful, beneath his precision.

Paris Beckons

"You mean to go, then?" I said at last.

"To Paris? Naturally."

He tapped the ash from his pipe and rose with that quick, birdlike motion I knew so well.

"Bees are excellent companions, Watson, but they are monotonous correspondents. They seldom write from Paris, and never about Spanish bulls. When a wounded young man, possessed of some talent and possibly of some importance, sends me a problem which he cannot place before any other living mind, I confess I feel a certain—what is the fashionable word?—responsibility."

"And you would like me to accompany you," I said, my heart already quickening with the old, familiar anticipation.

Holmes glanced sideways at me, and there was in his eyes that affectionate irony I had come to cherish.

"My dear fellow," said he, "I should be quite lost without you. Besides, someone will have to explain to me what on earth these people mean when they speak of jazz."

I laughed, the sound surprising me with its own youthfulness."Very well," I answered. "Paris, then. To consult on a bull and a book."

"And perhaps," Holmes reflected, turning his gaze once more towards the far-off line of the hills, "to determine what it is that a bronze animal in a foreign city can show a young man about himself, and an old man about the world."

The bees moved and shimmered in the golden air. Somewhere in the cottage, a clock chimed the hour.

The war, with its uniforms and its casualties and its muddy fields, felt, for an instant, very far away.

Yet I sensed, as I had so many times before, that we stood once more at the threshold of something whose consequences we could not yet foresee.

I did not know then that the bull Remington could not forget, the sculpture he had seen in Paris, and the unwritten book would draw Sherlock Holmes, Albert Remington, and myself into a mystery unlike any we had ever known—a mystery not of crime, but of courage; not of guilt, but of meaning.

But I did know this: when Sherlock Holmes rose from his bench and went into the house to send a telegram to Paris, the game, in whatever new form it had chosen to assume, was once again afoot.

CHAPTER II

The Writer at Harry's Bar

Arrival in the Jazz Age

Paris, June 1924.

A city syncopated by jazz, the chatter of typewriter keys, and foreign ideas fermented by domestic wine. Paris was a city shaking off the long fever of war only to find her new voice from a lost generation.

Holmes and I arrived beneath a drizzle, the colour of tarnished silver.

The cab rattled over the rough stones of the Rue Daunou before depositing us before an unassuming façade with a brass plaque:

HARRY'S NEW YORK BAR

SANK ROO DOE NOO

Holmes paused to survey the swinging half-doors: two varnished wooden panels of horizontal slats, opening in the middle like the entrance to a western frontier saloon.

"Curious," he observed."An American portal guarding a Parisian sanctuary."

Inside, the room was all dark, warm wood and soft amber light. The air held cigarette smoke, gin, rye whisky, and the worn comfort of expatriate longing.

The mahogany bar stretched long and high, its edge softly rounded and finely carved. Behind it gleamed bottles displayed like stained glass: Plymouth gin, Old Overholt rye, French cognac, bourbon, vermouth.

American college pennants hung along the walls, circling the room: Harvard crimson, Princeton orange, Yale blue—faded trophies of homesickness and ambition.

Beyond, the room opened into wooden tables and mismatched chairs. A padded bench upholstered in deep red and forest green stripes ran along the back wall, as if embracing patrons who did not know where else to sit.

The pianist at the far corner coaxed *St. Louis Blues* from an upright, his fingers rolling over the keys like someone telling his story one note at a time.

A trio of Americans near the bar argued loudly about baseball, gesticulating wildly as if every gesture might summon the spirit of Babe Ruth himself.

Holmes smiled faintly. "A more reliable national religion than any other," he mused.

"Holmes!" I whispered sharply. "Look, there he is."

At the bar sat a broad-shouldered young man, sleeves rolled to the elbow, forearms sun-browned and scarred in the way of men who have handled both oars and rifles.

He leaned over a notebook, pencil tapping in restless staccato. A half-finished rye whisky sat beside him, the ice melting slowly into the amber.

Holmes observed him for a long moment.

"He has already rewritten that page seven times."

"How can you possibly know that?" I asked.

I knew Holmes lived for moments like these.

"Note the indentation on the bar beneath his notebook—repeated erasures. See the stub of the pencil, newly sharpened, excessively used. And that stack of folded pages in his coat pocket, each creased twice along the same axis."

Holmes lowered his voice.

"A man reworking a phrase too large for him yet. A man writing towards his soul."

An American Dreamer

At the far booth, I noticed another figure, slight, elegant, restless, his fair hair falling in soft disarray, a pencil tucked behind his ear like the first budding antler of a stag.

James Fitzpatrick.

A glass of gin rickey sweating before him, his eyes drifting between the smoke-hazed room and the open volume of Petronius's *Satyricon* at his elbow.

He murmured something to himself, a line not quite right, a melody of a sentence he could not catch.

He did not look up.

Not yet.

Holmes, however, took note.

"Trimalchio," he said under his breath. "A character who reminds me of certain West London financiers. Excess without substance."

But before I could inquire further, Harry the bartender approached Remington to whisper something in his ear.

Remington Rises

Remington turned. Suddenly, intently, he locked eyes with Holmes.

He stood.

Straightened his shoulders.

Crossed the room with a soldier's gait.

"Mr Sherlock Holmes?"

His voice was low, steady, braced with the echo of battlefields.

Holmes inclined his head.

"Mr Remington."

For an instant, something passed between them, a recognition of souls carved by experience.

"May I buy you gentlemen a drink?"

"Only," Holmes said, "if it is not that deplorable beverage you were consuming earlier."

Remington barked a laugh.

"The gin rickey grows on you."

"So does fungus," Holmes replied. "Scotch, neat."

I ordered a whisky and soda, a drink with backbone, and we settled at a table beneath the pennants.

Fitzpatrick looked up once.

Briefly.

His doe-like eyes, wide with alertness, catching ours with the soft glimmer of someone who feels too much, too quickly, too deeply.

Then he returned to his Roman ghosts.

Conversation about Truth

As our drinks arrived, three other Americans drifted nearer—drawn, it seemed, by Remington's presence as much as by curiosity about Holmes.

The first man to approach our table possessed the sharp, hawk-keen features of a born critic, and eyes that seemed forever measuring, cutting, and rearranging the world into metre. A long, pointed moustache framed a mouth made for pronouncements, not hesitations.

Above it all rose his hair, a dark auburn tempest, swept upward as though caught in a permanent squall, and one doubted any comb had successfully navigated it in years. His hands moved as he spoke, quick and precise, as if tapping out stresses in some invisible line of verse.

"Eli Pond," Remington added.

"Editor. Storm in human form."

Pond gave us the briefest of nods, as if to acknowledge that we, too, were now part of his temporary republic of letters.

The second gentleman was of a markedly different cast. His dark hair was cropped close, disciplined and a neat moustache lent his face a faintly professorial air. Compact in build, with the sturdy self-assurance of a man accustomed to editorial battles rather than physical ones, he wore his tweed coat as though it were both armour and uniform.

He stood with one hand thrust into his jacket as if searching for a misplaced phrase, the other clasping a well-loved pipe, held not as an ornament but as an extension of thought itself.

"Malcolm Bennett," Remington said by way of introduction. "Poet. Critic. Chronicler of the tribe."

Beside him sat another American. His face was long and clean-shaven. His gaze was level, keen. A cigar rested between his fingers with the absent-minded familiarity of a man who often forgets he is holding one. He gave the impression of a man forever poised between detachment and indignation: a careful chronicler of humanity, studying us all through the wavering veil of cigar smoke.

Remington tipped his glass towards him.

"And this," he said, "is Dos Pasillos.

"Juan. Writer. Painter.

"The man who sees the gears turning even when the machine looks quiet."

Dos Pasillos inclined his head, polite, but with that quick, darting intelligence that seemed always to be mapping the room, recording its angles for later use.

The pianist slid into a softer chorus of blues. The chatter of baseball talk near the bar dimmed behind us.

Dos Pasillos leaning back, cigar already half-ash, exhaled a thin ribbon of smokeand continued the argument he had been advancing with Pond and Bennett.

"The thing about Paris, you see it when you've been around long enough, is that it runs on two fuels, hunger and illusion. You get the Americans coming in thinking the place is a cathedral for artists, but really it's a factory, grinding them down, fitting them into its gears. Everyone's got some myth they're chasing, something they're trying to plaster over the cracks. And the trick—well, the trick—is to know the machine is running even when you think the lights are soft and the wine is cheap."

He flicked ash gently, like punctuation.

Fitzpatrick, having at last drifted from his booth, hovered near our table, lifting his glass, a half-mischievous smile glimmering at the edges of his mouth. "Paris," he said flippantly, "is the only city where you can go bankrupt in money, hope, and self-respect, and still call it a splendid night out."

A ripple of laughter passed through the group: Pond's sharp, Bennett's warm, Remington's low and muttered.

A soft, appreciative hum came from Pond, a sound between a scoff and a purr.

He lifted his glass as though in salute. "My dear Juan," Pond said, "Paris is not a machine, it's a crucible. The weak melt. The strong distil. The rest evaporate altogether."

He twirled his hand in a flourish of rings and cigarette smoke. "If one is ground down, it is because one arrived as grain instead of gold."

Fitzpatrick chuckled softly, a quick, fleeting laugh that carried something unguarded beneath. "Gold?" he said. "My dear Eli, half of us arrived as tinsel. Paris is merely kind enough to let us glitter awhile before the tarnish sets in."

The remark earned a round of genuine amusement, even from Holmes, whose eyes glinted.

Bennett gave a small, amused sigh. "Trust Pond to turn a factory into an alchemical vessel," he said, voice warm with wry affection. "But Juan isn't wrong. Paris does sort people. You come here thinking you're building cathedrals, and discover you're really dismantling them stone by stone, trying to figure out what the foundation ever was."

Bennett sipped his drink and continued, "Hunger and illusion," he mused. "Yes. And also, recognition. Every writer who lasts here finds clarity, sometimes, usually bought at a price."

Fitzpatrick nodded, looking into his glass. "Clarity," he smiled mischievously. "In Paris it comes like a bill slipped under your door. And the total is always higher than you thought you'd spent."

Pond barked a short laugh. "Ha! Leave it to James to turn debt into philosophy."

Dos Pasillos flicked ash and nodded once. "He's right, though. Paris always collects."

Dos Pasillos said, "You know what Paris does? It strips the paint off a man. Leaves the grain showing. Fine if you've got good wood underneath. Hell on you if you don't."

Remington grunted. "I came here to write, Juan, not to be carpentered."

Holmes, who had been watching them with that serene acuity that made even the sharpest men shift in their chairs, spoke in a low, measured tone. "And yet each of you speaks of truth," he said, "as though it were an adversary rather than a companion."

Dos Pasillos turned to him, studying Holmes with sudden interest.

"Truth's not a companion, Mr Holmes," he said. "Truth is a blade. You use it, or it uses you."

Dos Pasillos drew again on his cigar, smoking like a man timing the burn.

Holmes watched them all, eyes half-closed, taking the measure of three futures wound tight as fuses.

Bennett took a pull from his glass. "Truth is the only thing worth chasing," he said. "Everything else is journalism."

Pond snorted. "Truth is form. Get the form right and the truth follows. Get the form wrong and you're just chattering."

Fitzpatrick leapt into the fray with that half-wild energy that clung to him whenever drink and talk ran too close to matters of art or failure. He set a hand on the back of an empty chair.

"Truth?" he said. "In my experience, one must write honestly, or the readers say 'so what.'"

Remington lifted his pencil and pointed it towards Fitzpatrick in agreement.

Next, he gaze turned to Holmes as if the floor had shifted beneath him.

"The bull in Spain," he said slowly. "That wasn't just a story."

Holmes shook his head. "It was no invention," he said. "It was the unvarnished thing. It was truth."

Remington looked down at his hands. He offered. "I thought I'd been running from it, all this time."

Holmes's expression softened—rare, almost paternal. "No, Mr Remington," he said. "You have not been running from it. You have been climbing towards it."

The words seemed to settle over the table like a benediction.

Pond was the first to speak.

"Well," he said gruffly, "if any of you intend to write all this truth, do it quickly. The age is not in the mood for half-measures."

Bennett chuckled, Fitzpatrick returned to his Romans, and the conversation dissolved into other matters, poems, publishers, rumours of books not yet written.

But Remington remained very quiet.

After a time, he turned back to Holmes, and this time there was no mistaking the purpose in his eyes.

"Mr Holmes," he said, "may I speak with you alone?"

Holmes inclined his head. "Certainly."

He glanced at me. "Watson stays. He is my second memory."

The others drifted back to their corners of the room.

The piano resumed its easy blues. The baseball argument rose again like a comfortable storm.

The Three Bulls

And at our small table beneath the Harvard pennant—*VERITAS* in bold white letters against crimson felt—our true case began.

Remington drummed his fingers once. Then plunged in.

"I appreciate you coming, Mr Holmes. I know you're retired."

Holmes waved this aside. "The bees can spare me. Tell me about the bull."

Remington exhaled sharply, as if he had expected Holmes to circle the subject rather than strike it cleanly.

He reached into his coat and withdrew a folded sheaf of papers, creased twice along the same axis, exactly as Holmes had predicted.

He placed them on the table.

"This is my book," he said. "Or what I have of it."

The pages were few, held together by a single clip.

The Bull in the Field.

Holmes lifted an eyebrow, surprised by the candour.

"You saw a bull in Spain," he pressed.

Remington nodded.

"I can't get it out of my head. A bull in a field outside Pamplona. Just standing there. Morning light. Breath in the cold air."

He swallowed.

"It wasn't a bullfight. Not even close. It was just... the bull. As it is. Before any man touches it."

His gaze drifted for a moment to the smoky mirror behind the bar as if searching for the reflection of that Spanish dawn.

"And then, in Paris," he said, "I saw the same bull, but sculpted in bronze. As if the real one had simply been cast in metal."

Holmes leaned forward. "And now something is missing."

Remington's jaw tightened.

"Two things." He tapped the manuscript.

"This, my original manuscript.

"And the sculpture.

"Both gone. Both taken."

A chill traced my spine.

Remington looked directly at Holmes. "I think whoever stole the bronze also stole my novel."

Holmes's eyes sharpened, not with excitement, but with a deeper, quieter intensity.

"Tell me," he said softly, "what does the bull mean to you?"

Remington sketched a small circle on the cocktail napkin, tapped the pencil a couple of times, and looked at Holmes with bewildered intensity.

"I'm trying to figure that out," he whispered. "That's why I wrote to you."

He drew a long breath.

"I saw a bull in Spain that I can't forget.

"I saw its likeness in a sculpture in Paris.

"And I'm writing a book about something I don't yet understand."

He met Holmes's gaze. "I think you do."

Holmes did not speak at first.

Then he raised his glass.

Slowly.

"To the bull," he said.

"And to finding them, both of them."

Remington clinked his glass against Holmes's.

"And the third," he added.

Holmes glanced up. "The third?"

Remington tapped his chest gently.

"The bull in here."

CHAPTER III

A Question of Courage

A Soldier's Gait, a Writer's Soul

The rain had thinned to a silver mist by the time we stepped back onto the Rue Daunou, settling upon coat-collars and lamplight like a shawl of silver netting.

Holmes paused beneath the awning of Harry's Bar, the warmth of its interior—jazz, smoke, and American voices—glowing behind us.

He drew a slow breath.

"Courage, Watson," he murmured, almost to himself, "is seldom what men believe it to be."

He was not speaking to me.

His thoughts lingered still upon the young American inside: the war-scarred writer with ink-stained fingers; the missing bronze, the stolen manuscript, and the bull that had stirred something deep within him.

Paris lay before us, a glistening maze of wet cobblestones and gaslight, its night streets humming with the muffled conversations of those who would rather not sleep.

Holmes stepped out into it, cane tapping once upon the pavement.

"Do you know what struck me most about Mr Remington?" he asked at last.

"That he sought you out?" I suggested.

Holmes shook his head, walked a few paces in silence before he spoke, not abruptly, but with the kind of measured gravity with which a sculptor first lays chisel to stone.

"He has a touch of genius—one he wields instinctively.

"But." He paused, the tip of his cane clicking once on the slick pavement. "He carries the war inside him still, quietly, tightly, like a shell fragment he refuses to have removed."

I studied Holmes's profile in the half-light. "And why do you suppose that is?" I asked.

Holmes did not answer.

We walked on.

A Walk Through Paris

We made our way towards the Place Vendôme, the mist turning each lamp into a blurred halo and each passing figure into a half-formed ghost.

From a nearby café floated the wavering piano strain of *Worried and Lonesome Blues*, played softly now, as if the pianist were confiding his sorrow only to those willing to lean in and listen.

Holmes moved with the stride I had come to associate with his most absorbing cases, that peculiar, feline, graceful rhythm of his.

"Remington," he said slowly, "is not merely hunting a thief, Watson. He is hunting meaning, trying to get back something the war took from him, to recover what he fears was lost."

"And the bull?" I ventured.

"The bull," Holmes replied, "is the axis upon which his experience turns. He has seen something that refuses to be tamed, diminished, or hollowed. That is why it haunts him."

We passed a bakery whose ovens already glowed for the coming dawn, shadows of bakers moving like silent priests behind frosted glass.

Two students hurried by, arguing about politics and love in a tumble of French and English.

A taxi splashed through a puddle, sending a sheet of water shimmering under the gaslight.

Holmes watched the ripples fade.

"Remington," he said softly, "I believe he desires to write a book that will make him

"Not the man forged by war.

"But a man sculpted by truth."

"And we?" I asked.

"We," Holmes said, "follow the trail of three bulls: the bronze, the book, and Remington's inner bull."

A Sudden Interruption

We were turning onto the Rue Cambon, the wet stones beneath our feet reflecting the pale façades of the great houses, when a man collided sharply with Holmes.

The impact was shoulder-first, deliberate.

Holmes rocked back a fraction but did not fall.

The stranger muttered something in a language too low for me to catch, and vanished into the fog-laden street with the swiftness of one accustomed to disappearing.

I hurried to Holmes's side.

"Holmes, are you hurt?"

He lifted a hand, not to reassure, but to hush.

"No," he said quietly. "Quite the contrary. We have just been contacted."

"Contacted?" I repeated.

Holmes slipped a hand into the pocket of his overcoat and withdrew something small and pale, wrapped loosely in a scrap of paper. It looked almost trivial until he tilted it beneath the nearest lamp.

It was a fragment of horn—the tip of it—its curve unmistakable. Near the point, a smear of darkened blood clung to the surface. Not much. Just enough to be seen.

"My word—Holmes, that's blood!" I exclaimed.

He merely turned it once between his fingers. As he did, I caught it too: a faint smell of iron, yes—but also something else. Fat. Smoke. The unmistakable ghost of a kitchen.

"What type of horn is that? Antler?" I asked.

"Bull," he answered.

"The blood—"

"Kitchen blood," Holmes replied at once, almost amused. "Meant to frighten. Crude. Practical. Intended to alarm. Poorly chosen for the task."

He studied it a moment longer, then smiled faintly—not with pleasure, but with appraisal.

"Whoever placed this wished me to be frightened," he said. "They lack the means, the vocabulary, or the patience to speak otherwise."

"And yet you say we've been contacted?"

"Indeed," Holmes said, rewrapping the horn and slipping it back into his pocket, "because the object itself is not accidental. Bulls are not selected casually. Not here."

"You mean—"

"I mean," Holmes interrupted gently, "that there are people in Paris who prefer silence, Watson, and who do not appreciate outsiders asking the wrong questions."

"And the bronze?" I pressed.

Holmes's eyes glinted briefly in the lamplight.

"Whether they have taken it," he said, "or merely wish us to step away from it, remains to be seen. But when a warning arrives in so clumsy a form, it is often because someone nearer the ground has acted on behalf of something far more disciplined."

Holmes's First Thread

"The facts, Watson," he said.

I knew my cue.

"Very well," I replied. "We have: a young American writer, recently from Spain, who sees in a field near Pamplona a bull that impresses him beyond any ordinary encounter.

"In Paris, he recognises the identical bull in a sculpture displayed in a small gallery.

"That sculpture is stolen, shortly before Remington's manuscript disappears from his room.

"And now"—I glanced at his pocket— "a bull's horn has been slipped into your possession by a foreign stranger in the Paris streets."

Holmes inclined his head.

"Admirably summarised, Watson."

"The sculpture," he said, "is our natural point of departure."

"The sculpture?" I asked. "More vital than the manuscript?"

"For the moment, yes," Holmes replied. "The manuscript is mutable; it exists in memory as well as on paper. But the sculpture is singular. It has drawn thieves, possibly a secret society."

Eyes half-closed, he continued.

"Consider, Watson: someone believes that what Remington saw in Spain is connected to what he recognised in that Parisian bronze.

"And someone has taken great pains to remove both objects."

"And the secret society?" I prompted.

Holmes tapped his cane on the walk.

"Men do not slip objects into a stranger's pocket for amusement, Watson.

"They have announced two things:

"First— that they are aware of my presence in this affair.

"Second— what they offer is no greeting, but a warning, cold, deliberate, and precise."

CHAPTER IV

Galerie Aubry

The Gallery's Door

The rising sun cast a rose hue over the sleepy city below.

It was early morning: the hour when the Left Bank shakes sleep from its bones, when painters open their shutters, when cafés grind their first serious coffee, when the Seine begins again its slow procession of thoughts.

The rain and clouds had gone, leaving behind a faint coolness of washed air.

Holmes and I walked beneath a narrow procession of wrought-iron balconies.

We turned onto the Rue de Seine.

Galerie Aubry was a narrow structure of pale stone, tucked between an antiquarian map-seller and a perfumer whose windows exhaled lavender and smoke.

The shutters of Galerie Aubry were already unlatched.

"She rises early," Holmes observed.

Holmes did not need to knock twice at Galerie Aubry. The door opened at the first tap.

Mademoiselle Evelynne Aubry

Mademoiselle Aubry stood in the threshold, a woman of perhaps forty something, composed—luminous in that restrained Parisian way—with dark hair swept into a loose chignon, and eyes of the extraordinary sort: the colour of the sky at midnight, a deep blue which, when the light from the window caught them, revealed a faint violet cast—so subtle one might have missed it without looking twice.

Her face was oval and finely proportioned, tapering gently to a well-defined chin set above a long, graceful neck. The cheekbones were cleanly defined, catching the light in a manner almost sculptural, as though shaped by a careful hand rather than by accident of birth. Her mouth was slightly parted, the lips full—particularly the lower—yet held in quiet composure. There was warmth in her complexion—not the pallor of London drawing rooms, but a softer tone, luminous and alive, like olives touched by the Mediterranean sun.

Simply put, she possessed the appearance of a woman who could stand beside a Degas and not be diminished by it.

It was not merely that she was beautiful. It was that she was attentive—and that, I confess, is a far more dangerous quality.

"Monsieur Holmes. Dr Watson," she said. "Merci for coming."

Her gaze lingered, not on Holmes, but upon me.

Holmes cleared his throat with unmistakable precision.

"Good morning, Mademoiselle," he said.

Holmes inclined his head. "Mademoiselle Aubry."

"You have come about the bronze," she said.

"The bronze," Holmes answered, "and the hands that took it."

Her breath caught—not audibly, but in the faint tightening of her shoulders.

"Enter," she said at last.

The Empty Plinth

The gallery was a long chamber, its white walls dressed in a hush of varnished canvases: pastoral French countrysides in deep greens and umber, a Breton fisherman rendered in strokes thick as rope, a twilight study of the Camargue marshes where horses rose like pale ghosts from the reeds.

Tiny landscapes in gilt frames glimmered like half- remembered dreams.

A trio of charcoal equine sketches—swift, searching lines—hung beside a pair of seventeenth-century monastic panels whose pigments had aged to the colour of old tobacco and candle soot.

Here and there, bronzes stood: stags bowing their crowned heads, a weary plough horse leaning into its harness, a panther frozen mid-stride.

But despite all this richness, the room felt unbalanced—its centre of gravity disturbed.

Holmes felt it too.

His steps slowed as he approached the plinth.

He motioned towards the empty wooden pedestal.

"It was my father's most beloved piece," she said. "He was a quiet man, a scholar of animal anatomies, a student of the animaliers. He said Bonheur sculpted not merely the form of an animal, but the heart and soul."

Holmes nodded once, almost imperceptibly.

"And have you received visitors," he asked, "men who showed a particular interest in this bronze?"

A flicker crossed her face.

"Yes," she whispered. "Several times."

Without speaking further, she crossed to a narrow cabinet, opened a shallow drawer lined in faded velvet, and withdrew a sepia photograph, a gallery catalogue plate, mounted on card, its corners softened by years of turning.

She held it between her fingers, and the image caught the lamplight.

The bull in the photograph stood majestically upon a low base of textured earth, one foreleg slightly in front of the other, head raised to survey a world that answered only to his will.

The head, broad, square, uncompromising, was set at a slight angle.

The neck was massive, carved with a natural architecture of strength, each fold of hide suggesting the latent torque beneath.

A ridge of coarse, matted fur crowned the shoulders, descending in rugged strata along the crest of the spine.

The nostrils flared gently, the lips drawn not in aggression, but in attentive calm.

His horns swept upward in arcs, not the symmetrical crescents of show stock, but the uneven, living curvature.

The tail, long and sinuous, hung in a natural, unstudied line, terminating in a tuft that almost brushed the earthen base like the stroke of a calligrapher's brush.

Here was no decorative ornament, but an animal rendered with an integrity so stern and unembellished.

And across the base, faint but unmistakable, ran the incised signature:

I. BONHEUR

—cut with the clean, exacting confidence of a man who knew precisely what truth he had beckoned from bronze.

"This is the missing Bonheur," she said.

Holmes breathed out slowly. He leaned forward sharply.

I felt my pulse rise at the sheer presence the photograph carried.

"Isidore Jules Bonheur," he said, "brother to the more famous Rosa Bonheur. A master among the animaliers—Bonheur, whose bronzes were prized for their fidelity, their dignity, their refusal to sentimentalise nature."

Mademoiselle Aubry nodded, moved.

"He captured animals," she said softly, "not as trophies, but as truths."

Holmes closed his eyes briefly, almost a benediction.

I felt my own heart stir at the strange grandeur contained in that photograph.

"Mademoiselle," I said, "it is magnificent."

She turned to me, eyes soft.

A faint warmth touched her cheeks, a rose, fragile and sincere.

Holmes's cane tapped sharply.

"Watson will examine the photograph later," he said. "For now—the visitors."

But Mademoiselle Aubry's eyes flicked to mine before she turned.

Her voice trembled, just once.

More Visitors

"In the weeks before the theft," she continued, "several men inquired about the bronze.

"One was English." She hesitated. "Or perhaps American. His accent was strange—heavy, direct."

Holmes's gaze sharpened.

"Remington."

"Yes."

She smiled. "Albert Remington. He came twice. He stood before the bronze for nearly an hour, saying almost nothing. When I asked if he wished to purchase it, he said 'the sculpture had already purchased him.' I did not understand."

She drew a slow breath, gathering the memory as one gathers a fragile piece of porcelain.

"Also, there were three of them," she said at last. "Spaniards. They arrived together, though they did not move like men accustomed to company. Quiet, exceptionally so. Their manners were impeccable, almost old-fashioned in their courtesy."

Holmes inclined his head. "Describe them."

"They wore good wool coats," she continued, "carefully brushed, but frayed at the cuffs. Their boots were solid but worn thin in the soles. When I greeted them, they glanced at each other helplessly until I addressed them in Spanish instead."

Holmes's eyes sharpened. "And then?"

"Relief," she recalled. "Gratitude, even. They relaxed. They spoke softly, very softly, as though afraid of being overheard. And they asked to see only one object."

"The Bonheur," Holmes said.

She nodded. "Nothing else in the gallery existed for them. They stood before the bull in silence for a very long time. Not admiring it, exactly... more as though they were searching the bronze for something."

Holmes exchanged a glance with me.

"They did not sign the visitor's register," she added. "I invited them to, but the eldest said they 'did not wish to disturb the book.' A strange phrase—but said with such gravity that I did not press the matter."

"And they made an offer?" I asked.

"Yes." She hesitated, almost embarrassed. "A modest sum. Far too modest. I believe they hoped, very politely, that I did not know its worth. When I declined, one of them bowed—truly bowed."

Holmes studied her.

"And how did they leave you, Mademoiselle?" he asked quietly.

"Somber," she whispered. "As though the refusal had wounded them, not in pride, but in purpose. They thanked me in Spanish... and walked out into the rain without another word."

She drew in a sharp, steadying breath.

"The third visitor," she said, "was... quite different."

Holmes folded his hands. "Different how, Mademoiselle?"

"German," she replied. "Unmistakably so. His voice filled the entire gallery before he had crossed the threshold—loud, booming, the sort of voice that believes the world must part before it."

I winced sympathetically; Holmes did not allow himself the indulgence.

"He was overdressed," she continued, "in a heavy black coat far too elaborate for the weather. Silk lining, velvet collar—everything made to impress, but nothing worn with ease. And though he tried to present himself boldly, there was something in his manner..."

She searched for a word that would not sound unkind.

"...as though his thoughts raced faster than his body could follow."

She continued.

"He moved about the gallery in sudden bursts, stopping sharply, starting again, never still for more than a heartbeat. He backed into a sculpture and tipped it on its side, but no harm was done."

Holmes nodded once, slowly. "Go on."

"He went straight to the Bonheur," she said. "Barely looked at anything else. He claimed he was purchasing it for an anonymous client, would not give a name, nor even a profession. He asked the price. I told him."

"And he haggled?" I asked.

A shadow of irritation flickered across her elegant features.

"Relentlessly. As though he were at a street stall rather than a gallery. When I refused to lower the price, he seemed... agitated. Not angry," she added carefully, "but strained, as though time itself pressed upon him. Then he presented his card to me, I think to impress upon me that he was of importance."

She pulled the card from the drawer. It read:

GUSTAV REICHENBACH

Verbindungsbüro Internationale Angelegenheiten

Représentation Privée - Paris,

12 Rue Bonaparte

Holmes's eyes narrowed, not at the words themselves, but at the hollowness behind them.

Holmes studied the card. "A liaison office for international affairs. Private representation.

"A man who hides behind titles," he murmured.

Holmes's eyes sharpened. "What did he do then?"

She exhaled. "He asked for the provenance papers. They are kept in my father's old files in the back office. When I returned..."

She stopped, visibly unsettled.

"Yes?" Holmes prompted gently.

"He was holding the bronze," she gasped. "Both hands wrapped around the bull's flanks, lifting it, weighing it, turning it toward the light. He had no permission to touch it. I asked him, firmly, to set it back.

"He apologised, but his voice cracked as he did so.

"There was sweat on his brow despite the cold."

Holmes leaned forward slightly.

"Which sculpture did he knock over?"

"A Barye," she replied. "A small panther study, quite sturdy, fortunately. He brushed against it in his... abruptness. It toppled but did not break."

Holmes's fingers drummed once upon the table.

"And the register?"

"Yes." She went to the drawer and removed a small, leather-bound visitor's book. "He signed it. The name was..." she flipped the page delicately, "...Herr Gustav Reichenbach."

Holmes's brow furrowed at once.

"And then?" he asked softly.

"When he left," she said, "I noticed my father's Montblanc fountain pen was missing from the table. A cherished one—black lacquer, gold nib. It had been beside the register for twenty years. I had used it that very morning."

Holmes's gaze lifted from the ledger with a sudden, quiet intensity.

"Mademoiselle," he said, "some men steal only what they are told to steal. Others... cannot help but take what their nerves demand."

A shiver passed over her.

"You believe he is the culprit?"

Holmes's voice dropped to a thoughtful murmur.

"I believe," he said, "that Herr Reichenbach bears watching—very closely indeed."

May Rose and Orange Blossom

Mademoiselle Aubry moved closer to the empty plinth, her silk sleeve brushing the walnut as lightly as a butterfly's wing crosses candlelight.

"It was the pride of my father's collection," she said softly. "His *trésor*. He said its shadow filled the room more completely than any man ever could."

I nodded, struck by the gravity in her tone.

Holmes observed her profile with quiet interest; I with something rather less guarded.

She turned then, and her gaze rested on me, not Holmes.

"You have seen many bronzes, Dr Watson?" she asked.

Her voice was low, velveted by the acoustics of the narrow room.

"A fair number," I managed.

"Though few with such... weight of presence."

A faint smile touched her lips.

"*Présence.* It is precisely how my father described it."

She stepped nearer, close enough that I caught the delicate fragrance of may rose and orange blossom.

Holmes coughed once—pointedly, but with amusement.

Mademoiselle Aubry continued, eyes not leaving mine: "He used to say that Bonheur understood the inward life of animals. That the sculptor captured not their muscles—but their memory."

Her fingers grazed the bare wood of the plinth as though tracing the outline of the vanished bull.

"When I was a girl," she said, looking up at me, "I believed the sculpture protected this room. Even now, without it, I still feel the absence...here."

She touched her palm lightly to her sternum.

I felt a warmth rise in my face that had nothing to do with the gallery's lamps.

Holmes, behind her, raised one eyebrow so high that it nearly joined his hairline.

"Indeed," I said awkwardly. "A piece like that would leave an impression."

"Yes," she whispered. "On those who see it clearly."

For one suspended moment her meaning hovered between us.

Then Holmes's cane tapped sharply on the marble floor.

"Mademoiselle," he said dryly, "perhaps tomorrow you would show Dr Watson the ledgers. He is, after all, eminently qualified to appreciate the finer nuances of your father's collection."

Was there laughter in his voice? A hint only, but unmistakable.

She inclined her head towards Holmes with perfect composure, yet when she turned back to me her smile returned—a gentler one, meant only for me.

"If you would, Dr Watson," she said, "there is much I would show you."

And Holmes, behind us, allowed himself one quiet, satisfied chuckle.

And with that, I lifted my hat, and Holmes turned towards the door.

CHAPTER V

The Apartment on Rue Bonaparte

A Door Left Carelessly Ajar

Paris in the late afternoon seemed like a city closing one eye. Clouds drew silently across the sun, and the boulevards dimmed to a troubled grey.

Holmes and I walked briskly along the Rue Bonaparte—Holmes with his long stride; I at something just shy of a military trot.

The address on the card—12 Rue Bonaparte—turned out to be a tall, narrow building of a faded Napoleonic yellow, its courtyard gate half-ajar as though recently disturbed.

Holmes paused.

"Observe, Watson. A man who wishes to appear important keeps his door locked. A man who wishes to appear unimportant leaves it open."

"And a man who is neither?" I ventured.

"Leaves it ajar by accident," Holmes replied. "I suspect we shall meet the latter."

We ascended the worn stone steps, each tread groaning underfoot, and reached a door on the second landing. It bore a small brass plate:

G. REICHENBACH

Représentation Privée

"*Représentation Privée*," Holmes read softly. "A private representation office."

Holmes rapped twice, with the air of a man knocking on the shell of something hollow.

A thunderous voice boomed from within.

"Ja, ja! One moment!"

The door flung open with such force that air rushed past us. Herr Gustav Reichenbach stood framed in the threshold, exactly as Mademoiselle Aubry had described:

Overdressed.

Overscented.

Overanxious.

He wore a burgundy waistcoat embroidered with gold thread, and a cravat tied in a style so elaborate it appeared to be strangling him.

"Guten Tag, meine Herren!" he exclaimed. "Good afternoon, gentlemen! What an honour! What a surprise!"

"It need not be a surprise," Holmes replied, stepping past him without waiting for an invitation. "We used your card."

Reichenbach blinked. "*Natürlich.* Yes. Of course. Please, come in."

An Apartment Entirely Too Much

The interior struck me first as an assault on the senses.

Heavy damask curtains the colour of crushed raspberries. A Persian rug so ornate it seemed almost dizzy. Porcelain figurines—scores of them—crowded on every surface like a porcelain parliament.

Holmes surveyed the room with slow, surgical interest.

"Do sit," Reichenbach urged, waving his arms so dramatically one figurine trembled.

I sat carefully on a stiff velvet chair. Holmes remained standing.

"You visited Galerie Aubry," Holmes said at once.

"Ja! A delightful establishment. Very tasteful. Very... small."

"Small?" Holmes repeated.

Reichenbach's hands fluttered. "Not small-small. Merely... intimate. Yes. That is the word. Intimate."

Holmes examined him the way one examines a clock whose gears are visibly slipping.

"Mr Reichenbach," he said, "a valuable sculpture vanished shortly after your visit."

Reichenbach paled. "Surely you do not think I—?"

"Think?" Holmes echoed. "No. I observe."

A Misplaced Montblanc

His gaze shifted.

I followed it.

On a small escritoire near the window lay a single object, glinting faintly in the afternoon light.

Black lacquer.

Gold nib.

Elegant.

Old.

A Montblanc.

Mademoiselle Aubry's Montblanc.

Holmes stepped forward, lifting it between his fingers.

“This,” he said, “appears to have wandered.”

Reichenbach emitted a strangled yelp.

“Ach du meine Güte! Oh my goodness! That—yes—I meant to return it—it was a mistake! Entirely a mistake!”

Holmes’s eyebrow arched to a perilous height.

“Mistake?”

“Yes! Absolutely! I... ah... I admired the pen. I picked it up. I thought to test it—the ink, you see! I have always valued a fine nib. Then Mademoiselle called to me from the back room, and I set it in my pocket without thinking! Without meaning!”

“You left with it?” Holmes asked.

Reichenbach clutched his cravat. “I am a fool! A fool of the worst variety, an absent-minded one! But a thief? *Nein!* Never!”

Holmes turned the pen in his hand, silently staring at Reichenbach.

“Your behaviour in the gallery was... energetic,” he said calmly.

Reichenbach winced. “I was nervous, Herr Holmes.

“The client who sent me—he is very demanding. Very impatient. I was under—how do you say?— *Zeitdruck.* Time pressure.”

Holmes studied him for a long, silent moment. “And your anonymous client—does he often employ you to evaluate bronzes?”

Reichenbach swallowed. “Not... often.”

“Or ever?”

The German wilted.“No,” he conceded.

Holmes nodded once. “As I suspected.”

Holmes stepped aside, gesturing for me to rise.

"Come, Watson. Herr Reichenbach's guilt extends only to poor taste and poorer judgement."

Reichenbach sagged in relief. "So... you do not think...?"

Holmes slipped the pen into his pocket.

"I think," he said dryly, "that you are entirely too clumsy to execute a theft of this precision."

Reichenbach blinked. "Is... that a compliment?"

"It is a reprieve," Holmes replied.

We reached the door.

"And Herr Reichenbach," Holmes added, pausing at the threshold, "if you encounter your anonymous client again—"

"Yes?"

"Do let him know that Sherlock Holmes is in Paris."

Reichenbach's eyes widened. "*Um Himmels willen!* Should I?"

"Yes," Holmes said, adjusting his gloves. "It will do him no good at all."

Holmes tipped his hat, and we descended the stairwell.

"What do you make of him?" I asked as the street air met us.

Holmes did not glance back.

"A red herring, Watson," he said. "Served very cold."

CHAPTER VI

Returning the Montblanc

Paris, in Her First Light

The morning light along the Rue de Seine had taken on a lilac hue. Paris, still half-dreaming in her unguarded morning beauty, was waving the last fragments of sleep from her shoulders. Bakers drew up their awnings, the warm breath of rising loaves drifting into the street, mingling with the lingering perfume of last night's revelries.

Flower-sellers were setting out their shallow wicker trays, brimming with peonies and early roses, so that the boulevard itself seemed a summer garden.

A small, long-haired kitten emerged from a flower bed along the curb, followed by a second.

A milk cart rattled past us, its wheels murmuring over cobblestones, while a solitary painter—scarf crooked, easel under arm—stopped to study the way the early sun caught the curve of a wrought-iron balcony like tufts of gold. The entire scene seemed to echo the quiet purpose with which Holmes and I made our way toward Galerie Aubry.

Holmes walked beside me with his usual quiet inevitability, the tip of his cane striking the pavement in that soft, precise rhythm that had become as familiar to me as my own pulse.

The shutters of Galerie Aubry were already unlatched.

Holmes walked ahead with that silent, purposeful tread of his, while I carried a small parcel in the crook of my arm, wrapped carefully in linen and tied with modest twine. The weight of it was slight; its significance, immense.

Holmes did not knock. He merely inclined his head toward the door.

I rapped once.

It opened at once.

Two Surprises

Mademoiselle Evelynne Aubry stood framed in the doorway, dark hair gathered loosely, wearing not yesterday's sober attire, but a dress of chartreuse flowing silk, so lightly woven that the morning light seemed to move through it like breath through a butterfly wing, her expression poised between expectation and something gentler.

"Bonjour, docteur," she said softly.

"Good morning, Mademoiselle. I... er... believe this belongs to you."

I placed the linen-wrapped parcel into her hands.

She loosened the twine, drew back the cloth, and there, resting against the pale fold, was her father's Montblanc.

The change in her face was instantaneous and profound: a brightness, a soft cry—near-silent—and then a rush of gratitude so sincere that before I could prepare myself she stepped forward, her hands warm on my shoulders.

"Merci," she whispered.

She embraced me, lightly yet entirely, and pressed a kiss to my cheek.

Not French politeness.

Not coyness.

Something warmer.

Sincere. Pure.

I confess the gallery blurred for a moment, or perhaps my glasses required adjustment. My pulse beat rather foolishly in my throat.

Holmes coughed behind me.

Once. Sharply. With amusement.

Evelynne stepped back with perfect grace, a faint rose in her cheeks.

"You have restored to me," she said quietly, "something of my father."

I bowed, awkwardly, I fear, and Holmes pushed past us with a sigh.

"Yes, yes—sentiment is the balm of civilisation, Watson, but if Mademoiselle will kindly direct us, we have work that cannot wait for hearts to settle."

The Locked Studio

Galerie Aubry's upper rooms were seldom used except for quiet cataloguing.

Mademoiselle Aubry led us through the gallery's long, familiar nave, the bronze statues gleaming, up a flight of stairs and down a narrow corridor to a door we had not yet been permitted to enter.

Evelynne said, her voice low. "You urged me, over the telephone, to touch nothing until you had seen the room yourself."

"My father's studio," she said, keys trembling faintly in her hand.

The key turned with a soft, reluctant click, and the door opened upon a chamber filled with that strange fusion of silence and memory found only in workrooms long since abandoned.

Long tables sagged beneath portfolios of correspondence. Tools lay arranged with the meticulousness of a surgeon's tray. Sketches—anatomical, muscular, precise—lined the walls.

Evelynne whispered, almost reverently, "I haven't been up here in many years."

Holmes stepped closer.

The air here was different—cooler, stiller—as though the dust itself had agreed to remain undisturbed out of respect for the man who once occupied these rooms.

"This is where my father worked," she said, gesturing to a long table strewn with brushes, pigments, folders of correspondence, and tools for examining bronzes.

Holmes surveyed the room with the alertness of a hawk.

"Your father," he said, "did not simply collect Bonheur's works. He studied them."

Aubry nodded.

Holmes, however, entered as though crossing the border into a territory long anticipated.

"Watson," he said, pointing, "observe the dust."

I looked. He was right.

A thin but unmistakable disruption marked the path across the floorboards, the faint track of a shoe dragging only slightly to the left.

"Someone has been here," Holmes said. "Recently."

Evelynne paled.

Holmes tapped his cane twice.

"Someone was here," he said, "not merely to steal, but to study."

He turned back to her. Holmes looked sharply at her

"Did your father ever express why he thought this particular bull held such significance?"

She hesitated, eyes dropping toward her clasped hands.

"He told me a good likeness shows form—but this one, he said, held something of the soul."

Holmes Discovers the Spanish Origin

Holmes moved to the great oak desk against the far wall. Its surface was crowded with notes in her father's hand, written in that deep violet ink that seemed to belong to another century.

In a shallow drawer lay small tools for inspecting bronzes: a jeweller's loupe, a bone-handled brush, a thin metal probe. Holmes lifted the loupe. Its lens was smudged with old fingerprints.

Aubry placed a heavy ledger before him.

"These are the records," she said, "of all acquisitions concerning the Bonheur."

Holmes turned to the marked page. I leaned in beside him.

Only a handful of entries concerned the bull. They were incomplete, oddly restrained—references without certainty. A Spanish estate. A Paris dealer who kept the piece out of public view. A transfer without bill of sale. And, three years ago, an inquiry from a gentleman from Seville who appeared shaken by the sight of the bronze and left without explanation.

Holmes closed the ledger without comment.

He sifted gently through the papers on the desk, then stopped. A thin notebook lay partly concealed beneath a folio. Its spine was softened by years of handling.

Holmes lifted it with care.

"Ah."

He opened it to a page where the ink had faded unevenly. Lines were struck through, rewritten, crowded with marginal notes.

At the top of the page was written:

Toro de Navarre—Modèle vivant, 1875

Bull of Navarre—Live model, 1875

Holmes did not look up at once.

"Your father believed," he said at last, "that the bull was sculpted from a living model."

Evelynne nodded, breath held.

Holmes turned the page. It was filled with various rough, quick posture sketches—the head of a bull, a three-quarter view, a bull from behind—the ears and eyes unnervingly alive.

Below it, in her father's hand, were notes on Bonheur's method: sketches made from life, rapidly, in fields and markets; observations of posture and tension; the way an animal carries its weight when it believes itself unobserved. Only later were these impressions translated into clay, then bronze.

One line stood apart:

This specimen, unusually imposing, was sketched, I believe, in Spain.

No date followed. No place.

Holmes closed the notebook and looked up at us.

Then he lifted the slim portfolio that had held her father's correspondence.

One envelope lay atop the others, heavy cream paper, unmarked, the flap slit cleanly open.

Holmes said, touching it lightly. "The envelope remains—its contents do not. Perhaps the letter was taken during the theft."

He lifted the envelope toward the window; no imprint of writing lingered except the name on the front, written in a script so old-fashioned it seemed almost formal to the point of ceremony, presented itself:

À Monsieur Henri Aubry

Galerie Aubry

Rue de Seine, Paris

—and upon the reverse flap, written in a smaller, measured hand:

Isidore Bonheur

Hôtel d'Étigny

Bagnères-de-Luchon—Pyrénées françaises

1897

Holmes's eyes narrowed with that particular intensity he reserved for objects bearing contradiction.

"Note the absence of text," he said softly, "yet the envelope had weight once, and purpose."

He turned it over, let his fingers glide along the interior fold—then stopped.

"Ah."

He angled the envelope so that the light struck it obliquely, revealing a faint, ghostlike darkening on the inner paper: the powdery residue of charcoal, a smudge that curved like the vestige of a horn or the arc of a massive shoulder.

"Mademoiselle," Holmes said, "your father did not preserve a letter. He preserved a drawing."

Evelynne stepped closer, a hand rising unconsciously to her mouth.

"A drawing? But my father never..."

"Not his drawing," Holmes said gently. "Bonheur's hand. A study in charcoal—quick, urgent—pressed flat inside this envelope for many years."

I bent nearer and saw it at once: the shadow of a powerful form of a bull, an impression only charcoal can leave when carried against paper for decades.

"Someone stole the bronze," Holmes said quietly, "and this drawing."

He closed the envelope with deliberate care.

Evelynne pressed a hand to her mouth.

"But who would care for a mere sketch?"

Holmes regarded her gently.

"It was never mere," he said. "Your father kept it apart. Bonheur sent it without words. That is why it mattered."

He laid the envelope on the desk.

Holmes did not pace. He stood very still.

"These were not thefts of chance," he said at last. "They were acts of pursuit. Someone wants the bronze, the manuscript, and the sketch—not for their worth, but for what they reveal together."

He tapped the desk once."The bull is the key. The living animal. What Bonheur saw. What Remington recognised."

His cane lifted slightly.

He motioned for silence.

Then he crossed the room with two slow, precise steps.

"Watson," he asked, "do you feel that?"

"What?"

"The air."

I felt nothing at first, only the cool draft from the window.

But Holmes's hand hovered before a narrow door set flush with the wall.

Aubry's breath caught. "That door leads to the old cataloguing room. It has not been opened in a very long time."

Holmes's fingers brushed the handle, and stopped.

"Someone opened it yesterday."

"That room hasn't been opened in years," Evelynne said.

"Yesterday," Holmes replied.

She shook her head.

Holmes tapped the lower hinge."A faint smear of oil. Fresh. And someone had oiled the hinges, perhaps to silence the door, no doubt, and to guarantee that it moved freely."

I felt a chill.

Evelynne shook her head. "But I... no one..."

Holmes pressed the latch and pushed open the door.

The door opened with a low, reluctant sigh, as though disturbed from a long and dreamless sleep.

The stale air shifted. Dust rose.

And inside—The room beyond was stark, its whitewashed walls cracked in vertical seams, its lone window shuttered. Dust lay heavy on the floorboards except for a single trail, disturbed, recent, leading toward the sill.

"Look, Watson," Holmes exclaimed.

I followed his gesture.

Holmes knelt.

Evelynne gasped.

Beneath the sill lay a small, dark object. He lifted it carefully: a pendant shaped like a bull's horn, broken cleanly in two.

Holmes turned it in his palm, studying the fracture.

"A talisman," he said. "Worn. Not displayed."

He examined the window latch. Scratched. The paint flaked inward. "Exit," he observed. "Not entry."

He turned the broken horn in his palm.

"This belongs to a secretive order," he said quietly. "The Brotherhood of the—"Holmes shook his head.

"A Brotherhood?" I questioned.

"The name escapes me. But I have seen this mark before."

He set the horn between us. "This is not an art theft, Watson," Holmes said sharply."This is erasure. This is *damnatio memoriae.*"

CHAPTER VII

The Bar at the Hotel Ritz

The Approach to the Ritz

The doors of the Hôtel Ritz did not merely open; they admitted one. The doorman—an elder statesman of buttons and braid—inclined his head with the solemnity of a diplomatic envoy before ushering us past the large wooden and glass doors.

What greeted us was not a hallway, but a gallery of opulence and grandeur masquerading as one.

The marble floor, polished to a mirrored lustre, reflected the chandeliers overhead—those vast constellations of crystal. Along the walls, immense gilt-framed mirrors multiplied the space into a succession of gleaming infinities. Between them hung canvases the size of altarpieces. Heavy draperies the colour of burgundy wine gathered in thick folds around doorways.

Footmen moved along the corridor with the silent fluency of well-trained ghosts, bearing silver trays laden with letters, cocktails, and discreetly folded newspapers.

Holmes, whose habitual disdain for ornament was momentarily set aside, surveyed the corridor with a slow, appraising eye.

"Paris," he mused, "is never content merely to welcome. It must stage one's arrival."

And on we proceeded, past mirrors, past marble, toward the bar.

The bar, set a little apart from the main lobby as if to shield its patrons from the mere fact of the outside world, was panelled in dark, honeyed wood; mirrors caught the lamplight and broke it into gentler fragments along shelves of crystal and cut glass. Brass rails gleamed. The air carried the mingled scents of tobacco, money, and possibility.

Behind the bar stood a man of middle years, spare of frame, with a nose like a hawk and eyes that had seen too much foolishness to be surprised by any amount of it. His hair, once black, had surrendered at the temples to a dignified silver.

"Gaston," Holmes inquired. "Or is it Gatz?"

The barman's mouth twitched.

"Here, Monsieur Holmes, I answer to both," he replied in excellent English, touched with only the lightest trace of French music. "Gaston to the hôtel. Gatz to certain Americans who cannot pronounce 'Gaston' without swallowing half of it."

He set two napkins upon the polished wood.

"For monsieur our specialty—a Sidecar?"

"Not tonight," Holmes said. "A dry sherry. Fino, if you have it. And for my friend—"

I opened my mouth to request something modest, but Gaston forestalled me with a knowing nod.

"Dr. Watson will have a whisky and soda. For English nerves, monsieur—better whisky than Cointreau."

Holmes shot me an amused glance.

"You see, Watson? Paris reads us as easily as an open file."

A Glimpse of Genius

At the far end of the bar, somewhat removed yet unmistakably present, sat James Fitzpatrick—a creature of uneasy grace, as if designed for a ballroom but condemned to sit at tables instead. Before him lay a scatter of papers, a fountain pen, and three small, nearly empty glasses bearing the ghostly remains of gin. His hair fell in a boyish wave that belied the tired set of his shoulders.

And just beyond, through an archway framed in rosetted plasterwork, a courtyard opened briefly to our view: a private Eden of clipped hedges, white hydrangeas glowing faintly under lantern light, and a single marble fountain whispering to itself.

I glimpsed Zennia Fitzpatrick there for a moment, her silhouette restless and radiant, turning a slow circle as if the courtyard itself were a ballroom she alone could hear the music for.

Holmes's gaze passed over them with the brief acknowledgement of a naturalist noting a rare species in its proper habitat. Then he inclined his head slightly toward a quieter table by the window.

Remington sat there, half in shadow, a bottle of wine and three glasses before him. He wore the same worn jacket I had first seen at Harry's Bar, but the set of his jaw was harder; the lines about his mouth had deepened into something that looked uncomfortably like resolve. He nodded as we approached and gestured to the empty chairs.

"Holmes. Doctor."

"Remington," Holmes returned. "You chose your ground well. This place is noisier than it appears."

"That's why it's good for talking," Remington said. "Noise gives privacy."

Gaston arrived with our drinks and set them down.

"Your American friend has already paid for the first round," he noted to Holmes. "He said it would offend him if you argued."

Holmes nodded toward Remington.

"Then we must not offend him. Thank you, Gatz."

The barman inclined his head and slipped away with the silence of a man who hears everything and repeats nothing.

The Unsigned Letter

Remington did not drink at once. Instead, he reached into his coat pocket and withdrew an envelope—plain, cream-coloured, its edges faintly roughened by travel. He placed it on the table with care.

"This came to my room at the George V this morning," he said. "No return address."

Holmes's fingers moved toward it with the same economy of motion I had seen him use when approaching a viper in a glass case.

"May I?"

"That's why I asked you here."

Holmes lifted the envelope. The paper, I noticed, was of a heavier stock than that generally used by hotels; the flap had been sealed—not merely gummed—and then opened with a knife.

On the back, faint but clear, was the mark of a Spanish post office. *Pamplona*, the stamp declared, in ink the colour of dried blood.

Holmes's eyes narrowed to their keenest line.

"Spain," he remarked. "And not Madrid, not Barcelona—Pamplona."

He slid the letter from its sheath and unfolded it carefully. The characters that met our eyes were unlike any hand I had recently seen: tall, ascetic letters, each curve and stroke shaped with the slow, reverent precision of a monastic scribe. The ink was a deep, unyielding black, without variation of haste or hesitation.

Holmes angled the page so that the light fell full upon it."Read it aloud, if you like," Remington said. His voice had gone flat. "I've already done it enough times."

Holmes cleared his throat softly and began.

Señor Remington,

You are writing of what must remain unknown. If you persist, you disturb what should remain undisturbed.

You harm what is harmless.

Leave this matter.

Do not return to it.

Do not ask for it.

Those who keep it are patient.

This is your only notice.

No signature.

Courage and Prudence

Holmes lifted his chin.

"It is a warning," he said. "An intimidation."

He glanced at Remington.

"But turned inside out.

"They assert that *you* are the threat."

Remington shook his head.

"Damnedest thing," he said quietly.

Holmes read the final line twice, his lips moving soundlessly. Then he laid the page upon the table between us and regarded Remington with a gaze that seemed to weigh not only the man before him, but the forces around him.

"How long," Holmes asked quietly, "have you been carrying that in your pocket?"

"Since eleven this morning," Remington replied. "Long enough to get drunk twice—and decide against it both times."

Holmes gave the faintest of approving nods.

"Curious," he murmured. "Very curious indeed. The hand is monastic—trained, disciplined, practiced in copying what must not be corrupted."

"A monastery, then," I ventured.

Remington poured himself a small measure of wine at last, then pushed the bottle toward us with a gesture that was half offer, half defiance.

"You see why I wrote you?" he said. "It's one thing to lose a manuscript, and a bronze I only saw for an hour. It's another to be told what I can and can't write—and where I can and can't go."

Holmes tapped the edge of the letter with a long forefinger.

"And yet," he said, "they are not entirely wrong. You do not understand—yet—what you have stepped into."

Remington's jaw tightened.

"I understand someone pinched my book," he said.

"I understand someone stole that Bonheur from Aubry's gallery.

"I understand someone thinks they can scare me back to Kansas. They can't."

Holmes's eyes glinted, not unkindly.

"Courage, we have already established you possess," he said. "The question now is whether you will marry it to prudence—or to stubbornness."

"And the difference?" Remington demanded.

"Prudence," Holmes replied, "selects its battles in order to reach the truth.

"Stubbornness selects them merely to prove it cannot be moved."

Remington almost smiled.

"You think you can tell which I am?"

"I think," Holmes said, "that you are a man who has already lost enough not to squander what remains on trifles.Which suggests that if you persist, it is because some part of you knows this is not a trifle."

He folded the letter once more, but did not return it.

"Tell me, Mr. Remington. Where, exactly, did you see this bull?"

The Bull in the Field

Remington tilted his head back and remembered. "Near Pamplona," he said. "North of the town. There's a road that goes out past a row of poplars and then breaks into open country. Fields. Stone walls. A river in the distance. On a rise beyond the fields there's a monastery, nothing grand—just old stone on older rock. The kind of place that looks like it was built to outlast whatever the world throws at it."

He took a breath, as though recalling something that had lodged beneath his ribs and refused to dislodge.

"I was walking alone," he continued. "Early morning. Mist burning off. And then I saw him—standing in a field separated from the road by a stone wall. No other cattle. No herdsman. Just the bull. He looked at me like he knew exactly what I was. And he didn't move. Didn't snort. Just stood there.

"Whole."

The word hung in the air like a bell-stroke.

Holmes's gaze sharpened, but his voice remained soft.

"And you are certain," he said, "that the Bonheur in Aubry's gallery was a likeness of that same animal?"

Remington nodded.

"As certain as I am of anything," he said. "It wasn't just resemblance. It was recognition. Like seeing a man in a uniform and then seeing his portrait without it—you know it's the same soul."

Holmes leaned back, steepling his fingers.

"Very well," he said.

"We have a bull in a field under the shadow of a monastery.

"We have a bronze in Paris that mirrors him.

"We have a manuscript missing, a sculpture stolen.

"A bloodied bull's horn fragment.

"A strange bull-horn pendant.

"And now a letter from Pamplona urging you to forget what you have seen."

Holmes smiled—a thin, dangerous line.

"You will not forget. I will not permit it. And our unseen correspondents have made their first mistake."

"Which is?" I asked.

"They have confirmed the importance of precisely what they wish to conceal," Holmes replied. "Nothing so advertises the presence of a secret as the clumsiness with which it is denied."

He turned back to Remington.

"You asked me, in your letter, whether I would take your case. I accept—with one condition."

Remington lifted his chin.

"Name it."

"That you accompany us," Holmes said. "To Spain. To Pamplona. To the very field where you first saw the bull. You will show me the place, the monastery above it, the paths by which one might watch such a creature unseen. If you are to be warned away, it is as well you understand what you are being warned from."

Remington stared at him for a long moment.

"At the monastery?" he said at last. "With you and the doctor?"

"With Holmes and Watson," Holmes corrected gently. "We have trod rougher ground than Navarre."

Remington's mouth curved in something that was not yet a smile, but no longer a grim line.

"I'll go," he said. "I want to see the bull again. I want to help Aubry get her bronze back. And if the men who wrote that letter don't like it—"

He shrugged.

"They can tell me to my face."

Holmes inclined his head, as though a bargain of some gravity had just been sealed.

"Then it is settled," he said. "We shall leave Paris for Spain as soon as arrangements can be made. The field, the monastery, the men, the Brotherhood—"

He paused, his fingers resting on the envelope.

"The bull," he said. "Always the bull."

I glanced at the broken horn on the table.

"You said you had seen that symbol before."

Holmes's eyes sharpened. He drew his hand back slightly, as though something had pricked him.

"Yes," he said slowly. "Yes... that is it."

He touched the envelope again — this time with deliberation.

"The Brotherhood of the Toro Bravo."

"The what?" I asked.

"A society," Holmes said."Ancient. Secret."

"You know of them?"

"Even London, at times, hears whispers."

"Toro Bravo?" Remington asked, setting down his glass.

"A society older than the modern bullfight," Holmes replied. "Very old. Very quiet. And very serious. Whether this letter comes from their hand—or from another merely borrowing their gravity—we shall discover."

Paris Insists

Holmes rose, setting a few neatly folded notes upon the table.

"Come, Watson. Mr. Remington. Tonight we sleep in Paris. Tomorrow, we begin to think in Spanish."

As we stood, Gaston appeared.

"Leaving us so soon, messieurs?" he asked.

"For the moment," Holmes replied.

Remington slid the envelope into his jacket, pushed his chair back, and stood.

"Spain awaits."

Gaston's eyes twinkled as he gathered the empty glasses with easy grace. "Then there is nothing more to discuss," he said lightly. "I hope you will return."

He paused, the faintest smile touching his mouth. "The die is cast. Paris merely insists on seeing how it lands."

CHAPTER VIII

Paris to Navarra

Train to Navarra

Morning found us at the Gare d'Orsay, where iron pillars rose like the ribs of some ancient beast, holding up a ceiling of pale Parisian light.

The station hummed with departures—boots on tile, whistles, vendors calling "Café! Pain! Journaux!"—but for Holmes, all sounds folded into a single purpose.

We were heading south.

Holmes carried only two cases: one small valise containing the essentials of his craft, and the violin case he had polished the night before, its wood gleaming like a secret he had decided to confess only to Spain.

As the train lurched forward, Holmes tilted his head and observed: "Listen, Watson. The rhythm is different now."

And indeed, the rails sang a harder song—less polished, more ancient—as though we were leaving the civilised lattice of Franceand entering a land carved not by elegance but by endurance.

Into the Rails and the Morning

Our compartment held its own silence—that intimate, almost ecclesial hush that settles upon travellers embarking on a road whose end they cannot yet imagine.

Holmes sat by the window, long fingers templed beneath his chin, the countryside flickering past in cool greens.

Remington—broad-shouldered, restless, carrying the scent of tobacco and red wine—claimed the opposite bench.

He travelled light: a battered leather satchel, a flask he pretended no one saw, and a notebook whose pages remained stubbornly blank since the loss of his manuscript.

Outside, France unfurled, then slowly contracted into hills, shepherds, stony terraces, and the long shadows of the Pyrenees preparing to rise like judgement.

The Spanish Passengers

We had scarcely crossed the frontier when the door to our compartment slid open with the soft decisiveness of wealth accustomed to admission.

A young Spanish woman entered first—not merely beautiful, but carrying herself with that unstudied radiance that suggests both lineage and danger.

Her eyes were dark, languid, unembarrassed; her gown a travelling dress of deep burgundy, its embroidery glinting like wine catching lantern-light. Her gaze settled on Remington; her smile was warm, while her eyes remained cool and aloof.

Remington returned the smile.

Behind her came her husband.

Tall.

Immaculately tailored.

A face carved with the aristocratic certainty of a man who expected doors—geographical, social, moral—to open before he reached them.

His hair was dark, his moustache neat, his manner irreproachable in that particular Iberian way which blends courtesy with an imperceptible hint of possession.

They spoke softly as they passed—Castilian, unhurried, with that noble cadence that transforms even pleasantries into declarations.

Remington's head lifted—and the woman's gaze caught his.

Recognition flashed. Not social—literary.

The husband turned.

"Señor Remington?" he asked in Spanish-inflected English, with a warmth so polished it gleamed.

Remington blinked, surprised."Yes."

The man bowed slightly, as though acknowledging a matador.

"I have read of you," he said. "Your writings of the *las ferias de San Fermín* last summer were much admired in Navarra. My cousin spoke of seeing you in Pamplona, fierce with notebook and questions."

Holmes's eyebrow rose imperceptibly.

The woman smiled a practised, courteous smile, the sort that guided conversation where she wished it to go and softened even her husband's austerity.

"We should be honoured," she said, "if you would join us for luncheon in the dining car. There is much in Spain you have seen, and much you have not."

Her voice was like a peeled grape—soft, lush, yet hiding something sharp.

Remington, drawn by admiration, beauty, and flattery (the three chords to which his soul was tuned), accepted with a half-smile.

Luncheon in the Dining Car

The dining car glowed like a miniature salon: white linens, brass fixtures, champagne in silver buckets, and sunlight turning the windows into gold-leaf panels.

Holmes and I sat at our table, strategically distant yet close enough that fragments of conversation floated towards us like petals torn from some clandestine flower.

The aristocrats introduced themselves as: Don Ramiro del Castillo and his wife, Doña Ysabel de Arriaga.

"Old Gold" to their marrow, though we did not yet know the name.

Their words drifted towards us, teasing sense:

"...your lost manuscript, señor... a terrible crime...

"...we know influential publishers—Madrid, Barcelona, Mexico City...

"...such a story deserves the world...

"...we can help you recover it...

"...our estate outside Pamplona—please, be our guest..."

At one point the woman's laughter, light as champagne bubbles, carried down the aisle.

I frowned, watching the exchange.

"I do not like this," I said.

"Nor do I," Holmes replied.

He was not watching the couple, but Remington's face.

"A man flattered is a man open. A man wounded is a man led."

And Remington was both.

Lunch ended in a flurry of courtesies. Hands were shaken, promises implied but unwritten, and at the last, Don Ramiro pressed something into Remington's hand.

A pendant.

A bull's horn—but cast in solid gold, its surface warm, luminous, and unmistakably costly.

"May this guide you," the Spaniard said. "A token of our admiration. And our welcome in Navarra."

Remington Returns

Remington dropped heavily onto the bench across from us.

"Well," he said, exhaling, "that was something."

He held up the pendant.

Holmes took it without asking. He turned the gold once in the light.

"Eighteen carat," he said quietly. "No one gives such a thing without expecting a return."

I nodded in agreement.

The afternoon light fell upon it, and the gold blazed.

I caught my breath.

For it was identical, in form, curve, and iconography, to the black alloy pendant Holmes kept hidden beneath his coat.

Holmes turned it over in his fingers.

"The same," he concluded. "Yet not the same. One cast for the flock, the other for the shepherd."

Remington frowned.

"You mean what, exactly?"

Holmes placed both pendants side by side on the table.

The contrast was startling:—one, iron, rough-forged, dark, secretive;—the other, pure gold, spotless, meant to be seen.

"Two factions," Holmes said softly. "Within the same brotherhood."

He leaned back, eyes half-lidded.

Remington swallowed.

"And which one invited me to lunch?"

Holmes's voice dropped to a near-whisper.

"The one that dresses danger in silk, and calls it hospitality."

Nightfall in Navarra

By the time the train descended from the mountains, evening had accumulated in the valleys of northern Spain like dark wine settling in a chalice.

Olive groves unfurled beneath us, silvered leaves trembling in the dusk. Distant shepherd bells carried on the wind.

The silhouettes of monasteries crowned the hills, stern and watchful, as if carved from the very rock they guarded.

Pamplona awaited, its lights flickering like small, stubborn stars refusing to be extinguished by the coming night.

Holmes rose, fastening his coat.

"Come, Watson. Come, Remington. Spain is ready for us."

Remington smiled, tipped his hat, and swung his battered satchel over his shoulder.

"Yes," he said, "but are we ready for Spain?"

Holmes did not answer.

He only glanced once at the gold pendant in Remington's hand.

"And she wastes no time choosing her players."

The train gave a long, low whistle and plunged us into the heart of Navarra.

CHAPTER IX

A Pamplona Welcome

The Navarra Night

Night pressed low over Pamplona—not storming, not raging, but quietly watching, with its hood drawn low upon the brow. The lamps along the Calle Estafeta flickered in an exhausted yellow, their light too thin to challenge the vast, star-pierced dark pressing down from the high Navarra hills.

As we proceeded onward, the city's alleys seemed to narrow.

"There's a place I use when I'm here for the bullfights," Remington said. "Not fancy. Not quiet. But it knows what a man wants after a long day in the ring. The Paisano. Two blocks ahead, up by the old square."

"Paisano?" I repeated. "That sounds almost... convivial."

"It's convivial until it isn't," Remington replied, his voice dry, flat as beaten copper. "Depends who comes down from the hills."

Holmes walked between us, hands joined lightly behind his back, his silhouette long and lean against the shuttered façades—the picture of a scholar moving through a foreign land with the indifference of one who already understands it.

"And what draws you there," Holmes asked, "beyond its proximity to danger and spectacle?"

Remington gave a slight shrug, half lost in the lamplight that trembled above us. "They don't ask questions," he said. "They pour strong wine. And if a man returns at dawn covered in dust, no one bothers to ask."

Holmes emitted a thoughtful hum, approval, amusement, or both.

"A hotel that respects silence," Holmes remarked. "Admirable."

Being Followed

Remington slowed a fraction, drawing in a breath as though testing the air. "You feel it too?" he asked.

Holmes did not break stride, though his head angled by the smallest degree—an instrument tuning itself to danger.

"Oh yes, Remington," he said. "We have been followed since the station doors closed behind us."

At this, I tightened my grip upon the handle of my valise.

"Followed? By whom?" I demanded.

Holmes did not turn. His profile, touched by the lantern's dim corona, might have been hewn in relief against the night.

We had scarcely crossed the threshold of the courtyard when Holmes halted—with the soft, almost imperceptible stillness of a hunting animal that has scented a shift in the wind.

"Gentlemen," he noted, "we are observed."

Remington stiffened.

I felt the prickle at the back of my neck that no rational faculty can dismiss.

From a narrow alley to our right, a figure detached itself from the darkness—a shape, more silhouette than man, moving with a purpose in the silence of its tread.

Holmes tilted his head.

"Do not look directly at him, Watson. You will see more by pretending to see nothing."

But Remington was already turning.

The shadow figure advanced to within ten paces, then—with a suddenness so violent it seemed to split the air itself.

The shadow lunged.

No weapon—only open hands, but hands that moved with the precision of one accustomed to discipline, ritual, and the cold resolve of necessity.

Holmes stepped back, drawing the man off-line.

The assailant swept an arm toward Remington.

Not to strike him, but to drive him back, to unbalance, to warn.

Remington, never one to retreat, met the gesture with a ferocity that surprised even me.

His fist shot out in a clean, brutal arc, a boxer's blow.

Not elegant, but honest.

It caught the stranger squarely beneath the eye.

A low grunt, more breath than pain, escaped the man.

He staggered backward a single step, one hand briefly covering the darkening bruise.

But he did not fall. He did not flee.

He straightened.

And then, in a gesture so chilling for its calm, he lifted two fingers touched his heart and drew them down through the air between us—a silent command to go no further.

A sign of warning, a benediction, or both.

Then the attacker stepped back into the alley and vanished as though swallowed by stone.

Only then did the echo of his parting whisper reach us, a sound closer to breath than speech:

“Volveos!”

Turn back!

Holmes’s cane lifted instinctively, but the man was already moving, slipping into the alley’s throat with the sure-footed swiftness of one accustomed to rough stone and mountain paths.

Something dropped as he turned, a small object rattling across the cobbles.

Remington bent to retrieve it.

Holmes’s hand shot out. “No. Allow me.”

He stooped and lifted it into the lamplight.

A single wooden bead—smooth, brown, worn by years of prayer-thumb and rain—a bead from a rosary, cracked cleanly in half.

Holmes closed his fingers around it.

“We are not threatened,” he said quietly. “We are warned.”

Remington rubbed his knuckles and muttered.

“Next time, I’ll finish the job.”

Holmes gave a thin, knowing smile.

“On the contrary, Remington. Next time—” Holmes let the broken bead rest in his palm.

“We shall listen.”

We walked on through the narrow streets of the town, the echo of the encounter still shivering in the air behind us like a cord that had been plucked and not yet stilled.

Navarra at night was a study in dark stone and darker silence, houses pressed shoulder to shoulder like penitents before confession, their shuttered windows catching the lamplight in faint, trembling shards.

Somewhere in the upper rooms, a guitar strummed a slow lament, and the scent of woodsmoke drifted low along the eaves as though reluctant to rise into the chill.

Remington flexed his bruised knuckles with the grim satisfaction of a man who has finally struck at something.

Holmes kept his hands clasped behind him, his gait unhurried, almost meditative.

"No police," he said softly, as we turned a corner. "Not yet. The man wished only to warn us. His purpose was not violence, but deterrence."

"Deterrence," Remington growled, "is what you try when you're afraid the other man might fight back."

Holmes gave no reply, but the faint upward movement at the corner of his mouth suggested agreement.

The street narrowed into a quiet bend. At last, the hotel appeared— half cloaked beneath an outcrop of ancient stone, stood Hotel Paisano.

Hotel Paisano.

Its façade had a rugged, old-world music to it: part Castilian dust, part aristocratic shadow, part frontier inn where secrets pass beneath the clatter of hooves.

A modest stone building, perched with its lantern swinging gently above the door, it seemed to murmur its welcome to travellers who dared the mountain night.

Holmes paused, lifted his gaze to the upper windows, their shutters half-drawn, their panes reflecting a thin ribbon of candlelight, and gave a satisfied nod.

"This will do," he said.

Inside, the air was heavy with the aromas of red wine, slow-cooked lamb, oak smoke, and the faint mineral coolness of mountain water carried in earthen jugs.

A small, stoop-shouldered clerk emerged from behind the counter, his spectacles glinting like twin moons in the lamplight.

"Buenas noches, señores. Rooms? Luggage?"

Holmes inclined his head with the careful courtesy he reserved for the unassuming but competent.

"Three rooms," he said, "quiet, if possible."

The clerk nodded briskly.

"You are fortunate. The hill-town is calm this season."

He slid three heavy brass keys across the worn mahogany.

Remington handed over the luggage receipts, and two young porters—thin as reeds, their eyes bright with the curiosity such travellers always stirred—lifted our cases ineptly, but managed to carry them all.

"Your bags will be in your rooms when you return from supper," the clerk assured us.

Holmes gave a faint smile.

"We shall only require the bar for now."

The Hotel Bar

The bar of the Hotel Paisano lay just beyond a low archway, a chamber of stone and timber, lit by two pendant lamps whose glow flickered like captured embers.

A few patrons sat about in reflective silence: a pair of shepherds nursing red wine; an elderly woman knitting, her needles clicking like faint castanets; and a black-clad priest murmuring over a worn book of hours.

We took a table near the hearth, where a small fire whispered against the iron grate.

The proprietor—a genial man with a salt-white moustache and the bearing of one who had served wine to pilgrims for forty seasons—brought us a bottle of Navarra tinto, the colour of garnets steeped in shadow.

Holmes raised his glass, examining the surface of the wine as though expecting it to reveal to him the nature of Navarra itself.

Holmes poured sparingly. “To caution,” he added.

Remington raised his glass with an unfazed grin. “To hell with caution.”

The proprietor drifted away.

“It is curious,” Holmes mused, “how some places declare their intent before one has drawn breath. Navarra is one such—not hospitable, not hostile, but... watchful.”

Remington drank deeply, wiped his mouth with the back of his hand.

“She’s a land that likes to size a man up,” he said. “Sees what’s beneath the coat.”

Holmes inclined his head. “Well observed.”

I could not help glancing toward the windows, where the wind pressed its cold fingers against the glass as though testing the seams of our shelter.

A moment of quiet fell over us—not companionable silence, but the taut stillness of men waiting for something unnamed.

Holmes felt it too.

His eyes narrowed slightly, tracking some faint, invisible disturbance in the air.

"Watson," he whispered, "do you perceive—"

He never finished the sentence.

The lamplight sputtered.

Then the room fell into darkness.

Suddenly, a single scream—high, startled, feminine.

A chair scraped violently across the floor.

A glass shattered.

"Watson, remain seated," Holmes breathed, his voice steady in the void, as though he could see through it.

Something brushed my elbow—soft, swift, purposeful.

Then a faint tap upon our table.

A slip of paper, dropped into the darkness.

Remington rose half a second before the lights returned, his chair toppling backward with a crack.

Light flooded back into the room in a sudden, almost accusatory blaze.

The waitress—young, startled, her apron askew—was on the floor near the bar, one hand pressed to her breast, her breath trembling in quick, frightened gusts.

Holmes was beside her before anyone else could move.

"You are hurt?" he asked gently.

She shook her head no, though her eyes were wild.

"S-sir, I... someone—someone brushed past me. From behind."

Her voice wavered.

"It felt like a shadow. And when I turned—nothing. Nothing at all."

Remington crouched beside her.

"What did he look like?"

"I—I don't know," she said. "I never saw a face. Only... movement."

Holmes gave a single, grave nod. "Of course. Shadows seldom keep their appointments with the eye."

He returned to our table.

The slip of paper lay where it had been placed, white against the dark wood.

Holmes opened it.

Three words—written in a rough, hurried hand, as though carved rather than penned—stared back at us:

NO SOIS BIENVENIDOS.

Beneath it, a second line:

REGRESA.

HAY PELIGRO CERCA.

YOU ARE UNWELCOME.

RETURN.

DANGER NEAR.

Holmes folded the note slowly, the quiet of his movement more ominous than any outcry.

"Gentlemen," he said, his voice as calm as winter steel, "our arrival has not gone unnoticed."

He set the folded warning beside the bottle of red wine, its presence between us like a small, dark oath.

Outside, the night deepened—and somewhere in the hills above the town, a bell tolled once, then again, as though measuring the hours before dawn would bring us to the bull.

CHAPTER X

Morning in Pamplona

San Telmo

Morning in Pamplona arrives like a velvet curtain lifting, in a slow, ceremonial grace. The city was waking, but reluctantly: shutters creaked open like eyelids rubbed of sleep. A faint magenta light washed along the rooftops, softening the clay tiles to rose, while the mist that clung to the Arga River drifted upward to kiss the trembling bells of the cathedral towers.

Holmes, Remington, and I crossed the Plaza Consistorial just as those bells tolled the hour, a deep, bronze rolling sound that seemed to stir the pigeons and the dust. The streets narrowed around us into a maze of whitewashed walls, red-wood balconies, wrought-iron railings tangled with drying laundry. The first slow knot of mule-carts clattered across the square.

Holmes, with the stride of a cat, walked with a particular focus, chin lifted, eyes half-lidded not in weariness but in concentration.

"In which direction do we find your bull, Remington?"

The American shifted his shoulders beneath his worn jacket, glancing up the slope where the morning light gathered in pale gold pools among the rooftops.

"There's a rise beyond the town," he said, "a long shoulder of hill. I saw the bull grazing below it, in a field of dry stone and broom. And above that field—" he pointed with a curt, almost reluctant gesture"—a monastery built into the rock. White walls, red roof, a tower."

He added, with a thin, hard smile:

"I remember it because the bells startled the bull. And because I thought, at the time, that monks must sleep like anchors—once dropped, they don't rise for anything short of a storm."

Holmes fixed Remington with a narrow, probing glance.

"Which is precisely why monasteries—when they speak at all—should be listened to."

Holmes said calmly, glancing toward the rising ground. "Yet you will observe, Watson, that increasing proximity to this animal is accompanied by a corresponding rise in hostility—an attack in a darkened alley, a warning note, the extinguishing of lights. Danger rarely gathers without design. That alone makes the bull our proper starting point. Any secrets the monastery has should not be ignored. If we must wake sleeping monks, then so be it."

I frowned, feeling the weight of impropriety settle upon me like a damp London fog.

I lowered my voice out of instinctive reverence.

"Should we really trouble the brothers of a monastery? The place is consecrated ground, Holmes. It feels... unsound. Improper. We ought to be questioning the local tavern-keepers instead, men who know the smell of danger the way they know the smell of wine."

Remington gave a brief grunt of agreement. "Watson's right. Bars are where men talk. Monks don't talk at all, in my experience."

Holmes stopped walking.

We halted with him, two sceptics and one detective standing beneath a shuttered balcony hung with drying basil.

He turned his face slightly, as if aligning his thoughts with some invisible compass.

"My dear Watson," he said quietly, "if danger hides in taverns, then fear hides in monasteries. And fear, Watson—fear—is often the better witness."

He gestured toward the rising road.

"The brothers of San Telmo may speak little, but silence, when listened to properly, tells us far more than chatter ever could."

He resumed his stride, long and inexorable.

A Door That Watches

The monastery appeared without warning: a low arcaded structure nestled on a hill, sandstone worn smooth by centuries of prayer and mountain wind.

Above the wooden door was a small carving—a bull, stylised and ancient, its head bowed, its stance resolute.

Holmes studied it.

"A medieval Navarran emblem," he said softly. "But stylised in a way... older—a hint of something brought here long before the bulls ran on festival mornings."

He touched the carved horn.

Holmes knocked once.

The sound echoed like a footstep in a crypt.

The extra-large, ancient, carved oak door opened without creak or ceremony.

A man stood framed by candlelight: thin, narrow-shouldered, face etched by sun and contemplation, robe brown as earth, eyes deep-set and alert.

Brother Santiago regarded us through a small crack of the door, his face half-lost in the morning's uneven light, his hands folded in the sleeves of his habit. He stood so still he might have been carved from the stone itself.

Holmes inclined his head with that particular courtesy he reserves for genuine austerity.

"We come not as intruders, Brother, but as men seeking clarity in a matter that has touched both Paris and your own hills. Your order may hold a fragment of what we require."

The friar's eyes narrowed at once—not in simple caution, but in that deeper mistrust born of a man whose life has been spent guarding thresholds, spiritual and otherwise, from intrusion.

"Who are you?" he demanded, the words clipped, flint-edged.

Holmes inclined his head with the barest courtesy.

"I am Sherlock Holmes. These are my companions, Doctor John Watson and Señor Albert Remington."

The friar's gaze moved over us in a swift, appraising sweep—not the glance of hospitality, but the measuring of trespassers.

"Why have you come to San Telmo?" he asked. "What is it you seek?"

Holmes answered with his quiet steadiness, the tone he reserved for suspicious men whose hostility he found unsurprising.

"I am a detective by vocation. Certain matters—missing, mislaid, or concealed—have drawn me to Navarra. Those same matters now draw me to your monastery."

A faint scowl crossed the friar's features, swiftly suppressed but not lost on Holmes.

"We know who you are, Señor Holmes," He said, bitterness just barely checked. "Even here, we hear whispers from the world beyond. But reputation alone grants no passage at San Telmo."

He gathered his robe closer, as though guarding something more than warmth, and glanced toward the cloister arch where the shadows were thickening.

"You will find no answers here," he said. "And it is nearly *Lauds*. I must return inside."

He made a slight bow—formal, dismissive, final—and stepped back as though to close the world off.

As the giant oak door thudded shut, its iron bands groaning into place, I confess a peculiar breath of relief escaped me. Something in my upbringing protested at the notion of interrogating holy men; the very stone beneath our feet seemed to murmur that such inquiries were seldom welcome within cloistered walls.

Holmes, however, did not share my ease.

He stood very still, his gaze fixed upon the heavy door with a knitted gravity.

"Watson," he said, "when a man bars information, it is seldom piety that prompts him—more often fear."

Remington was already halfway down the worn stone steps, shoulders set with that purposeful stride of a man who prefers open fields to closed answers. I suspected he meant to orient himself toward the hills and the remembered pasture where the bull was.

Holmes turned then, descending two measured steps after him.

But before we had taken a third, the oak door swung open with abrupt force—its hinges crying out like startled birds.

The friar stood framed in the threshold, but the hardness had vanished from his features. His smile was strained, unnatural; his eyes no longer sharp with suspicion, but wide with a troubled urgency—almost supplication.

“Please, Señor Holmes,” he said, the words released on a breath that trembled at its edges,“please... enter.”

The friar gestured inward.

“Enter. You will be safe here.”

Holmes murmured as we stepped inside:

“Watson—note he said *will be safe*, not *are safe*. The distinction matters.”

The Hall of Echoes

The interior was austere: stone walls, wooden benches, a long corridor lit with narrow slits of sunlight.

Every footstep echoed, not loudly, but with a strange roundness, as though the monastery itself listened.

On one wall hung a tapestry: a simple depiction of a woman in a blue robe holding a small scroll.

Holmes slowed.

“That,” he said softly to me, “is not a saint commonly honoured in Spain.”

The friar heard him.

“No,” he said quietly. “She is honoured here for what she carried.”

Holmes’s eyes flickered.

“Truth?”

The friar nodded once.

“*La Verdad.*”

As we walked on, my eye caught another image upon the opposite wall—a modest oil painting in a dark wooden frame, half-lost in shadow, yet unmistakable in its subject:

San Fermín himself, rendered not as the triumphant martyr of cathedral altarpieces, but as a quiet bishop in red vestments, his features grave, almost scholarly, one hand raised in blessing, the other holding a narrow palm branch that seemed carved from the very silence of the room.

Holmes slowed just perceptibly.

"A local devotion," he said.

The friar nodded once, his voice lowered as though the saint might overhear.

"He watches over our home," he said.

Holmes's gaze lingered an instant longer, his expression unreadable in the cool, filtered light.

"My name is Friar Luis Santiago," he said at last, his voice low.

He extended a hand—hesitant, uncertain whether to trust.

Holmes accepted it with a courteous incline of the head.

"A pleasure, Friar Santiago. Tell me, how long have you served at San Telmo?"

"Oh, nearly thirty years," Santiago replied, and here a fleeting pride warmed his tone.

"Thirty?" Holmes lifted an eyebrow. "But you cannot be much more than thirty yourself."

A shy smile touched the friar's features, softening them.

He appeared to be in his mid-to-late thirties.

His face was long and lean, with a vertical emphasis rather than width. It tapered gently from a broader forehead to a narrower chin. There was very little softness in the planes of it; even when relaxed, the structure read angular rather than rounded. It was a face that suggested intensity—stretched, searching, almost ascetic.

His eyes were an olive-green, darkened at the rim with a trace of deep blue, as though shadowed by long thought. They were large, rounded, and expressive, and they dominated his face, drawing immediate attention. His gaze, however, was sidelong and guarded—almost appraising.

There was sensitivity in the eyes, but steel in the jaw.

This combination of intensity and vulnerability in Santiago's face revealed a man capable of strong leadership, yet marked by interior strain.

"I grew up here, Señor Holmes. As a boy I tended the stables... the orchards... the cattle. When I was old enough, I took the habit of Saint Francis. One does not leave the mountain once it has chosen him."

Holmes touched a thoughtful finger to his lips, nodding slowly.

"Yes. We have come to see the bull."

Remington stepped forward, unable to mask the impatience in his voice.

"I'd like to lay eyes on it, friar, before any more words get between us and the trail."

Santiago's breath faltered; the composure he attempted to summon slipped from his grasp.

"Please, Señor Holmes—no more small talk."

His voice trembled, and the pleading in his eyes was no longer veiled. The olive-green shifted like coastal water before a storm, the blue at its edge deepening into shadow.

"I must ask for your help. The bull you seek... is missing."

Holmes stiffened almost imperceptibly. "When did you first suspect theft?"

"I learned only moments ago," Santiago continued. "Brother Mateo, his keeper, returned from the upper pasture. He did not find its tracks where they should be. That is why I called you back. Something is wrong at San Telmo... gravely wrong."

He looked from Holmes to Remington, then to me—measuring, perhaps, the strength of the men he had just confessed to.

"Missing?" Remington asked sternly.

Holmes questioned next. "Missing—escaped, you mean?"

Santiago hesitated, still not truly wanting to trust Holmes, but at this point he had no choice.

"Not missing, señor—but stolen, we believe."

"Where was the vaquero, the keeper of the cattle?" Holmes asked.

"Brother Mateo—he was on a small errand," Santiago replied sheepishly.

Santiago lifted his head quickly—too quickly—as though Holmes's mention of the missing *vaquero* had struck a nerve he meant to hide at once.

"It is... complicated, Señor Holmes," he said, forcing steadiness into his voice. "Brother Mateo—yes, yes, he tends the herd—yet his absence is not the heart of the matter."

Holmes arched a single eyebrow.

"It would seem very much the heart of it."

But Santiago pressed on, almost desperately—folding his hands together as though trying to hold his composure in place.

"Please, señor," he said, the words tumbling out in controlled urgency,"do not trouble yourself with Mateo at this moment. We—we are simple men here. We are not equipped to face those who have done this. What matters is that the bull is gone."

He took a breath, then another, as if bracing himself.

"You are a detective unlike any other," he said softly, eyes fixed on Holmes with a mixture of hope and terror. "And I... I beg you, use your skill, your science, your method—find our bull. Find him before the thieves take him farther into the hills, where not even God keeps the same watch."

Remington's posture tightened, fists rigid at his sides.

"He'll find him," Remington said. His voice was low, carved from something fierce and personal. "And I'll see for myself where the trail leads."

Santiago's gaze flicked to Remington, then quickly away—uneasy, but resigned.

He turned back to Holmes with a look that was not trust—not yet—but the closest thing a frightened man can offer when hope is his only refuge.

"Please, Señor Holmes. Help us."

Holmes drew in a long breath, his eyes sharpening until they seemed to take in every grain of the cloister stones.

"We shall begin," he said, "with the corral."

Santiago paled, but he stepped aside.

"The corral," he said. "Come. I will show you."

And the door creaked open further, admitting us into the shadowed inner world of San Telmo.

Holmes Examines the Corral

The monastery grounds unfolded before us: low cloisters wrapped around a central courtyard, tiles the colour of old wine glistening faintly in the morning damp, olive trees planted by hands long ago whispering above us like tired sentinels.

As Santiago led us inward, our steps echoed beneath the arcades, a slow, solemn rhythm that seemed to disturb the very air, as a faint perfume of incense drifted from the chapel.

At last the cloister opened into a larger yard, ringed by weather-worn wooden fencing and low stone troughs.

"This," Santiago explained with a stiff gesture, "is the corral."

Holmes stopped three paces from the gate and inhaled once, deeply—the breath of a man reading a terrain the way others read manuscripts.

"Watson," he called, "observe the dust."

I bent nearer.

The ground was churned into irregular furrows, as though something massive had turned in agitation.

Holmes crouched—fluidly, without haste—and touched his gloved fingers to the disturbed earth.

"A struggle," he said quietly. "But not of a bull resisting its herdsman. No... this is different."

He traced a faint arc with his hand.

"Here—the hind hooves dug deep. The animal was pulled, not guided."

Santiago stiffened as though the truth had struck him across the face.

Remington's jaw clenched.

"I knew that bull wouldn't go easy," he muttered.

Holmes rose, dusting his hands.

Holmes turned from the churned earth and fixed Santiago with that thin, surgical gaze of his—the kind that could unlace a man's composure without ever raising its voice.

"Brother Santiago," he said softly, "bulls do not simply vanish. Nor do thieves enter monastery grounds without knowledge of their paths, their timings... or their risks."

Santiago swallowed.

His eyes drifted—first to the chapel, then to the distant hills—as though seeking absolution from anything but the men before him.

"There are... people," he said cautiously, "men from the villages... or the hills...who covet strong cattle. Sometimes for breeding. Sometimes for sport."

Holmes waited.

He did not blink.

Santiago continued, his voice tightening:

"You might find answers there, Señor Holmes—among the... ah... *ferias*, the small livestock fairs. They trade animals quietly. At night. Off the old road toward Estella."

Remington frowned.

"Fairs? At night? That sounds like smuggling."

Santiago lifted both hands, palms outward, a gesture of helpless innocence.

"I tell you only what we hear," he said.

"We monks... we do not ask questions.

"We pray. We tend the land. We keep to our vows.

"And always"—his voice faltered—"we are called to walk humbly, and to seek what is holy."

Holmes stepped closer until the friar seemed to shrink beneath the weight of being seen.

"And if we go to these fairs," Holmes asked mildly, "will we find the men who took your bull?"

Santiago's breath caught, in the sharp, honest fear of a man imagining what might happen to an animal he loved.

His voice trembled, but his resolve did not.

"Señor Holmes... yes," he said. "If they mean to sell him, the night fairs are the first place.

"The traders move quietly

"The money is quick.

"A stolen bull is easier to hide there than anywhere in Pamplona."

He lifted a shaking hand and pointed toward the dark rise of the hills.

"That is where such men go. If you search, you must start there."

Holmes bowed his head—a gesture not of courtesy alone, but of understanding.

Santiago exhaled shakily, relief and dread mingling in his eyes.

"I pray you find him, señor," he whispered. "He does not deserve the fate these men will give him."

Holmes turned to us.

The morning light, cold and pale, caught the lines of his face and made them seem carved rather than living.

"Come, gentlemen," he said. "Our path, it seems, begins in the hills."

Santiago watched us go, his lips moving in a silent plea.

Thus ended our first encounter at San Telmo, in the quiet plea of a monk—Santiago—who had placed the fate of his bull, and his hope, into Holmes's hands, and had no one left to turn to but us.

"Come, gentlemen," Holmes said again, "there is a bull somewhere in the night fairs of Pamplona, and if we would find him before those who stole him decide to sell him, we must quicken our step into the dark before it closes over him for good."

CHAPTER XI

The Night Fairs

Toward the River Arga

The morning sun had reached its noon peak as we climbed a little higher along the flanks of Navarra when we left the monastery behind us, its whitewashed walls receding. The bells of San Telmo spoke a low, humming note.

We walked in silence at first.

The path descending from the monastery twisted downward between terraces of olive and wild rosemary. The scent of both rose thickly in the air, stirred by a breeze that still carried the faintest chill from the Pyrenees.

Remington walked ahead, his stride impatient, as though each unused second was one stolen from the pursuit of the bull he named El Toro.

Holmes followed with his chin lowered, the manner of a man listening to the earth beneath his feet for whispers it had not yet decided to offer.

At last he broke the silence.

"Watson," he said, "you observed the friar's hesitations?"

"I observed several," I replied. "Too many. As though he feared the words he would speak."

Holmes walked on a few more paces before answering, his tone thoughtful rather than suspicious.

"Not fear of us, Watson," he said. "Fear of what lies beyond the monastery walls. These 'night fairs' may be more than rustic gatherings."

Remington stopped short, turning his gaze toward a cluster of distant hills where low clouds drifted like slow herds.

"If these fairs are where the cattlemen trade," he said, "that's where we'll hear talk—real talk. Men loosen their tongues with wine and fire."

Holmes nodded.

"Precisely. Rural commerce is seldom written down, but always spoken. If a bull was moved by strangers, someone at these fairs will have seen something—footprints in the dust, a cart leaving at the wrong hour, a horse lathered when it ought to have been cool."

I glanced from one to the other.

"Do we even know where these fairs are held?"

"The friar spoke of the western valleys," Holmes replied. "Near the River Arga. A few hours' walk, perhaps less if we follow the shepherds' paths."

Remington adjusted his hat against the rising sun. "Then that's where we go. Trails like that... men don't forget what they've seen out there. And if someone took the bull—someone bragged about it."

Holmes's eyes narrowed slightly, not in distrust, but in calculation."Let us proceed, then," he said. "Spain is a land where truth often travels by rumour, not by parchment. If we listen well, the land itself may begin to speak."

And with that, we set our steps toward the west—toward the River Arga, toward the so-called night fairs.

And as Holmes would later remark: "Even the clearest truth, Watson, becomes perilous when pursued in darkness."

The night had thickened by the time we descended toward the valley where the night fair smouldered like a trembling fire. Lanterns dangled from crooked poles; shadows swayed beneath them with the weight and gait of beasts and men alike. The haggling of shepherds drifted through the air along with the sharp cry of a tethered goat and the metallic clank of cattle-hooks.

Remington's stride lengthened.

"This is where men talk," he said. "And where they hide what matters."

The noise of the fair rolled outward in warm, dusty gusts—drums, clapping, the rise and fall of excited voices—yet Holmes seemed to hear none of it.

He tapped his cane once against the packed earth and fixed Remington with a look both courteous and surgical.

"Before we proceed," he said, "tell me again: the creature you saw. Not the bronze—the bull itself. Describe him exactly as memory will allow."

Remington drew a long breath, the kind a man takes before stepping into a ring.

"He was dark," he said. "Not brown, not bay, darker. A blue so deep it passed for black unless the sun hit him just right. Then you'd see it... a kind of cool fire along the hide."

Holmes inclined his head.

"Go on."

"The shoulders were massive," Remington continued, gesturing unconsciously with his hands. "Not swollen, not show stock, just there. Like the beast had been carved out of pressure and earth. His neck had that ridge, the fur there stood coarse, almost weather-beaten."

Holmes's eyes flicked briefly toward the distant corral.

"A resemblance of line and proportion," he said, "but that alone is insufficient. What of distinguishing marks?"

Remington nodded, lowering his voice as though the fair itself might overhear.

"There was a mark on his left flank. White. Clean-edged. Not a star or a blotch. It looked..."

He searched for the word.

"...like a triangle. Tall and narrow. Pointing down. I thought at first it was chalk from a herder's hand, but it didn't fade. Not with sweat, not with dust. It was part of him."

Holmes's eyes sharpened as though a match had been struck behind them.

"A downward-pointing triangle," he repeated softly, "on the left flank."

"Yes," Remington said. "A brand, maybe, but not one I've ever seen."

Holmes's voice dropped into a register I had learned, over long years, to trust for its ominous accuracy.

"No, Remington. Not a brand."

He looked toward the fairgrounds, where the air shimmered with heat and noise.

"A sign. And signs are seldom accidental."

"And if we find him?" Remington asked.

Holmes gave a faint, enigmatic smile.

"Then, my dear fellow... we shall see whether memory or myth casts the larger shadow."

Holmes's eyes took in every booth, every shifting silhouette.

"Ask plainly," he said in a low tone. "We will hear the truth only when we speak in truth."

We entered the fair.

A cluster of cattlemen stood around a pen of beef cattle. Remington stepped forward, addressing them in simple, precise Spanish.

"Señores, have any of you seen a great black bull taken from the hills two nights ago? A bull stronger than the others. A bull that would not be mistaken."

A long silence followed.

One shepherd spat into the dirt, eyes narrowing as he studied Remington's face.

"And why," he said slowly, "would three strangers come asking about such a beast?"

Holmes cut in, voice smooth as velvet laid over steel.

"Because it was stolen. And because theft leaves tracks."

The shepherds exchanged glances, quick, nervous.

Another man, older, with a crooked nose and the flat stare of one accustomed to danger, stepped forward.

"There was movement on the mountain road two nights ago," he said. "Oxen. Two carts without lanterns."

Holmes's eyes sharpened.

"Heading where?"

The shepherd pointed toward the darker slope beyond the valley.

"To the ravines above the old mill. No one uses that road. Too steep, too narrow. Only fools or men who wish to disappear."

Remington stiffened. "Could they have taken a bull that way?"

The shepherd snorted. "With oxen and rope? Yes. If they had many men. And courage. Or desperation."

Before Holmes could question further, a heavyset butcher shoved through the small gathering.

His apron was smeared with blood.

A short-handled bull-ring hook swung from his belt.

He was clutching a nearly empty wine bottle in his left hand.

The butcher lurched forward, wine heavy on his breath, eyes bleary but burning with a misplaced certainty. He jabbed a blunt, meaty finger toward Remington.

"You," he growled, "I know you."

Remington blinked, caught between confusion and rising temper.

"I've never seen you before in my life."

One of the younger shepherds shouted, "*Está borracho otra vez, ¡ojo!*"

He is drunk again — watch out!

The butcher's laugh was harsh and ragged. He stumbled backward a couple of feet.

"Mistaken?" the butcher spat.

"I may be drunk, but I'm not blind. Liar. You're the foreigner, the sewing machine seller, who took my wife from me last summer. You remember that, Americano?"

Remington's jaw tightened.

"I did no such thing. And I was in Paris last summer. You have mistaken me for someone else. I am not a salesman."

The butcher swayed side to side, eyes narrowing to vicious slits.

The wine bottle fell from his hands.

He steadied himself on a nearby stool.

"Don't play games with me. You have the same face. The same voice – *alto... norteamericano... bigote"*

Tall. American. Moustache.

"Sir," he said evenly, "you are mistaken. My companion has insulted no one here," Holmes interrupted.

He planted a broad hand on Remington's chest.

"You think I don't remember *Yanqui*? I see you mock me. You think I forget?"

Remington slapped the hand away. "Touch me again," he said, low and steady, "and I'll put you through your own table."

The butcher lunged.

A stool clattered.

A knife flashed in the butcher's fist, not brandished in malice, but in the sloppy, impulsive way a drunk waves whatever is at hand.

Holmes moved like a whipcrack, one hand snapping to fix the man's wrist, the other guiding the blade harmlessly downward.

The butcher staggered, overbalanced,

Remington's fist caught him squarely on his nose, a clean, brutal punch that dropped the man to one knee.

"*¡Carajo!*" he exclaimed. "*¡Ay, mis narices!*"

Damn – oh, my nose!

Gasps and laughter rose from the nearby stalls.

A lantern swung.

Someone muttered, "*¡Basta, hombre!*"

Enough, man!

The butcher, clutching his swelling nose, glared up with wounded pride more than pain.

"You people bring trouble," he slurred.

"Leave Navarra be."

Then he stumbled back into the shadows of the crowd, swallowed by voices and smoke and the restless pulse of the fair.

Toward the Ravines Above the Old Mill

The little circle of night-fair men dissolved as swiftly as it had formed, walking away and melting back into shadow, each man retreating with the furtive precision of someone who had said too much, and regretted even the saying of it.

Within moments the fair was soundless save for the flicker of a dying torch and the distant, irregular bleat of a goat tethered somewhere behind the tents.

The butcher, dazed and dabbed with a handkerchief by a sympathetic stout woman, sat upon an overturned crate muttering into his cup; but none of the others so much as looked at us now.

The night had drawn its curtain.

Holmes stood quite still, listening, not to the fair, but to the silence gathering around it.

"The ravines above the old mill," he said, turning the shepherd's words over as though testing their tensile strength. "A road too narrow for commerce, too steep for pilgrimage... yet used, two nights past, by men with oxen and darkness for company."

Remington adjusted his collar, jaw tight.

"We follow it," he said. "If they took a bull up that way, it would leave marks."

Holmes gave a small nod, pleased, not by the certainty, but by the instinct behind it.

"Yes, Remington. A bull does not vanish into the mountains like a pocket-watch into a coat. It leaves weight behind. It leaves disturbance."

We stepped away from the fair and its waning lanterns, the dirt beneath our boots crisp with the cool of evening and the faint, resigned scent of trampled thyme rising as we walked.

The path the shepherd had indicated was little more than a scar cut slantwise between two stone terraces.

Above us, the mountain loomed enormous and unlit, its ridges drawn in the ink of encroaching night.

I felt a stir of unease, that familiar awareness that grows in travellers who sense that even the air is watching.

"Holmes," I ventured quietly, "if this road is so seldom used, surely the villagers would avoid it for a reason?"

Holmes's reply came after a pause, measured, reflective.

"Villagers avoid it because thieves do not," he said.

"But fear does not alter the fact." Holmes stopped walking. "The fact is, Watson, two carts passed here in darkness, bearing something heavy enough to require oxen, yet precious enough to move without lanterns."

He crouched near the first bend in the trail, gloved fingers brushing the ground.

A faint scrape—metal upon stone. A crushed briar. A rope-burn on the bark of a low-hanging branch.

"Here," Holmes whispered.

Remington leaned nearer.

"That's drag," he muttered. "Something large."

"Indeed," Holmes answered. "Dragged uphill. With difficulty."

He rose slowly, his eyes narrowing toward the dark ridge above us, where the old mill lay unseen, all angles and ghosts and forgotten industry.

"We continue," Holmes said.

And with that, we pressed on into the increasing silence of the mountain.

The Old Mill

The ascent to the old mill proved far more punishing than the shepherds had suggested. The path narrowed into a treacherous ribbon of shale and dry earth. Its edges crumbling beneath our boots with each upward step.

The night had deepened; no stars guided us now and the quarter-moon hid behind clouds.

Remington forged ahead with the grim determination of a man following a memory through the dark, while Holmes moved with that curious feline exactitude that allowed him to seem both swift and unhurried.

I alone slipped twice, catching myself against thorn and rock and cursing silently the stubbornness of mountains and the men who choose to climb them.

"Ascent," Holmes asserted without turning, "is always a dialogue, Watson, and the mountain always wins."

At last the path widened, and a cold wind swept across us with the metallic scent of water and forgotten machinery.

The silhouette of the mill emerged, a hulking mass of abandoned stone perched precariously at the edge of a ravine.

Its wheel, vast, skeletal, rotted, hung crooked over a black trough where a stream once ran with enough force to turn its paddles and warrant human effort.

Now only a thin trickle remained, slipping over moss-dark stone with the sound of someone whispering secrets to the earth.

Holmes lifted his lantern.

The yellow glow struck the façade of the mill, its shutterless windows yawning like blind eyes, its door sagging inward upon a broken hinge, the heavy lintel above it carved with initials long eroded into anonymity.

"Oxen pulled something heavy this way," Holmes murmured.

He ran his palm over the earth, bringing up a smear of flattened grass and grit.

"Dragged... not wheeled. The tracks end here."

Remington exhaled through his teeth.

"Then let's see if they left him alive."

He pushed forward before either of us could answer, shouldering the warped door.

It groaned inward with a slow, reluctant cry that echoed through the empty mill and returned as a hollow lament.

Inside, the darkness gathered thick as wool.

Dust floated in our lantern's path like ancient spirits disturbed from their vigil.

In one corner, a collapsed stack of grain sacks; in another, rusted tools whose handles had long since surrendered to rot.

And then

Remington stopped so abruptly that I nearly collided with him.

"Holmes," he whispered, the word roughened by hope and dread.

The lantern swung forward.

There, in a crude pen assembled from broken planks and lengths of frayed rope, stood a bull.

Large.

Dark.

Breathing in slow, heavy pulses.

Its coat, though dark, was red-brown.

Its horns curved handsomely, but with the common symmetry of stock breeding, not the uneven, weather-written arcs that had burned themselves into Remington's memory.

Holmes stepped closer, lantern angled so the creature's flank caught the light. "No mark," he said quietly. "No triangle. No scar. No white sign at all."

The bull snorted, pawed once, as though offended by our disappointment.

Remington's shoulders fell, not with despair, but with the grim resignation of a man whose hope had sprinted too far ahead of fact.

"This isn't him," he murmured. "This isn't even close."

Holmes crouched, examining the pen's construction.

"Recently assembled," he observed. "The nails are new. The rope... recently cut."

His hand found a splintered board, still fragrant with sap.

"And the animal has not been here long."

"Then why bring this bull," I asked, "to an abandoned mill? To hide it?"

Holmes's expression shifted—not surprise, but realization's first shadow.

Holmes brushed his hand over the rough planks of the makeshift pen.

"Why hide a bull in a mill?" I asked.

"Because, Watson," Holmes replied, "cattle thieves are like any other criminals: they require a pause in which to vanish. This mill offers shelter, darkness, and—most importantly—silence. A stolen bull can be held here until the night is deep enough, or the road empty enough, to move him again without witnesses."

Remington nodded angrily. "It's a halfway house for stolen flesh."

Holmes gave the faintest smile. "Precisely."

Remington laughed. "So this fellow is stuck in the middle of somebody else's fight."

Holmes inclined his head. "As are we."

Holmes turned slowly, his lantern sweeping across the mill's vast interior, the rafters, the shadows, the door through which we had entered.

And outside, carried faintly on the wind from the ravine, came the sound of something moving.—slow, deliberate, heavy—as though a large body had brushed against stone.

Holmes's eyes lifted sharply.

"Gentlemen," he whispered, "we may not be alone."

The boards outside creaked once more.

Remington reached for the latch. Holmes raised the lantern higher and drew the door open in one swift motion.

A broad, pale face regarded us placidly from the dark. Wet nostrils flared. A long breath steamed in the lantern light.

There followed a soft, unmistakable low: "moo."

For a moment none of us spoke. Then Remington laughed first. "Well," he said, wiping a hand across his mouth, "hello, beautiful."

The cow shifted her weight, unimpressed by our relief, and lowered her head toward the scent drifting from within.

Holmes regarded her thoughtfully. "Madam," he said at last, "your interest is understood. Ours is strictly professional."

The bull in the corner snorted and pawed the ground.

"They may hide a bull from men," Holmes observed, "but from animals—another matter altogether."

I laughed. "She had merely followed her nose."

Remington gave the cow a small, courtly tilt of his hat. "Let's leave Romeo and Juliet and head back to the hotel. I'd welcome a drink."

CHAPTER XII

The Market

Our Daily Bread

Morning in Pamplona did not so much rise as unfurl: a slow exhalation of silver light along the eaves, a stirring of shutters, a murmur of hooves upon the stones, as the city shrugged off its dreams and remembered its errands.

From the adjoining room came a single thread of sound—a violin, softly drawn, a fragment of a Sarasate melody, only a phrase tested and released.

It rose.

Paused.

Returned, altered by the smallest degree as though Holmes were turning an idea in his hands.

The violin has always been a tool of cognition for him—like pacing, like chemicals, like his pipe.

I lay still and listened, understanding that he had not slept much, and that something we had seen the night before had not yet found its proper shape.

When the phrase resolved at last, the bow lifted, and the silence that followed felt deliberate—as though a decision had quietly been made.

Later that morning, as we gathered our coats, I said lightly,"I heard your violin."

Holmes did not look up as he fastened his cuff. "Yes."

"That usually means something has occurred to you."

He gave the faintest smile. "It means," he said, "that thinking indoors has reached its limit."

Remington raised an eyebrow. “And the remedy?”

“The market,” Holmes replied. “Men who steal cattle must still eat. They must buy rope, bread, and salt. And we must listen.”

He reached for his hat. “One learns a town quickest where it feeds itself.”

Holmes, Remington, and I walked beneath the mellow glow of the earliest sun along the Calle Curia, where the walls leaned inward as though conspiring with one another.

Bread ovens had already begun; the scent drifted around us—warm crust, rosemary, a suggestion of woodsmoke.

Somewhere nearby, a butcher’s cleaver struck against a block, while a woman poured buckets of water into the gutter, sending little silver rivers running beside us.

Remington walked with the impatient stride of a man who mistrusted mornings for their slowness, his eyes restless beneath the brim of his hat. Holmes, on the other hand, moved with the silent, long-shadowed grace of a heron, alert to currents of meaning invisible to other men.

I confessed myself most attentive to the stalls that were beginning to open, platters of olives glistening like polished obsidian, peppers heaped like small bonfires, and wheels of cheese the colour of pale gold.

“Food first,” I suggested hopefully. “Deduction, Holmes, is seldom improved by an empty stomach.”

Holmes did not smile, but his cane gave one faint, approving tap. “Even the brain must find its bread, Watson.”

Remington muttered, “Bread’s no good unless a man’s earned it,” but he followed us toward the market square.

The Market Square

The Plaza del Castillo had begun to quicken, though it was still early enough that the shadows cast by the arcades clung close to the flagstones.

Vendors laid out their wares in temporary stalls, setting up before next week's fiesta.

Chickens clucked irritably from wicker cages.

Two old men argued over the price of cider apples.

A dog slept beneath a table, dreaming of sausages.

The scent of fresh *pan de maíz* did nothing to improve my discipline, and everything to improve my appetite.

We threaded our way toward a cluster of women selling oranges and pottery.

Holmes scanning the periphery with that distant, almost musical concentration that came upon him when the world had begun whispering.

"Holmes," Remington said, "what's our plan?

"Ask strangers if they've misplaced a bull?"

Holmes inclined his head.

"One asks about carts, Remington. One asks about men. A bull is much like a story—you find its outlines by studying its footprints."

We might have pushed on toward a baker whose loaves steamed fragrantly upon his counter, but at that moment Holmes stopped so abruptly that I nearly collided with him.

"Watson," he exclaimed.

"Look ten paces ahead."

I followed his gaze.

The Curious Monk

There, bent over a basket of monastery bread, his hood pushed back just enough to reveal a violet bruise blooming across his cheekbone, stood a Franciscan monk with a blackened eye. He had not yet seen us.

Holmes's voice lowered to a surgical whisper. "Observe the bruise, Watson. The curvature suggests a right-handed punch delivered at very close quarters."

"Remington?"

Remington's jaw tightened. "I recognize my own work."

The big American took a breath as if to speak, and that was the moment the monk looked up.

Recognition struck his face like lightning.

Terror followed.

He dropped the bread.

The basket overturned; round loaves rolled across the stones like startled animals. His hand flew to his cheek, as though the memory of the blow had risen from beneath the skin.

"Stop!" I called instinctively.

But the monk had already stumbled backward. His sandals skidded. He turned and ran—not with the steady stride of a cloistered man accustomed to quiet paths, but with the frantic, stumbling haste of someone who had seen a ghost and knew it might follow him.

Holmes watched him vanish into a narrow side street. Then he straightened. His face, usually composed, aloof, almost ascetic, was sharpened now by something rarer: controlled indignation.

"Watson," he said, "that man was terrified."

"Of?" I ventured.

Holmes lifted his cane. "Exposure."

Remington exhaled sharply. "Looks like Santiago was playing a game of dodges. Well, he sure didn't tell us the whole damn truth."

Holmes nodded once, curtly. "A monk with a blackened eye is a very curious thing indeed.

"And San Telmo dispensing threats like alms.

"Yes, gentlemen, we have been treated as fools—a discourtesy I do not easily forgive."

He turned toward the road leading back toward the hills.

"Holmes, where are you going?" I asked.

He did not slow his step. "Back to San Telmo," he said. "Where, this time, we shall leave with the truth."

Remington pulled his coat tighter, his eyes gleaming with something between anger and relief. "About time.

I'm tired of smoke and shadows, saints with secrets, and waking up every morning with a new bruise."

CHAPTER XIII

On the Trail of a Blackened Eye

San Telmo's Secrets

The sun stood high and large over Navarra, a great burning disc that glared down at the world with something close to temper. Its heat hammered the road in blows, hard, bright, and punishing.

Holmes walked ahead of us in a silence that burned no less fiercely. His cane struck the stones at an even pace, but there was nothing easy in it. The sight of a Franciscan monk's bruised eye—Remington's blunt signature. I had seen that set in his shoulders before: the posture of a fencer on guard—blade raised, body angled—silently warning the world: *En garde!*

Today, Holmes would have the whole of the truth, stripped of shadow, stripped of omission, as bare as the roads boiling beneath that Spanish sky.

Remington matched him step for step, jaw set, eyes forward, the restless impatience of the night's frustration transmuted into something harder, keener.

San Telmo clung to the hillside, whitewashed walls glaring under the noon sun. And from the tower above, the bells broke the air with hard bronze strikes, each one leaving behind a long, lingering echo—like an old chant pleading for help.

When we reached the great oak door of San Telmo, Holmes did not immediately knock. He stood before it, studying the iron bands, the sun-scorched grain, the faint scrape marks at the threshold—as if the wood itself might confess more readily than the monks behind it.

At last, he lifted his cane and gave three sharp, deliberate raps.

A narrow hatch slid open.

A pair of young, anxious eyes blinked out at us—eyes that flicked first to Holmes, then to Remington, then to the blistering noon behind us, as if weighing escape routes.

There was a rustle of cloth, a whispered exchange we could not quite catch, and then the door opened only a hand's breadth—just enough for a novice, thin and pale, to squeeze into the gap.

"Brothers are at prayer," he murmured, though his voice carried an unmistakable tremor.

Holmes regarded him with that quiet, surgical stillness that has undone stronger men.

"We shall wait," he said.

The novice swallowed—audibly.

Then, glancing over his shoulder into the gloom beyond, he stepped back.

A second figure appeared behind him.

Santiago.

His posture was straight, his expression serene, but the strain in his eyes betrayed him instantly.

"Doctor... Señor Holmes..." he said softly. "This is not a good hour."

Holmes stepped past the threshold before the novice could think to bar his way.

"On the contrary," he said. "It is the perfect hour."

The Refectory

Brother Santiago stood beneath the dim glow of the oil lamp set before the icon of Mary Magdalene, its golden surface catching on the sweat along Santiago's brow. His expression—meant to be neutral—betrayed itself at once: embarrassment at what had happened, and a fragile, flickering hope that Holmes might already have found the monastery's missing bull.

Holmes's tone hardened by a degree.

"There are matters we must discuss, Brother Santiago. Matters that cannot wait. And questions"—he tapped his cane lightly against the flagstones—"that will have answers before this hour is done."

"Come," Santiago said. "You may speak with me in the refectory."

We followed Santiago through the cloister. Somewhere deeper within, chanting rose and fell—steady, indifferent—like the monastery's heart refusing to quicken for any visitor.

The refectory of San Telmo stretched long and narrow beneath its vaulted ceiling, a cool stone chamber carved by chisel. Rows of heavy wooden tables ran the length of the hall, their surfaces worn smooth by centuries of elbows, bowls, and folded hands. High windows admitted narrow shafts of light, dust swimming lazily in them. A crucifix hung at the far wall above a battered lectern, marked with old candle drips and ink stains long since dried.

Our footsteps sounded too loud.

Santiago motioned us toward the table.

Holmes did not sit.

He let his gaze travel the room once, slow and exact—taking measure of nail heads, cracked plaster, and the long shadows beneath the beams—then turned back to Santiago.

"Brother Santiago," he said, "I bring news."

A tremor crossed the friars's face and vanished. "What news?"

Holmes allowed silence to do its work.

"We found the bull."

The words were calm—too calm.

I knew the tone.

He was not offering a fact; he was placing a piece upon the board. Holmes was playing chess now, and Santiago was the man across the board whether he knew it or not.

And so, when Holmes said, "We found the bull," I felt no shock. I understood. It was the bull we had found last night in the abandoned mill—not ***the*** bull, not yet—only a bull that would serve as the piece Holmes needed to advance.

Santiago's composure broke in a single breath.

"You—" His voice caught. "You found him?"

Hope—raw, unguarded, almost childlike—flared across his features. His fingers gripped the table edge.

"Where? Is he harmed—?"

Holmes watched him as a cat watches a mouse—not for cruelty, but for certainty.

Then, very gently, as though placing relics on an altar, Holmes reached into his coat pocket and set two bull-horn pendants upon the table.

First, the crude rusted iron—black, simple, weathered by many hands.

Second, a solid gold pendant, the sort of token a thief might favour.

Their contrast was stark.

The friars's face drained of colour.

Holmes had the poor friar in a kind of checkmate.

Holmes stepped closer; his voice did not rise. "You seem," he said, "to have misplaced something, Brother Santiago."

For a long moment, the only sound in the refectory was the faint clatter of a distant censer and the quiet racing of Santiago's breath.

He tried to speak. He failed.

He tried again.

Santiago stared at the two pendants.

His breath hitched.

His hesitation was brief.

And then, with a reverence that betrayed far more than speech, Santiago reached out and closed his fingers around the rusted iron pendant.

Holmes's eyes gleamed.

"Thank you, Brother," he said softly. "That was the move I needed."

The Price of Silence

Santiago's voice cracked.

"You must not show those here. It is not permitted."

Santiago closed his eyes, as though bracing himself.

Holmes leaned a fraction nearer.

"Who steals bulls in the night?" he asked. "Who watches trains? Who sends threats and whispers disappearances?"

"I cannot speak of such things," Santiago said hoarsely. "It is forbidden."

"My dear Brother, forbidden," Holmes said, almost gently.

"So is theft—and yet here we are."

Santiago looked up. Not defiant now—only desperate.

"I beg you... do not force me."

Holmes's expression softened, but only by a hair.

"I need not force you," he said. "You have already begun."

Brother Mateo

Suddenly a sound came from the corridor—quick footsteps—then Remington reappeared in the refectory doorway.

He was not alone.

And behind him, shoulders hunched, habit disordered, one eye swollen into a bruised confession, stood Brother Mateo.

Remington's voice was tight.

"Look who I found wandering the halls," Remington said. "Recognize the handiwork, Watson?"

The monk shrank beneath Remington's stare, hood dropping forward like a penitent curtain.

Here stood a young man in his mid- to late twenties, clad in a dry, dust-covered brown habit, yet with one eye swollen and bruised, still wet and darkened to deep plum.

He had the face of—not a loud revolutionary nor the comic companion—but a shepherd who must read weather before it arrives and see movement in grass before the flock does.

Mateo's expression carried a quiet interiority. He did not react outwardly to whatever surrounded him; instead, he appeared to be processing something privately. The slightly lowered gaze and relaxed mouth suggested thought rather than tension. There was no visible anger, no obvious fear, no performative bravado.

Mateo's lips were set but not tightened. His jaw was not clenched. Even his ears had the quiet curve of a musical clef. His eyes, from what I could ascertain behind the bruise, were deep hazel. Sun-caught. Quiet. Green-brown with gold in them. His eyelids sat heavy, giving him a look of fatigue or contemplation rather than alertness.

What stood out most was a restraint and detachment. He would be the one who watched. The one who absorbed. The one who was apart from the group even while physically among them. Possibly the one who carried the weight of something not yet spoken.

It felt as though he were listening—not to the people around him, but to something inward or upward.

Even then, I had a difficult time reconciling this rather quiet young monk as our assailant.

Santiago paled.

"Mateo," he whispered, horrified. "*¿Por qué estás...?*"

Why are you...?

Holmes extended a hand, halting the space between them.

"No theatrics, Brother Santiago. The hour for those has passed."

He turned his gaze fully upon Santiago.

"You have deceived us once," Holmes said, "and attempted to hide a witness whose face proclaims a truth you would rather conceal. We stand at the threshold of your secrets—and I assure you, Brother, we will cross."

Santiago's breath shuddered.

His palms pressed flat against the table behind him, both for balance and—perhaps—for absolution.

"I am not sure if I can trust you, Señor Holmes," he said at last, voice trembling.

Holmes nodded once, cool and grave.

"The feeling, I assure you, is mutual."

A thick silence fell—heavy, whole.

Santiago's eyes moved between us—Remington's clenched jaw, my own steady stare, Holmes's pale, unblinking certainty.

At last his resistance cracked.

"There are those," he said quietly, "who care for the bull... and others who would misuse it."

Holmes did not blink.

"Ah," he nodded slightly, "so the factions exist."

Santiago closed his eyes, realizing too late how much he had admitted.

Holmes stood perfectly still, a man who had just heard the hinge of a great door open.

Then Holmes's eyes glinted like steel drawn from a sheath.

Holmes regarded him for a long, still moment, that terrible stillness he wielded like a scalpel.

Then he stepped closer, his shadow falling across both monks.

Holmes spoke first—quietly, sharply, like the flick of a blade through silk.

"Brother Santiago," he said, "am I correct in assuming you stole Señor Remington's manuscript?"

The friar froze.

The rosary halted mid-bead.

Even the dust in the rafters seemed to pause its drift.

"I—I did not, Señor," Santiago stammered, the tremor unmistakable in his voice.

Holmes's eyes narrowed—a raptor's gaze settling upon a trembling hare.

He did not move, but something in the room seemed to tighten around Santiago, as though Holmes's scrutiny were a physical force.

At last Santiago swallowed, his throat working painfully.

"It was... it was my brother," he whispered. "My brother who is living in Paris...with his wife and children."

Holmes tilted his head, studying the man as if inspecting a fracture in a relic.

"I am uncertain," he said at length, "whether I ought to ask why...or where it is now."

The silence cracked.

"Where is my manuscript?" Remington thundered, his voice filled with anger, shock, and that naked desperation of a writer whose only copy of his own soul has gone astray.

Santiago flinched.

His hands clenched around the rosary until the beads clicked sharply.

He looked from Holmes to Remington with the despair of a man cornered by truth.

"It is... missing," he said, barely audible.

Remington surged to his feet, his chair skidding backward with a scrape that jarred the ancient stone.

He strode toward Santiago, the set of his shoulders rigid, the breath ragged in his chest.

"Where," he repeated, low and deadly,"is it?"

Santiago could not meet his eyes.

His voice cracked open like a vessel dropped upon stone.

"My brother..."He drew a shuddering breath.

He closed his eyes, turned his head and looked away.

"My brother burned it."

The words fell like the tolling of a bell, rolling outward in slow, devastating waves.

Holmes closed his eyes—just once.

Remington stood motionless.

As though struck in the chest.

And Santiago, pale and trembling, clutched the rosary to his heart as though it were the only thing anchoring him to the world he had just set aflame.

There is an old adage that when a boxer takes a heavy blow, he is never quite the same afterwards.

For Remington, the blow came cleanly to the gut.

The hit was

Quick.

Hard.

And final.

The world collapsed at once.

I had seen men take such hits before—men who folded, and men who reached for anger because it was easier than balance.

Remington did neither.

He did not move.

His hands remained flat on the table, fingers spread, as though feeling for something that was no longer there.

The fury that might have followed did not come.

It hovered—and then—

He looked at the friar, slight, fragile in his brown habit, clenching his beads tight, eyes shut as though bracing for a blow.

Remington knew that posture. He had seen it in men who stayed on their feet because they could do nothing else.

The anger went out of him.

In its absence came intensified clarity.

He saw the friar for the first time—he saw the beads trembling in his hand, the jaw set despite it.

His fear was plain. His steadiness was plainer.

The contrast was startling. Out of proportion.

Remington drew a breath and let it out slowly.

He looked again at the small friar—and did not look away.

When he spoke, his voice was low, still rough with loss.

"All right," he said. "At least you told it straight."

And then Remington shook his head.

And walked out the door.

For a moment, no one spoke.

Santiago stood unmoving, the rosary still clenched in his hands, his shoulders bowed—not in defeat, but in something nearer to penance. He did not look after Remington.

Holmes remained where he was, eyes fixed on the closed door.

A Reckoning of Bulls

Santiago lowered his head.

Holmes adjusted his cuffs with deliberate calm.

"Come, Brother," he said. "We have done enough damage for one afternoon. Let us ensure at least one truth leaves this room intact."

"Am I correct in assuming you removed the Bonheur statue from Galerie Aubry?"

The rosary beads in Santiago's hand stopped.

The silence that followed did not feel like refusal.

It felt like collapse.

Santiago did not speak.

Mateo did not speak.

Neither needed to.

Their eyes—wide, stricken, guilty—said everything their vows would not allow them to utter.

Holmes nodded once, as though confirming a theorem.

"Then," he said, "we find ourselves in a most curious symmetry."

He drew himself upright, hands clasped behind his back, a posture both judicial and damning.

"You have my bronze bull,"

Holmes continued, "and I have your living one."

Santiago flinched as if struck.

Holmes leaned forward—not threatening, but implacable, like a weight placed upon the scales.

"Shall we then," he questioned,"trade bulls?"

CHAPTER XIV

The Shepherd's Watch

Remington's Room

Holmes and I descended into the narrow corridor of the Hotel Paisano, boots tapping softly against tiles that still held the night's cold, the air scented faintly with stale wine and stone dust.

When we reached Remington's door, Holmes paused and rapped once, a light, precise tap.

Silence answered.

Holmes tried the handle. It yielded.

The room within was neat—too neat—the bed stripped of any trace of habitation, the writing desk barren save for a single matchbook from the hotel bar, and the air carrying that peculiar emptiness left behind only when someone departs with intent.

At the foot of the wardrobe: no valise. No boots. No shirts rolled in haste.

Remington had not gone out. He had gone away.

Holmes stepped inside slowly, his gaze travelled over the room.

"His sactchel is gone," I said.

"Yes," Holmes replied. "And with it, his doubt, his hope, and his better judgment."

I turned toward him. "You believe he fled?"

Holmes shook his head.

"Not fled, Watson. A man does not flee from what he intends to reclaim."

He lifted the matchbook from the desk, examined it, returned it to its place.

"No—Remington has gone to seek the bull on his own terms. And perhaps to prove that the creature he saw was not merely the residue of youth or hunger or dream."

Outside, a church bell sounded Terce, its note a low bronze shiver that seemed to settle upon the very floorboards beneath us.

Holmes looked toward the shuttered window.

"We shall follow him," he said simply. "For without the living bull, we cannot bargain for the Bonheur."

I nodded. "And how do we begin?" I asked.

Holmes gave a small, faint smile.

"By doing here in Spain what we could not do in a city like London, Watson—speak with the men who rise before the sun, retire long after it sets, those who work the earth, tread the hills, and know far more than they ever realize."

The Taverns of Pamplona

We descended through the twisting lanes of the old quarter, past shuttered balconies and iron lamps whose glass still held the night's shadow.

Holmes entered each tavern with the ease of a man who seemed merely to be passing through.

We questioned the baker's boy, the mule-driver with dust in his beard, the tavern girl sweeping last night's sawdust into neat, defeated piles.

Most shrugged, some lied with unnecessary vigour, and a few simply looked away, while others questioned us.

But in the fourth tavern, a low, timbered place that smelled of garlic and yesterday's wine, Holmes found help in an unexpected quarter

A young shepherd sat alone at a table near the rear, hunched over a bowl of *caldo*, steam curling against his weather-flushed face. His rough hands cupped the wooden bowl as though warming more than fingers.

His rope-soled sandals were worn nearly to threads, and his rough wool cloak bore the mud and dust of the very hills that had confounded us. His rustic staff leaned within reach against the scarred wooden table.

Holmes approached him without formality, as though joining an acquaintance he had always known.

"You were at the night fair the other night," Holmes said. "What is your name?"

The shepherd's spoon froze mid-air.

The boy glanced up, wary but not insolent.

"Miguelito," he said quietly, after a beat. "Señor."

Holmes continued,his voice gentle as a doctor's:

"And you saw something."

"A shadow," the shepherd muttered.

"A bull?" Holmes asked.

The boy hesitated—not the hesitation of deceit, but of fear.

"I don't know," he whispered. "It moved like one...but there were men with it. Three? Four? No lanterns. No voices."

Holmes leaned forward.

"Where?"

The shepherd lifted a trembling hand and pointed toward the north—

"Toward the Barranco del Silencio," he said. "The gorge where the water runs thin. No one goes there, señor. No one."

"Watson," Holmes said, "we have our road."

Holmes regarded the shepherd boy for a long moment—not unkindly.

"Your eyes," Holmes said softly, "see farther than most. And your ears listen to what the land whispers when the rest of Pamplona sleeps."

The shepherd's shoulders tightened. His spoon hovered, trembling.

Holmes reached into his coat and placed several folded notes, crisp and discreet, upon the scarred tavern table.

"This," Holmes continued, "is not a bribe, but a retainer, for vigilance."

The shepherd looked up, startled.

"You would hire me?"

"Not hire," Holmes corrected. "Enlist."

The shepherd boy stared at Holmes—first in disbelief, then with something far more delicate. His mouth parted, but no sound came, as though gratitude itself had tangled in his throat. At last he managed a small, bewildered nod.

"Me, Señor?" he whispered. "As... as one of your men?"

"Yes," Holmes said gently. "To watch for a bull unlike any other—deep blue, so dark it passes for black, bearing upon its left flank a white triangle sharp as a shard of moon."

At that, the shepherd's breath drew in sharply, his gaze darting toward the tavern door as though expecting eavesdropping shadows.

Holmes leaned in, voice low, urgent:

"If you see him—if anyone whispers of him—you come straight to us."

The shepherd boy stared at Holmes, eyes widening, breath caught between doubt and wonder. No one had ever enlisted him for anything but toil. His fingers curled around the notes as if afraid they might dissolve.

"I... I will not fail you, Señor," he said.

The shepherd sagged into silence.

Then, with a solemn nod, he scooped the notes from the table and tucked them inside the lining of his cloak.

"I will watch," he said. "For the bull... and for those who move with him."

CHAPTER XV

El Toro

The Ravine

By the time we left the village behind, the day had slipped toward its quieter hour. The sun was lowering imperceptibly; the shadows stretched long across the road. The air carried that peculiar stillness that comes just before dusk—when even the wind seems to hold its breath, and the heat of the day clings stubbornly to the stones.

Holmes walked ahead with a purpose sharpened by the shepherd boy's clue, his silhouette lengthening across the ground like a dark, deliberate arrow. The shepherd had spoken the name with a shiver—Barranco del Silencio—as though the gorge kept not only silence but secrets.

The road narrowed as we travelled, and the hills grew steeper, their edges carved by centuries of water. Somewhere ahead, beyond the folds of rock and shadow, lay the place where the boy said the bull might be driven, or hidden.

Holmes did not look back. He seldom does when the truth pulls him forward.

We climbed northward toward the Barranco del Silencio, where the land narrowed into a jagged throat of stone.

The ravine swallowed sound. Even our footsteps seemed reluctant to echo between its blackened walls.

A thin stream trickled along the base, more memory than river, its silver thread catching stray shards of daylight that filtered through the gash above.

Holmes knelt by the bank.

"Watson," he called.

I crouched beside him.

There, pressed into the damp clay: a broad, heavy hoofprint, deeper than any ox, wider than any domestic bull.

Beside it, the scar in the earth where a rope had dragged under great strain.

Holmes brushed his fingertips across the track.

"The creature struggled here," he whispered. "And men—strong men—forced it forward."

He rose at once, as if the ground had already told him all it could.

His eyes moved rapidly now—too quickly for comfort.

"Note the depth of the impressions," he continued. "Not merely dragged—checked. They halted him twice. See how the mud pools here, then again there. A rope slackened, then tightened."

He stepped aside and crouched near a scrub of thorn and broom.

"Here—fur."

A small tuft clung to the thorns, blue-black, coarse, unmistakably bovine.

"Pressed free, not torn. That tells us he was possibly weakened."

Holmes straightened, eyes narrowing at the ravine walls.

"Observe the stone," he said. "No scarring. No scrape. He was not hauled upward. And yet—"

He pointed with his cane.

"No blood. No broken stride. No sign of collapse."

He advanced several paces, then stopped abruptly.

"And here—boot marks. Four men, possibly five. One limps. Another favours the right foot. All similarly shod."

He tapped the earth once.

"The heels are reversed."

Holmes straightened and glanced toward the mouth of the ravine, where the land fell gently toward the distant roofs of Pamplona.

"They were not driving the animal into the countryside," he said quietly. "They were bringing it down from the country—toward the town."

Holmes watched the descending track.

"They intended to deliver him."

He lowered his cane.

"To whom—or to what—remains the question."

He lowered his cane.

"And that," he finished, "is where the trail ends."

He rose, scanning the escarpments.

Then—a voice behind us.

"I have seen him."

The Shepherd Returns

The shepherd emerged at the mouth of the ravine, cloak flung back, breath sharp with haste.

Holmes studied him with razor attention.

"When?" he asked.

"Not an hour ago," the shepherd panted. "Near the edge of town. But he is hidden."

Holmes exchanged a glance with me, a glance that told us both the shepherd was not lying.

"Lead us," Holmes said.

"Not now," the shepherd insisted. "You must come at night—when the lamps burn low."

"Why wait?" I asked.

"Because," the shepherd replied, "there are eyes during the day... eyes that will not welcome strangers."

The Arena

Night fell. The moon was full, round, silver, and silent.

The shepherd guided us through Pamplona's back streets, lanes so tight the moonlight could not enter. A labyrinth of streets unfolded like secrets between shuttered homes.

We passed the river, the tannery, the silent blacksmith forges where tools slept in embers.

At last he stopped at a wide, iron-gated structure that rose before us like a Roman ghost revived by moonlight.

The Plaza de Toros de Navarra.

The bullfighting arena.

Empty.

Cold.

Its arches breathed the faint odour of blood long dried and dust that remembered the roar of crowds.

Without a word, the shepherd slipped through a side postern where the lock had been recently broken.

We followed.

The great corridors of the arena stretched out before us, arched, echoing, their walls painted in old reds and ochres that seemed to vibrate in the darkness.

Then—a sound.

A low, resonant exhale, not quite breath, not quite thunder.

Holmes lifted a hand for silence.

We rounded the final arch into a small, dimly lit training stall.

And there, standing in the straw, massive shoulders rising and falling with the calm certainty of a sovereign creature, was

The bull.

Remington's bull.

The bull Remington had named

El Toro.

The deep-blue, white-marked titan Remington had seen, broad, proud, unharmed, alert, its flanks gleaming like onyx.

"That's him," Holmes whispered.

He stepped closer to the stall bars.

"Who steals a bull from monks," Holmes murmured, "only to hide him in the very heart of Pamplona's blood sport?"

The shepherd made the sign of the cross.

Holmes's eyes narrowed.

"Someone hid him here—in the arena," he said. "Which raises a question indeed."

He turned to us, voice low, resolute.

The bull shifted its weight in the stall, a quiet, ponderous movement, but in the hush of the night it sounded like the settling of a stone colossus.

Holmes had just bent closer to examine the lock when a new sound cut cleanly through the straw-laden silence:

Footsteps.

Unhurried.

Measured

Heavy strides,

That fell one by one.

Unmistakably human.

Growing nearer.

The shepherd stiffened beside me, hands clutching his cloak, eyes gone wide and white as an animal caught in sudden light.

"Señor Holmes..." he whispered.

Holmes lifted a hand for silence.

A figure passed between two arches, a broad silhouette, strong, bull-like, with a purposeful stride heading towards the stall.

We stepped back from the bars, Holmes placing himself fractionally ahead of me with that precise, almost ritual instinct he possessed when danger entered a room.

Then—

The figure crossed into the moonlight.

Holmes spoke, low and firm, without the faintest tremor of surprise:

"You have returned."

The moon poured its cold silver across him now—across the face we knew, the jaw set like quarried stone, the coat dusty from long travel, the expression strained with something between shame and stubborn resolve.

Remington.

He paused before us,breathing hard, as if he had walked far and fast to overcome a decision he had nearly let ossify.

The shepherd stood half in fear—for Remington looked, in that moment, larger than life, broader, taller, and all commanding.

Holmes regarded him evenly.

"You were at their house," Holmes said, "the aristocrats from the train."

Remington gave a curt nod.

"Since yesterday."

I stepped toward him.

"I thought you had left Navarra entirely," I said.

Remington gave a rough exhale—half laugh, half disgust at himself.

"They told me many things," he muttered. "Things about the Brotherhood. About the bull. About the manuscript. Things I thought—God help me—I wanted to hear."

He ran a hand through his hair, frustrated, chastened.

"But sometimes a man listens to the wrong voices for the right reasons."

Holmes's gaze narrowed.

"And what brought you back, Remington?"

Remington looked at the bull—his bull, El Toro—his shoulders thrown back, and his voice softened to something honest, stripped raw.

"I changed my mind," he said quietly. "Or maybe my mind changed me. Either way... I'm back."

Holmes inclined his head—not quite approval, but acceptance.

"And they told you the bull was here?" he asked.

"They told me much else," Remington replied bitterly. "Enough to know I needed to choose my own path—not theirs."

Holmes stepped beside him, his eyes shifting once more to the stall.

The Hand He Follows

The bull stood motionless in the half-dark, an obsidian monolith of breath and muscle.

Remington rolled up his sleeves, crouching at the lock with a grunt of annoyance.

"This is nothing but a cheap provincial padlock. Give me ten seconds and a nail, and I'll have the damned thing open."

Holmes studied the mechanism quietly.

"I suspect, Señor Remington, that the metal is not the true obstacle here. The chain may yield, yes—but the creature behind it..."

I stepped back a pace.

Holmes lean over beside him, studying the bull with that meditative stillness which always preceded one of his soft deductions.

"I suspect, Remington," he said, "observe the eyes: not frightened... merely aware. He knows we are intruders."

I peered past them and took another step back. The bull stood motionless, his hide a dark sheen in the lantern's glow, his breath rising in slow, heavy pulses from cavernous lungs. A cold knot tightened in my chest.

"For goodness' sake, Holmes," I said, "he's larger even than the accounts suggested. If he charges in this cramped stall, no wall—no prayer—will save us."

The bull shifted—one slow, deliberate movement. The sound of his hoof against packed earth reverberated like a muffled drum.

Remington laughed.

"Everything with four legs can be coaxed or driven. Give me a rope, and I'll—"

But he broke off, for a voice drifted out of the shadows behind us—soft, young, weathered, and carrying that curious authority possessed only by those who spend long years in open fields and say little while doing so.

The shepherd stepped forward. His cloak smelled faintly of lanolin and mountain air; his hands, roughened by work, rested easily at his sides as he surveyed the animal. His eyes rested upon the bull with something halfway between affection and awe.

"No rope will do," the shepherd said, stepping into the half-light. "No man here will make him move. Not by force. Not by tricks. This one yields only to a certain hand."

Holmes regarded him with interest.

"You speak as one familiar with him."

"Familiar?" The shepherd's mouth bent into a knowing smile. "I watched him from the day he staggered on new legs beside his mother. But I am not the hand he follows."

Remington straightened, irritation flaring.

"Then who in blazes is?"

"Only one," said the shepherd. "The man who fed him from a pail, who calmed him in storms, who walked him across the Arga when he first learned the scent of the water. Brother Mateo."

I blinked in surprise.

"Mateo? The quiet monk? I should never have imagined."

"That monk? With the black eye?" Remington asked.

"Aye, Doctor," the shepherd said, smiling knowingly. "Mateo was raised among cattle and calves. He knows their ways."

The shepherd gave a small shrug.

"This bull was born in a blizzard," he said. "Not a gentle snow, but the kind that blinds the hills and drives the ewes against the stone. His dam went down before dawn, and the calf lay half-frozen before any of us reached him."

He shifted his weight, eyes still on the bull.

"Brother Mateo carried him inside the monastery kitchen. Set him near the hearth where the bread is baked. Dried him with old wool blankets. Fed him warm milk from a bottle—every few hours, day and night. For three days he would not stand. Mateo would not leave him."

The shepherd's voice softened.

"When the storm passed and the calf found his legs, they put him back with his dam in the lower pasture. But by then the scent had fixed. The bull knows his mother, yes—but he knows Mateo as the hand that kept him in the world."

He lifted his chin toward the animal.

"That is not a thing a rope can untie."

The bull shifted—the faintest turn of the head. He snorted again, softer this time, as though the shepherd's words had stirred some buried recognition.

Holmes nodded slowly, absorbing the revelation. "Then the conclusion is simple," he said. "We cannot lead the bull by cunning, nor by strength. We must persuade Brother Mateo to do what logic and leverage cannot."

"Aye," the shepherd said. "He will lay his hand upon the bull's brow, and the beast will follow him as a child follows its father. But until then..."

His gaze flicked to Remington, who still held the nail.

I looked at Remington. "...I would put away your tool," I said. "This lock stays closed tonight, unless you wish to see us all pressed flat into the straw."

Remington grumbled but tucked the nail back into his pocket. "Fine. I'll leave the miracle-working to monks and detectives."

Holmes allowed himself a thin smile, stepping back, eyes thoughtful.

The bull stamped his hoof and breathed—slow, heavy, deep.

CHAPTER XVI

The House of del Castillo

Temptation and Consequence

The sun was gliding low over Navarra in slow, deliberate inches, steeping the sky in violets and rusted gold.

We found our privacy not in any tavern, nor beneath the watchful eaves of Pamplona's cramped streets, but beyond them, in a fallow field where the stubble of last season's harvest rasped faintly underfoot, and a low stone wall, half-collapsed, traced a crooked boundary against the darkening hills.

Holmes chose a flat stone and seated himself with the air of a man settling into an armchair in Baker Street. I took my place upon the wall itself, while Remington remained standing for a time, bottle in hand, as though reluctant to anchor himself in any one position.

At last he uncorked the wine with a practised twist, drank once, and handed it to me without ceremony.

"Well," he said. "You wanted to know what I saw."

Holmes inclined his head.

"I am always interested in what men see, Mr. Remington," he remarked. "Even more so in what they wish they had not."

Remington gave a short laugh.

"That about covers it," he said. "All right. I'll tell it straight."

He leaned back against the stone, his face turned partly toward the fading light, partly toward us.

"I went because they made it sound," he began, "like a door opening."

"Who?" I asked.

"Don Ramiro del Castillo and his wife," Remington replied. "They sent a car—a big, dark thing, with a driver who looked like he'd been carved out of the same hillside as the road. Up through the cypresses, past stone walls older than anything I've seen outside Italy. Iron gates with their crest—castle tower, lions, all that good old-story nonsense. I've seen rich houses in Paris, but this place—"

He gave a long, low whistle.

"It sits on the land," he said at last, "the way a man sits in a chair he thinks was made for him."

"And you went," Holmes said, "because flattery is a key that can open even the most stubborn of locks."

Remington did not deny it.

"They'd read something of mine," he went on. "A little piece about the fights. Nothing big. They talked about translations in Madrid, in Barcelona—maybe Buenos Aires. South America. They said Spain ought to have writers who understand her. They talked about 'helping the right voices find the right readers.'"

"And you," said Holmes, "are fond of right readers."

"I am fond of being read," Remington answered bluntly. "And of paying my bills without pawning my typewriter."

The Blight Beneath the Vines

"Before we drove to his house, he chauffeured me along the terraces of his vineyard in a big Hispano-Suiza that purred like a cat stuffed with money. He talked about heritage, about pride, about how his family's wine once graced courts from Madrid to Vienna."

Holmes gave a small, noncommittal hum.

Then Remington paused.

"He was trying to impress, no doubt. But I grew up around fields. Northern Michigan. You learn what sick crops look like. And his vines..." He shook his head slowly. "Leaves freckled yellow. Downy fuzz under the veins. Bark splitting where it shouldn't. Clusters turned to rot before they hit full fruit. And the soil—thin, eaten from below. I'd bet my last dime on phylloxera."

Holmes's gaze sharpened.

"A blight above and a parasite below," he observed. "A ruin no proud landowner admits."

"Oh, he admitted nothing," Remington said. "Kept calling them his jewels. His legacy. But a farm boy knows when land is dying.

"And I heard something else—from a servant who didn't mean to speak in my hearing. Three months ago an agricultural inspector came by. Declared the whole vineyard 'unfit for production.' Said it needed to be replanted. Expensive work. Ten years minimum. Maybe more."

Holmes was very still.

"Begin with the land," he said quietly. "Men lie; soil does not."

Then Holmes's expression shifted almost imperceptibly.

"And the lady of the house?" he inquired. "What of Doña Ysabel de Arriaga?"

Remington gave a short exhale that might have been amusement or bitterness.

"Oh, Doña Ysabel de Arriaga. Hard to miss. She carries herself like she owns not only the house but the century. Silk, jewels, the whole old-world arsenal. Her people were grandees back when half of Navarra was scrubland. She likes people to remember she's a distant relation of Queen Isabella. Says it softly, like it's nothing—but she watches to see if you flinch. She outranks Ramiro, and she knows it."

He paused, rubbing the back of his neck.

"She's polite as a cathedral statue and twice as cold. You get the feeling she expects worship. And that Ramiro—poor bastard—is always two steps behind the life she thinks he deserves. You can see him sweating under the weight of her expectations."

"A man may endure poverty," Holmes said. "But to be judged for it at his own table..."

He let the thought trail away.

"Poor devil. He's scrambling to keep pace with a woman who thinks the century owes her a throne."

The Man of the House

Remington continued, "Then we arrived at the main house, a long loggia with cool tiles underfoot, the courtyard, all stone and sun, with a single lavish fountain working in the middle, the stables smelling of good hay and better horses, servants moving like quiet machinery in the background.

"I was met at the front door by an icy German. At first he did not speak; he only watched. I mistook him for a butler and handed him my hat.

"He handed it back to me.

"He then introduced himself—Dr. von Helldorff, a veterinary surgeon from Munich. Tall, blond, built like a linebacker. His height and too-upright posture placed him uphill from the rest of the room. His suit was impeccable, straight from the haberdashers, not a blemish on it; his shoes polished like mirrors. He wore black gloves, immaculate, as though he expected the world to be untidy.

"We shook hands. He made sure I felt it.

"Next, I saw Doña Ysabel at the top of the stair, in red silk, smiling as though nothing could surprise her and everything, secretly, bored her. Her gaze lingered—intently—on von Helldorff.

"He did not seem to notice her at all; his attention remained fixed on me, measuring me, I suppose. Then she glanced toward me briefly before she descended, gliding rather than walking, with that smile people wear when they're about to give you something expensive that actually costs them nothing."

He mimed a little courtly gesture, dry as dust.

"She welcomed me 'as a friend of the house' and said they hoped I would honour them at a ceremony on the opening day of the fiesta. The usual civic theatrics—speeches, medals, a parade of egos in their Sunday best.

"Then Ramiro entered the room, puffed himself up like a rooster, talking about dignity and lineage. Said the Ayuntamiento and half the city's grandees would be there.

"Then he paused and looked at me with a hungry sort of pride.

"'An honour worthy of being witnessed. And recorded.'"

Holmes lifted his eyes.

"A public stage."

Remington's mouth twisted.

"Then he let the real bait drop. Said the Ayuntamiento intended to name their house *Protectores de la Tradición Navarra*—Protectors of Navarrese Tradition. A ribbon-and-seal sort of honour. But he said it with the hunger of a man who expects the whole city to kneel when they're done applauding."

Holmes's eyebrow rose a fraction.

"A public coronation."

"Exactly," Remington said. "And right on its heels, Ysabel leaned in, close enough for her perfume to do half the talking, and said they'd be presenting their 'prize bull' that same evening in a *corrida*—a bullfight.

"Then, Von Helldorff spoke, staccato, enunciating every syllable.

"'A demonstration of what lineage can achieve.'

"I didn't like the way he said 'demonstration.' Or the way Ramiro smiled when he did." He winced."You could see what it meant to them. It read more like a desperate attempt to reclaim the grandeur."

Remington's lip curled.

"That little ceremony? It's Ramiro trying to prove to his new wife—and to all of Navarra—that he's still the man at the head of the table. That he's in command of something... anything.

"Meanwhile, Miss Doña gave old Helldorff the big-eyes-and-smile treatment, Ramiro completely oblivious—or acting as such.

"Then I felt a flicker; my mind drifted back to El Toro.

"They were talking bulls now. Hell, there was something in the way they talked about bulls that didn't sit right.

"Ramiro talked the way old, foolish men talk—loud, broad, confident in memory rather than fact. But von

Helldorff listened, cold and exact, and when he spoke it was to measure, to correct, to reduce the animal to angles and limits. Weight. Muscle. Temperament. No poetry at all. Ramiro nodded in submission.

"Ramiro went on, describing the bull as aggressive, 'hot-blooded,' a creature that would charge at the first provocation.

"Von Helldorff shook his head once.

"'No,' he said quietly. 'He hesitates. Two beats, sometimes three. The bull prefers the left when pressed. That is not aggression. That is calculation.'

"Ramiro faltered, then laughed as if the distinction were trivial. 'Yes, yes—temperament,' he said, waving it away.

"But von Helldorff did not follow him.

"'A bull like that does not spend his strength proving himself,' von Helldorff said. 'He lets others exhaust themselves first.'

"Ramiro nodded then, slower this time.

"I understood it in that moment—that Ramiro paid him, yes. But it was Helldorff who shaped the thing, who decided what the bull would do before it ever stepped into the ring.

"Helldorff was in command. He was the architect of it all."

Remington gave a brief chuckle.

"Then von Helldorff took his shot.

"I felt it before I heard it.

"'You write about bulls, Señor Remington,' von Helldorff said briskly. 'But you observe them as a spectator. The animal does not know you are there.'

"It was clear enough what he was doing. He was trying to draw me in—make me commit early, make me charge.

"I stayed where I was."

Holmes spoke almost to himself.

"A vineyard dying... a wife from higher stock... whispers of incompetence—"

He closed his eyes for a brief moment.

"Yes, Watson. That combination could drive a proud man straight into the arms of folly—or worse, into the arms of a parasite bleeding him of wealth and dignity."

Remington nodded.

"Yeah. Exactly that. Whatever game Helldorff is playing with El Toro, Ramiro is going to get the worst of it."

Saints for Sale

"Only then," he added, "did they invite me into the portrait-laden salon.

"They sat me down in a room with too many portraits on the walls. Dead men with good chins and bad consciences, all of them holding swords or wearing medals.

"Ramiro strutted to a painting above the mantel, arms spread as though he meant to embrace it. Doña Ysabel glided to his side and rested her head lightly against his shoulder. He seemed to swell with pride.

"'Nice painting,' I said.

"'This is not just a painting—this is an El Greco!' Ramiro said, his voice rising with excitement.

"'A St Francis,' he added. 'Early. From Toledo.'

"'Dr. von Helldorff has many connections on the continent,' Doña Ysabel said, her smile gleaming. 'He acquired this rare piece for us. He understands the art world—as well as the artefacts of antiquity.'

"Von Helldorff turned his cold gaze on me. 'Do you appreciate fine art?'

"I did not answer at once. I read the brass plate affixed to the frame—

SAINT FRANCIS IN MEDITATION

"Then my eyes moved to the signature, bold and confident in the lower corner.

"I said nothing.

"Helldorff said the Germans understand these things. 'The face alone—look at it. Peace. Authority.'"

Remington tilted his head slightly, remembering the angle of it, the way the light sat on the paint.

"'The saint did look peaceful,' I agreed.

"But I was also thinking—

"'Well fed.

"'Comfortable.

"'And plump.'

"Something was off. The El Grecos I've seen—especially the saints—they're usually gaunt.

"Ascetic.

"Stretched thin.

"Almost skeletal in spiritual tension, like the soul pulling the body upward."

He shook his head once, a small, private gesture.

"I thought about saying it. Right there. But when I saw old Ramiro beaming like a schoolboy, I decided against it."

He glanced up at Holmes.

"And what were you thinking?" I asked him.

He shook his head again, faintly amused.

"'A chubby El Greco,' I was thinking, 'is probably a fake El Greco.'"

Holmes gave a short, dry laugh, and I could not help but follow it.

Remington allowed himself a mischievous smile—took a sip of wine and continued his story.

"Then Von Helldorff stepped forward, just enough to place himself between me and the painting. One gloved hand rested lightly on the frame, possessive rather than protective.

"'Art,' he said evenly, 'is often misunderstood by Americans—who require a dollar sign to recognise value, and whose national taste has a regrettable tendency toward the superficial.'

"I met his eyes and said nothing.

"I think," he said, "Helldorff didn't care for the idea that I was onto his grift."

Holmes added, "Quite," he said, smiling. "The art market is an ideal instrument for a man of peculiar talents. Subjective values. Private sales. Reverence replacing verification."

"I didn't say anything at the time," Remington said. "But I reckon he has the Del Castillos so hypnotized he could sell them the Brooklyn Bridge."

Holmes inclined his head.

"Those who attempt to purchase authority," he said softly, "betray how little of it they possess."

Order and Ownership

"Don Ramiro poured the wine himself, which is supposed to make you feel honoured. It just made me watch his hands."

"And what did those hands do?" Holmes asked.

"They pointed," Remington said. "At maps. At me. At documents. At a painting of a bull that wasn't as good as Bonheur's bronze."

Remington sank down onto the low wall then, forearms on his knees, bottle dangling from one hand.

"Then I asked them about the gold bull's-horn pendant," Remington said. "Not straight out. I let it sit between us."

Holmes nodded. "And?"

"Ramiro said it was a 'mark of distinction. Old families. Old blood.'" Remington said, shaking his head as corked the wine bottle.

"Doña Ysabel said she thought I'd 'wear it well.' Said I had the 'look of a man who respected strength.'

"La Sociedad del Oro Antiguo," Remington stated. "That's what they called it."

"The Society of the Ancient Gold," I said.

"I asked what it was for," Remington explained.

"And they told you?" Holmes inquired.

"Not exactly, the Del Castillos spoke of the bull as if it were a title," he said. "'Our bull. The Castillo bull.' An animal 'fit to bear the name of the house'—that's how he put it.

"He talked about bloodlines—how the monks at San Telmo were 'simple men' who didn't understand what they had, how an animal of that quality belonged under the care of people who could 'present it properly to the world.'"

"Present it," Holmes repeated. "Interesting verb."

Remington glanced at him, a hard light in his eyes.

"Oh, he dressed it up," he said. "Talked about tradition. About the honour of Navarra. About how the foreigners would come and see a true Spanish bull in the ring and remember it all their lives."

"And you objected?" I ventured.

"Not at first," Remington admitted. "I know what bulls are for. I've watched enough tardes in the sun to understand that. But something in the way they talked..."

He searched for the phrase.

"They talked about the bull," Remington said slowly, "the way some men talk about a woman they plan to marry for her dowry. All prize, no respect.

"All the while, von Helldorff said nothing. As Ramiro rambled, he watched me instead with a predatory stare—quiet, steady, piercing—long enough that I noticed, and long enough that I knew he wanted me to notice.

"Ramiro, who had been drinking excessively, laughed too loudly and reached for his glass. It slipped from his hand and shattered at von Helldorff's feet.

"Von Helldorff looked down at his shoe—

"Polished.

"Creaseless.

"Black leather.

"And frowned.

"He bent, selected a shard from his shoe, brushed the rest aside with the edge of his gloved hand, and straightened.

"He crushed the glass shard between his fingers and thumb. There was a soft sound. Nothing else.

"He dropped what remained into the ashtray and and turned only his eyes toward Ramiro, who was still rambling."

Remington removed his hat, brushed his fingers through his hair, and continued.

"...rambling on about how they wanted the bull—shown to the world as 'their bull.' Owned, branded, displayed in the arena like 'a family crest in motion.' And they wanted my words to paint them as 'guardians of tradition, noble house, ancient rights,' and so forth."

Remington paused, then said more flatly, "Mind you, this is the same Ramiro who couldn't keep a vineyard alive for five years running. Now he talks like he's been raising bulls all his life."

He gave a half smile.

"Back home we'd call a man like that all hat and no cattle."

He drew a breath.

"And later?" Holmes pressed.

"Later," Remington said, "they stopped talking in specifics and started talking in metaphors. 'Strong symbols must make strong impressions.' 'A great bull deserves a great death.' That kind of thing. They didn't say they'd put him down in the ring. But you could hear it under the talk."

Remington, stopped and raised his eyes toward the distant outline of the arena, just visible against the dying light.

Then Remington continued. "Straightening his cuff, von Helldorff said, 'The world would read it and see there was still strength here, still discipline, still... order.'"

The last word landed between us like a weight.

"Order?" Holmes repeated.

"Von Helldorff," Remington said. "He's the one who kept using the word. Strong hands. On the land. In the ring. In the state. He never praised dictators outright—he's too careful for that—but he spoke as if disorder were a disease. Said people were 'like children,' better governed by firm fathers than noisy assemblies

"Von Helldorff said, clipped, brushing an invisible speck from his sleeve, 'The monks have no right to keep something so "important" hidden away in a field like a fat ox.'"

Remington paused and took a sip of wine, then continued.

"I asked if they meant to ask the monks, at least.

"To buy him. Deal fairly.

"Ramiro laughed. Ysabel smiled. They said the monks had already shown themselves unworthy, taking the bull without 'proper guardianship.' That they had 'simply corrected a wrong.'

"They talked about the monks as thieves. About peasants as animals. About the bull as a banner they could wave over all of Navarra. They said with my book, when I rewrote it, they could help it into Spanish, into South America. They said a writer needs patrons.

"I nodded anyway. You nod, sometimes, when you need to see the inside of a thing before you decide how to blow it open."

Holmes's fingers steepled, the familiar gesture at once contemplative and sharp.

"And you?" Holmes asked again. "Where did you fit in their design?"

Remington took another drink before answering. His mouth tightened.

"That," he said, "is where the wine turned sour."

He drew a breath.

"Von Helldorff told me I was wasting myself," Remington said. "That I had talent enough to matter but not discipline enough to be useful. I could stop circling the margins and write something that would endure. He said a man doesn't build anything of substance sitting in cafés."

Remington looked down at the bottle of wine in his hand.

"Then they started talking about how a man like me should be grateful for the backing of a great house. That I could stop wasting my time with little magazines and 'lost boys' and write something that would 'last'—something that made the right people look good.

"They didn't want a story," Remington said. "They wanted *their* story. I was just their typewriter."

"And you," I asked quietly, "are not willing to do that."

Remington looked at me—steady, unflinching.

"I don't mind writing about blood," he said. "I just won't lie about whose blood is being spilled."

The Bull and his Keeper

Remington's fingers tightened slightly upon his knee.

"And here's where I finally decided I was done with them all," Remington said, shaking his head.

"Von Helldorff had already turned away. Someone spoke to him in a low voice near the doors, and he went out without excuse or apology, his attention shifting as easily as a man changing tools.

"Helldorff went to speak with their ranch hand," Remington added. "A real piece of work. Big bastard. Hands like hammers. Missing his left ear."

Remington's jaw clenched.

"He stood there like he owned half the mountain. He glared at me through the doorframe, like he was measuring how hard I'd bounce if he threw me down the hill."

He spat dryly into the dust.

"I didn't like him. And he didn't bother hiding that he didn't like me.

"Earlier, I watched him shove a brittle old servant aside. The man nearly dropped a tray of wineglasses."

Holmes nodded, his eyes closed.

"And later the brute," Remington said, "kicked a stable dog out of his path. Harmless old mastín, grey around the muzzle, tail wagging like it thought every man was its friend. The bastard lifted his boot and sent it yelping." He paused, his breath tightening.

"I saw red. Felt like a bull in the chute waiting for the gate to crack open. I was halfway to charging the man when Doña Ysabel called my name—sharp, practised timing—like she'd seen the whole thing and didn't want her rugs spoiled."

Holmes's gaze sharpened, the faintest narrowing of the eyes. "Such men," he noted, "betray more than temperament. They reveal the character of those who employ them."

I felt my stomach tighten. "A man who mistreats the weak will do far worse when no one is watching."

"The dog," Remington said with a wry smile, "was the only member of the house I liked."

He spat into the dirt beside his boot.

"God help any animal under that bastard's care," he growled.

"It got me thinking about a creature like El Toro—thinking and worried.

"That's why I came back. We need to free the bull from this bastard before he breaks him."

Holmes was silent for a moment, weighing the words.

He rose, brushing dust from his coat with an absent hand. "Come," he said quietly. "We must return to the monastery.

"Santiago deserves the good news—that his bull lives—and the bad, that others have already laid claim to him."

CHAPTER XVII

Iron and Gold

The Battle Line

Dawn rose divided above the hills of San Telmo. To the east, a thin blade of gold cut the horizon; to the west, night lingered in heavy indigo folds. The monastery walls caught the first light, while the valley below remained in shadow. For a brief and uneasy interval, darkness and day stood side by side upon the stone.

Holmes walked ahead of us, the two pendants—iron and gold—tucked into his coat pocket, the riddle that drove him onward.

Remington strode beside him, silent and taut, a man whose trust in reason had been jarred by the strange hospitality of the Del Castillos a couple of nights before—their charm, their champagne, their unsettling talk of bulls, blood, and lineage.

And I followed, feeling as though we walked not toward a monastery but toward the heart of a labyrinth.

The great oak door of San Telmo opened at our approach before Holmes could lift his hand to knock.

Brother Santiago stood framed in the doorway, eyes shadowed, lips tight.

Holmes did not greet him.

He stepped into the monastery without invitation, Santiago forced to follow.

Holmes did not sit.

"Brother Santiago," he said, "I have returned to determine whether we should help you retrieve the bull."

Something shifted in the friar's face. His eyes widened with hope and concern.

Holmes did not so much as pause.

"We have found your bull.

"Yet what we have not found is truth."

Santiago shifted his weight, his gaze drifting upward over Holmes's shoulder toward the sixteenth-century triptych—Christ kneeling in the Garden of Gethsemane, dawn approaching.

"Truth," he repeated quietly.

"Consider our position, Brother Santiago," Holmes said, his gaze narrowing with that surgical lucidity which unsettled far sterner men. "We stand, through no intention of our own, between two opposing forces."

Holmes took a breath and continued.

"Your brethren have—

"Stolen a Bonheur sculpture of no small significance.

"Destroyed a manuscript belonging to our companion.

"And conveyed their displeasure by way of nocturnal threats and furtive violence.

"Yet those who have taken your bull prove no more virtuous." He removed the gold bull-horn pendant from his jacket pocket.

"Thieves as well—only of an eighteen-karat variety.

"Purchasing allegiance with bribery,

"Seducing it with charm,

"And sealing it with champagne.

"If you desire the return of your creature—alive and uninjured, as it presently remains—then I must insist upon the truth.

"For the moment, Brother Santiago, I cannot say upon which side of this battle line a man of reason ought to stand.

"One faction," Holmes continued,

"Steals in the night.

"Hides in cloisters.

"Destroys manuscripts.

"Issues its warnings by shadow and shoves."

His fingers turned the pendant once—no more—and let it fall back against his palm.

"The other," he went on,

"Steals in daylight.

"Rides in fine automobiles.

"Issues commands,

"And drifts above society—purchasing coercion at every level."

Santiago did not move.

His eyes, however, had not left the gold bull-horn pendant.

Then his eyes gazed upward toward the painting. He was muttering something that sounded like prayers.

Holmes leaned toward him.

"What we have is iron against gold—gold against iron. Both factions of the Brotherhood," Holmes went on, "have enlisted our help."

Santiago turned back toward Holmes, his face exhausted and paled by the inquiry. He attempted to compose himself.

"Señor Holmes," Santiago began, his voice trembling with the weight of confession.

"We are not thieves.

"Nor men who delight in force.

"We are men of peace.

"Formed for prayer, not for shadows."

Brother Mateo, his eye still bruised, hurried into the room.

"*¿Todo está bien, hermano Santiago?*" Mateo asked, his voice low but urgent.

Is everything all right, Brother Santiago?

Santiago crossed himself.

"*Hermano... la Casa del Castillo ha contactado a este hombre. ¿Qué haremos ahora?*"

Brother... the House of Castillo has contacted this man. What shall we do now?

Santiago's head dropped quickly to meet Holmes's gaze. His eyes were wide with fear.

His hands tightened around his rosary until the beads clicked softly.

"What we did—*Dios nos perdone*—was not done with pride, nor with ease.

"It was a grievous choice, made in fear, not malice. And yes... a poor choice."

He bowed his head.

"For that, señor, I offer you my apology with all the humility I possess."

Santiago drew a deep breath.

"I was told the sculpture would be kept safe."

He lifted his hands, palms upward.

"I will bring the Bonheur sculpture back with my own hands. And if there are other wrongs standing between us...allow me the chance to mend them, to make them right, as far as a flawed servant of God is able."

"First," Holmes said, "you will tell me everything—about the two factions of the Brotherhood of the Toro Bravo, and why I should help yours at all."

Santiago did not answer at once. He stood very still, hands folded within his sleeves.

"There are matters," he said finally, "that are not spoken of freely—even among brothers."

Santiago bowed his head.

"For generations," he said quietly, "we have kept silence. Not because we are ignorant, Señor Holmes—but because knowledge, once shared, demands allegiance."

Holmes's eyes hardened a fraction.

"Allegiance," Holmes repeated.

Santiago sighed.

"For your sake, Señor Holmes," he said at last, "and for his " he nodded toward Remington—"I think you must hear it."

He hesitated.

"But not from me."

Holmes raised an eyebrow.

"Because you cannot—or because you will not?"

Santiago looked up then, meeting his gaze squarely.

"Because I am forbidden," he said. "And because if I speak, I fear the bull you hold will never return to us alive."

Then Santiago turned toward the cloister door.

"There is one," he said, "who may speak of this without breaking his vows."

He glanced back once.

“He knows more than I do.”

Santiago exhaled.

“Brother Elías.”

Holmes straightened.

“Then lead us,” he said.

CHAPTER XVIII

Zezen isilak

The Silent Bulls

Below us, in a narrow fold of the ravine, the Archivo Diocesano de Navarra came into view, a long, rectangular building of pale limestone, its exterior worn by centuries of wind.

Above the main doorway, set into a shallow façade niche, stood a weathered stone effigy of San Fermín. His mitre was chipped, the crozier worn smooth by wind, yet the posture retained an unyielding dignity, as if the saint had been appointed to watch over the Archive.

Even Remington lifted his head to regard it, and for a moment the restless American stood as still as the stone saint above us.

Santiago pushed open the heavy wooden door.

We stepped into a chamber cool as a crypt, its air faintly tinged with vellum, dust, and the subtle sweetness of old beeswax left undisturbed for centuries.

Shelves climbed the walls to impossible heights, stacked with ledgers bound in flaking leather, parchment rolls tied with unraveling cords, manuscripts whose edges were curled like dried leaves.

A single candle burned at the far end, near a desk cluttered with quills, a chipped bowl of ink, and a pile of scrolls weighted by a river stone.

There sat Brother Elías de Órbigo, wearing the white habit of the Cistercians—over it hung the long, narrow black scapular.

He raised his head slowly as we approached.

His face was long and pale; his eyes magnified behind owl-like spectacles.

"Santiago," he rasped, "you bring guests."

"These men come under my protection," Santiago replied.

Elías regarded each of us in turn, not with welcome, but with scrutiny.

"This Englishman is Señor Holmes," Santiago continued, "a seeker of truths. This is Dr Watson. And the tall one, Señor Remington. They have come to learn of los toros,"

The monk considered this a moment.

"Very well," he said at last.

"Let the archives speak."

Holmes inclined his head with a formality that I recognised as his salute to intellect.

Without further ceremony he unlocked a drawer and removed several ancient ledgers.

"These," he said quietly, "are the herd records of Navarra."

Holmes leaned forward at once.

"Show me the earliest."

Elías opened a volume whose brittle pages bore the date 1573. The script was angular and severe—Basque characters pressed into the page like knife marks.

Holmes traced the ink with a long finger.

"Watson," he said quietly, "observe the phrase written here."

I leaned closer.

"Zezen isilak."

"What does it signify?" I asked.

"The silent bulls," Elías translated.

"A term used by those who tended a line of bulls raised in the high Pyrenees—long before Pamplona bore its present name."

Remington stepped nearer.

"You're telling me the bull I saw in the field belongs to a line older than Spain?"

"Older than her crowns," said Elías. "Older than her cathedrals."

He turned another page.

"These bulls bear a name among the mountain people 'Los Toros del Silencio.' The Bulls of Silence."

A hush settled upon the room.

"They make little sound," Elías said. "Even as calves they watch more than they cry. The bulls are gentle by nature—almost contemplative creatures."

Elías exhaled slowly.

"Los Toros possessed a rare temperament—"

He held up one finger.

"Intelligence."

A second.

"Courage."

A third.

"Strength tempered with an astonishing calm. They follow a trusted hand like dogs.

"They are peaceful when unprovoked, but when wronged"—Elías raised his voice as he tilted his head back—"when cornered or threatened, they become utterly wild—the fiercest animals in Spain."

Elías continued. "Monks and herdsmen prize them for their sweetness. Toreros prize them for their ferocity. Only the rarest matador survives such an encounter. Breeders covet them for profit."

Elías closed another ledger and rested his hand upon it. "But the lineage is dying. Our cows have died off. Our bulls, once a dozen, are now but one. Only El Toro remains."

Remington's jaw tightened, his voice scraping low in his throat. "Only one left?" he exclaimed. "How in hell does that happen?"

"Not suddenly," Elías replied.

He lifted his eyes. "Last season, there was a winter in the high Pyrenees unlike any in memory. It also reached Pamplona. Relentless snow. Harsh, unforgiving winds. Followed by ice that did not thaw."

Santiago added, "Before the big winter, we had a herd of two dozen cattle and three bulls. One week after heavy snow, the roof of our barn at San Telmo collapsed. Some cattle were injured, some worse. Yet we managed to..."

Santiago crossed himself.

"...to save what we could," Santiago continued, "we brought the survivors down. Near villages. Near estates. Under roofs not our own, crowded lowland barns where foreign stock had already brought disease.

"When the winter ended," he said quietly, "the line had already broken."

Elías folded his hands within his sleeves and spoke next. "The cattle lost in the storm were the last of the San Telmo herd. El Toro remains our only survivor." He hesitated. "There are whispers of another herd, protected high in the mountains."

He exhaled, as though setting down a burden long carried.

"The females of this ancient lineage—those born in the Pyrenees long before the Brotherhood existed—produced a milk so pure it was spoken of in Navarra with reverence. A blessing in quiet times. A danger in desperate ones."

Santiago folded his hands.

"A bull such as this draws men," he said.

"Not all of them honest."

Santiago drew a sharp breath—the breath of a man gathering courage.

"I should have told you sooner, Señor Holmes. But as you are English, and you, Señor Remington... American, I hesitated."

His hands folded slowly. He lifted his eyes then, first to Holmes, then to Remington, and something like resignation settled across his features.

"And so," he said, "I will speak plainly."

Santiago drew a breath.

"I will tell you why we took your—"

Holmes spoke without looking up from the ledger.

"Because you feared it."

The monk stopped.

Holmes turned a page of the ancient record with delicate fingers.

"Not the manuscript itself," he added mildly.

"What it would set in motion."

Santiago stared at him.

"You believe we feared... a book?"

Holmes finally lifted his eyes.

"No," he said.

"I believe you feared the men who would read it."

Silence filled the archive.

Santiago continued."Señor Remington, your country is vast, wealthy, and hungry for legend. Your book, once published in America, would ignite imaginations across the Atlantic."

A silence followed, long, taut, and strangely reverent, as though some unseen door had just swung inward upon darker corridors.

Remington stood there aghast. "You fear... readers?"

Santiago rose, paced once, stopped.

"Yes," he said. "Readers such as these."

He gestured faintly toward the ledger.

"Ranchers. Breeders. Speculators. Men who, after reading your book, would seek to purchase a bull, or the cows, and carry them to North America... to Mexico... to the far reaches of Central and South America. A single novel could make Los Toros del Silencio a global obsession, more famous than any Spanish festival."

Santiago bowed his head.

"If these bulls cross the ocean, Señor Remington... they will not survive long as themselves. The land will change them. The breeding will change them. American ranchers would come and seek these bulls—Texas, Colorado, Kansas... places where the lineage would be bred in careless abundance. American ranchers mixing the line with Angus, Hereford, or Longhorn stock."

Elías shook his head, gaze lowered. "And now perhaps you understand our fear—strangers scouring the high mountains, taking the few cattle that still live."

He drew a slow breath.

"The American threat is simply this, in two generations—three at most—what remains will be only the shell, a silhouette masquerading as heritage. The calm intelligence... the winter endurance... the curved Pyrenean horn...All gone."

Holmes tapped the ledger lightly.

"And abundance," he said, "kills rarity."

Holmes leaned back slightly, his eyes reflecting the candle's blue-gold flicker.

He paused, looking directly at Santiago.

"So you took the sculpture," Holmes went on, "not to profit from it, but to conceal it from the world.

"Bonheur provides the visual image of your bull," Holmes said. "Remington's book would have given the bull an international voice."

Remington drew a slow breath.

Santiago nodded.

"Señor," he said, "we are not thieves by habit. But we are guardians. There is a difference."

Holmes did not blink.

Santiago continued, his hands—those weathered, pasture-roughened hands—tightening around the rosary at his belt.

"My brother lives in Paris," he began. "He works at a café near Montparnasse... a place where many Americans dine. Writers. Painters. Travellers. He hears much."

He hesitated, ashamed.

"He overheard Señor Remington speaking of two things: his book...and a bronze bull he admired."

Remington looked intently at Santiago.

Santiago stepped closer.

“Understand this Señor Holmes: the Bonheur bronze is not merely a statue. It is the most accurate likeness ever made of the ancient Pyrenean bull.”

Holmes said nothing.

Santiago continued, his voice tightened.

“If that sculpture were bought by an American—if copies were cast, shown, photographed, displayed in some magazine—it would ignite curiosity far beyond Spain.

“The manuscript would create desire in the mind. But the statue...”

He raised his hand as though holding the bronze in the air, the statue would create desire in the eyes.”

Elías added. “And the eyes are the master of the passions.”

Remington agreed with a smile, “Once a man has seen a thing, he’ll cross an ocean to have it. Hell—they launched a thousand ships for Helen of Troy.”

CHAPTER XIX

The Man Without an Ear

The Deed

Brother Elías had scarcely finished speaking when a heavy blow struck the archive door.

The sound echoed along the stone chamber like a hammer striking a tomb.

No one moved.

A second blow followed by another—slower, more deliberate.

The candle flame trembled.

Brother Elías turned toward the door, his spectacles catching the wavering light.

Before he could speak, the latch lifted.

The door swung inward with a heavy, deliberate force.

A man entered.

He was of formidable build, broad through the shoulders and thick in the neck, with the slow and confident gait of one accustomed to obedience rather than conversation. A dark riding coat hung from his frame, and at his belt rested a long knife whose horn handle had been polished by years of use.

But what struck the eye most forcibly was the left side of his head.

Where an ear ought to have been there remained only a rough crescent of scarred flesh.

Santiago stiffened at once.

The man's gaze passed over us one by one with a sort of lazy contempt, as though he were counting cattle rather than men.

At last his attention settled upon Remington.

The American returned the look without moving so much as a finger.

The fellow smiled slightly.

It was not a pleasant smile.

Without greeting or apology he stepped forward and placed a folded parchment upon the table before Brother Elías.

"For you. For the records," he said.

His voice was low and coarse.

Elías looked at the document but did not touch it.

"What is this?"

"Ownership," the man replied.

Holmes had already lifted the parchment.

He opened it slowly and studied the page by the candlelight.

I observed his eyes move across the seal, the signature, and the elaborate flourish of script beneath it.

For a moment he said nothing.

Then, very softly—so softly I doubt any man but myself heard it—he murmured:

"Forged."

The brute's head turned.

"Did you say something, Englishman?"

Holmes folded the parchment with care and returned it to the table.

"Nothing addressed to you," he said calmly.

Brother Elías adjusted his spectacles and examined the document with trembling fingers.

The seal of Don Ramiro del Castillo shone red and official upon the parchment.

Santiago crossed himself.

"El Toro... belongs to them now?" he asserted.

The brute hit his palm with his fist.

"The law has spoken."

Santiago looked stricken.

"But the bull—"

"The bull," the man interrupted, "belongs to who holds the deed."

His hand drifted casually to the horn handle of the knife at his belt.

"Del Castillo."

Holmes said nothing.

But I saw the faintest tightening in his expression.

The brute now turned his attention fully toward Remington.

"And you," he said slowly.

"You are the American who writes stories."

Remington did not answer.

The fellow leaned forward slightly.

"Tell me something."

He tapped the parchment.

"Does your book explain how quickly a bull can die?"

The air in the room seemed suddenly to grow colder.

Remington rose.

Not abruptly.

But with the slow deliberation of a man who has decided that sitting is no longer an option.

He was taller than the brute by nearly half a head.

The two men regarded one another across the narrow table.

"I've seen bulls die," Remington said quietly. "Have you?"

The brute's smile widened. "Many."

"Then you should know something," Remington replied.

"What is that?"

"That bulls are not the only things that bleed."

For the first time the brute's eyes hardened.

His fingers tightened slightly upon the knife handle.

Santiago stepped between them at once.

"Señores—this is a house of God."

The brute glanced at him as one might glance at a troublesome child.

Then he released the knife.

He straightened and looked again toward Holmes.

"Three days," he said.

His voice had lost all trace of amusement.

"On the seventh... the bull will stand in the arena."

Santiago whispered hoarsely, "The feast of San Fermín..."

The brute's eyes moved once more to Remington.

"And if any man interferes with that arrangement..."

He let the sentence remain unfinished.

Holmes, who had thus far remained silent, spoke at last.

"In my experience," he said mildly, "arrangements founded upon false documents tend not to endure."

The brute stared at him.

He kicked the old chair aside with his boot and slowly drew the knife from his belt.

For a moment I thought he meant to strike.

Instead he drove the blade deep into the soft wood of the table between them.

The candle toppled over and went out.

The brute leaned close to Holmes, his ruined ear catching the last trace of light.

"Well, Englishman... I find foreigners what overstay their welcome don't endure much themselves."

Then he tore the knife free from the table and strode from the archive. The heavy door closed behind him with a hollow reverberation.

A deep scar remained in the old wood where the blade had struck.

For several seconds none of us spoke.

Then Remington exhaled slowly.

"Well," he muttered.

"That fellow certainly improves the atmosphere of a room."

Holmes reached once more for the parchment.

"On the contrary," he said.

"He improves the clarity."

He studied the seal again and allowed himself the faintest smile.

“Yes,” Holmes murmured.

“Quite forged.”He said calmly.

Holmes tapped the page.

“The ink is new.”

Another tap.

“The parchment artificially aged.”

Another.

“...and the seal,” Holmes continued, “is particularly unfortunate.”

I asked.“Unfortunate?”

Holmes smiled “...for the forger. It belongs to a bishop who died twelve years ago.”

CHAPTER XX

Three Days

Ancient Gold

Remington reached up, removed the gold bull-horn pendant from around his neck, and turned it once in his fingers.

Then he tossed it into the waste bin beside the desk.

"Well," he said, dusting his hands together, "good-bye fame... good-bye fortune."

Santiago spoke. "Señor Holmes... the pendants are not ornaments. They are allegiances."

Holmes stopped pacing. "Two rails of the same train," he said. "Running toward us."

"At the beginning," Elías said, "there was only the Brotherhood of the Toro Bravo—keepers of the cattle, united in a single purpose.

"But as the years passed—centuries—men began to see the cattle differently. As wealth. As power. As something to be traded... and bred for the ring. They concerned themselves with status, and with how the outside world might judge our land. The bulls became symbols.

"And so the Brotherhood divided. Irreconcilable. Two opposing visions.

"One iron... the other gold.

"In the Pyrenees, before the Romans set foot in Navarra, before roads and legions, there were Basque shepherd families who guarded the bulls. They were an inheritance—passed on as one passes a prayer, unchanged. These families called themselves Los Hermanos Custodios—the Custodian Brothers.

"The other," Elías continued, "call themselves La Sociedad del Oro Antiguo—the Society of Ancient Gold. They are men of nobility and high birth. They believe the bulls are meant to be shown, to be traded—and to fight. That Navarra should be known by its strength. That what is hidden is wasted."

Remington frowned.

"Old Gold... that's the del Castillos' game, isn't it?"

Both Elías and Santiago nodded.

Holmes's gaze remained fixed upon them—waiting.

"These men look upon the bulls," Santiago said, his voice thinning as if the air itself had tightened, "not as trust... but a sacrifice for the arena."

Remington's hand slapped the table. "The arena," he said.

"The arena," Santiago echoed, and made the sign of the cross again—but this time it looked less like piety than warding.

Holmes drew a slow breath and stepped nearer to the table, fingers grazing its edge.

"Brother Santiago," he said quietly, "you need not search the hills any longer. Your bull is not in the mountains."

Santiago's head snapped up.

"El Toro is in Pamplona," Holmes continued, his voice low but unyielding, "at the arena. The stalls of the Plaza de Toros."

For a heartbeat the friar did not breathe.

"We found him there two nights ago," I added. "Locked fast. Guarded—though clumsily."

Santiago pressed a trembling hand to his mouth.

"In the arena?" he whispered. "But... how? How could they move him so far, so quietly?"

"I do not yet know," Holmes said. "Only this—El Toro would not follow us. He stood as a mountain; even Remington could not coax him. The beast would not take a single step."

"He waits for one hand, and one alone. Mateo's." Santiago grinned slightly.

"Yes," he said. "He raised the bull from a calf. Fed him from his palm. Led him through storms. El Toro trusts no other living man."

Santiago's face blanched.

"Three days," he cried. "Only three days... and then..."

He broke off.

"They will wound him."

He gripped the back of a chair as though steadying the earth beneath him.

"They will kill him."

Remington nodded angrily. "The del Castillos want to sacrifice El Toro so that they can have their day in the sun and crown their lies with his blood.

"From that moment," Remington said, "the del Castillos possess more than an animal. They possess the story."

"A great bull slain before the eyes of the city," Holmes added. "His lineage sealed not by pasture, but by blood."

A sick unease settled in my stomach.

Then Remington rubbed his eyes in frustration and said bitterly, "Then they will name him the greatest bull of his generation and praise his heroic death before all Spain."

Santiago sank into the wooden chair as though his strength had suddenly left him.

"Well," Remington growled, "we'd better drag El Toro the hell out of there before the seventh."

And no one disagreed.

How Do We Fight Money?

Elías nodded.

Santiago turned stricken eyes toward Holmes.

"What are they doing? Why?"

Holmes looked from Santiago to Remington, then to the parchment, and finally toward the shuttered windows, where the wind of the Pyrenees pressed softly as an unseen witness.

"They are doing," he said, "what desperate men always do when power slips from their grasp. They seize. They falsify. They claim. And they sacrifice what does not belong to them."

His voice sank to an inevitable conclusion.

"And unless we intervene, they will sacrifice your bull, your legacy, to restore a name already collapsing under its own rot."

Remington pleaded,

"But how do we fight money?"

Santiago folded his hands, and when he spoke again his voice carried that tremulous weight which only a man of faith can summon when reason begins to fray.

"Señor Remington, we fight with a force more powerful than money."

He lifted his rosary slightly.

"We fight with faith."

He looked from Holmes to Remington, then finally to me, as though seeking the agreement of every soul present.

"Señor Holmes... we, all of us, must go to Mass this Sunday, July sixth."

Holmes lifted an eyebrow in a questioning arch.

Remington breathed out a sigh.

"At the Cathedral of Santa María. The great one. The whole of Navarra walks beneath its vaults on feast days. The del Castillos will be there... their allies of Ancient Gold... all men standing before God," Santiago pleaded.

Brother Elías lifted his pale, hooded head.

"And the Brotherhood will be there as well. We must show ourselves—openly. If we ask for a miracle, it must be asked beneath God's roof."

Santiago's voice lowered.

"And there is... another matter. In recent months, the del Castillos have brought offerings to the Cathedral—relics, they claim. Bones of obscure martyrs. Fragments of vestments."

His eyes darkened.

"Too many. Too suddenly. I dare not accuse them, not without proof, but these objects... they are not right. I would have your eyes upon them, Señor Holmes."

Holmes did not answer at once. His gaze shifted slightly, as though arranging the facts upon some invisible grid.

"You have handled them?" he asked.

"Only briefly."

"And their provenance?"

Santiago gave a faint shake of the head. “Uncertain. They arrive with stories—but no history.”

Holmes’s fingers steepled. “Relics without lineage are curiosities at best,” he said quietly. “At worst—contrivances.”

He paused—only a fraction—but in that instant something aligned.

“Curious,” he murmured, almost to himself. “First an El Greco of improbable proportion... now relics of saints of equally dubious origin.”

A thin smile, without mirth. “Then we are not dealing in faith—but in theatre.”

He rose slightly, as though the matter had already advanced in his mind several moves ahead.

“Then Sunday Mass becomes essential. A spiritual necessity for you; an evidential one for me.

And afterward...”

Santiago finished the thought with a whisper.

“Afterward, in the shadow of the Cathedral, we shall speak of how to free the bull. Not here. Not now. Not where walls may listen.”

Remington gave a grim, short nod.

“Fine. Mass it is. I’ve prayed before in stranger places. But if we’re asking for miracles...”

He lifted his hand as if holding a glass of gin in a half-sardonic salute.

“...let’s hope the saints of Navarra are still taking requests.”

CHAPTER XXI

Saints and Sinners

False Relics

The rain had fallen hard the night before, not in passing showers but in long, unbroken sheets that hammered the roofs and washed the streets raw.

By morning the downpour had ceased, yet the city had not recovered; the stones of Pamplona still drenched beneath a sky the color of dull tin. The plants and flowers slumped under the weight of the rain. Water lingered in the gutters, moving slowly as though reluctant to depart, and the air held a dense humidity, an unmoving heat, that pressed against the lungs, drawing sweat to the brow like tears.

There was not the freshness that follows a storm, but a heaviness—the kind that settles before something breaks.

The bells of Santa María had a different timbre on this Sunday; or perhaps it was only that my own nerves, strung tighter now upon the pegs of danger and impending decision, heard in their iron tongues not merely a call to worship but the slow, insistent tolling of a city being drawn, step by step, toward a reckoning it neither fully understood nor desired.

We came to the cathedral early, before the great tide of Pamplona had yet poured through its doors—Holmes and I by one street, Remington by another, the brothers Santiago and Mateo by a third, in their brown habits walking with that peculiar mixture of humility and prayer.

The façade of Santa María rose from the square with that sombre assurance which only many centuries can give: twin towers, darkened by time, weather, and incense, flanked a portal whose sculptured saints had watched kings and beggars alike wear grooves in the flagstones with their petitions.

Incense drifted faintly from within, a dry, resinous ghost of countless burned grains; the crowd in the square was already thickening—women in dark lace mantillas, men in Sunday jackets that smelt faintly of camphor and stored cedar, children fidgeting in their best boots.

Holmes slowed as we approached the great western façade, his gaze lifting with that peculiar blend of aesthetic appreciation and analytic detachment.

"The face of reason," he murmured.

I looked at him in puzzlement.

He gestured toward the towering portico with its classical columns and serene triangular pediment.

"A neoclassical mask," he said quietly, "laid atop a far older soul."

And indeed, as the sunlight carved clean lines along the façade, I could sense behind it the weight of centuries—the hidden Gothic skeleton of the cathedral, with its ribbed vaults, narrow lancets, and shadowed arches burrowed deep behind the Enlightenment calm of the exterior.

"A Renaissance mind," Holmes added, "built upon a medieval heart."

Remington smiled beside us.

"Like half the men in this town," he said.

"Or all the saints."

Holmes gave no notice of the remark; his eyes were fixed on the doors.

"Architecture, Watson," he said, "is confession in stone."

Inside, the Cathedral expanded around us in cool, dim vastness; the air was full of that peculiar amalgam of age and devotion—stone, wax, human breath, and something else indefinable, perhaps echoes of centuries of whispered prayers. Shafts of coloured light from the stained-glass clerestory windows stitched themselves across the pillars and the dust, weaving a sort of immaterial tapestry above the heads of the slowly gathering crowd.

We took our agreed position in a side aisle, not far from a small chapel dedicated to San Fermín. There, beneath a muted fresco of the saint in his episcopal mitre, a glass case had been arranged on a narrow table, the candles before it already lit, their flames trembling like little saints in the morning air.

Holmes's gaze travelled along the line of apostles carved into the cathedral wall, each bearing an ancient attribute.

"Peter's keys... Bartholomew's knife... Andrew's cross," he whispered. "Signal after signal of authenticity. These were carved by men who believed what they depicted."

Then, softly: "Remember them, Watson, when we examine the relics. Truth leaves fingerprints. So does forgery."

Brother Santiago's gaze flicked toward the case holding the relics and then away, as though he could not bear to look directly, while Elías's neck tightened.

Brother Santiago touched my sleeve.

"That is Deacon Honesto," he murmured. "He keeps the keys."

I noticed a deacon near the sacristy door—short, sparely built, though not frail—his posture upright with the quiet discipline of a man who had spent a lifetime standing through long services. A polished bald crown caught the lamplight, circled by a thin ring of iron-grey hair, that resembled a quattrocento halo in oil. He must have been in his mid-seventies, yet there was nothing diminished about him. His movements were careful, yes—but deliberate rather than uncertain.

He was watching not the altar, but the reliquary. When our eyes met, he looked away at once, as though caught thinking aloud.

The deacon hovered near the case, hands clasped too tightly, as though he wished to explain the relics—or hoped they might vanish first.

Santiago inclined his head slightly.

"*Buenos días, diácono Honesto.*"

Good morning, Deacon Honesto.

"*Dios le bendiga, hijo mío,*" the deacon replied.

God bless you, my son.

Santiago inclined his head slightly.

Deacon Honesto looked quizzically at Holmes, myself, and Remington, then offered a broad, welcoming smile.

"*Este es el señor Holmes, el doctor Watson y el señor* Remington," Santiago said. "*Nos visitan desde muy lejos.*"

This is Mr Holmes, Dr Watson, and Mr Remington. They are visiting us from very far away.

We shook hands.

The deacon's friendly smile remained, but his eyes betrayed a quiet calculation, as though he were measuring not our words, but our purpose.

Remington shook his hand and said, "Glad to meet you, Father."

The deacon smiled, said nothing, and did not correct him.

Holmes bowed his head slightly and said, "We have come to have a closer look at the relics of Santa María—quite interesting indeed."

At this, Deacon Honesto stepped back, muttered something about preparations still to be made, and withdrew toward the side chapel.

Holmes, by contrast, moved at once toward the case, hands folded loosely behind his back, his posture that of a man entering not a sanctuary but a laboratory.

Within lay the relics.

To an untrained eye, they might have appeared impressive enough: a small gilt reliquary ostensibly containing a bone fragment; a sliver of wood said to be from the saint's staff; a medallion bearing a cross and an inscription; a strip of vellum with a faded script; two or three minor objects whose labels proclaimed them to be associated with this procession or that miracle; and, at the back, an almost ostentatiously simple wooden box, upon which a small card named the donors in flowing copperplate:

DON RAMIRO DEL CASTILLO Y DOÑA YSABEL DE ARRIAGA.

Holmes bent closer, his keen gaze taking in not the sentiment but the surfaces.

"Ah," he murmured, so softly that only I heard. "How refreshingly clumsy."

"What do you see?" I asked, though I knew the answer would be a litany of minutiae which, in his hands, would form an indictment.

He obliged me with a faint inclination of the head toward each object in turn.

"The gold leaf upon that reliquary," he said, "has been applied by machine; note the evenness of the edges, the lack of hand-tool marks, the uniformity of the brilliance. Late nineteenth or early twentieth century at most.

"The screws on the underside are of modern thread, unsuitable to any date earlier than the last few decades.

"The glass of the case—too clear, too flawlessly cut—has the cold perfection of the factory, not the slight waviness of older panes."

He tapped a finger against the glass case, pointing to the ancient text. "The ink," he went on, "is a synthetic aniline mixture—not unknown in Spain, but certainly not of the tenth or eleventh century in whose name these objects pretend to speak. The script imitates older hands, but the spacing betrays a modern clerk."

"*El hueso, Señor Holmes*?" Brother Elías whispered, his voice roughened with a peculiar anxiety. "The bone?"

Holmes's eyes slid to the fragment in its little gilt box.

"Cow," he said, with clinical certainty. "A small piece, taken no doubt from the refuse bin of a butcher's shop. The porous structure is all wrong for a human phalanx. I have seen too many corpses to be mistaken there."

Santiago made a small, involuntary sound, as though the words had struck him physically.

"And this," Holmes added, indicating the medallion, "bears a cross whose arms are ever so slightly flared at the ends—a peculiarity which, if you consult your own diocesan heraldry, Brother Elías, you will find to be identical to the private crest of the del Castillo house. It proclaims its origin almost indecently."

Elías drew in a sharp breath through his teeth.

"To falsify relics," Elías gasped, "is to falsify holiness itself."

Holmes rested a hand for the briefest instant on the archivist's white sleeve—a gesture of solidarity so fleeting that another man might have missed it.

Remington added, "That points to desperation. Or greed. Usually both."

"I concur," Holmes said quietly. "Desperate, and clumsy. They sought to buy sanctity with new gold and borrowed bones; instead, they have purchased only evidence."

The Brute in the Nave

Before any of us could answer, the measured hush of the Cathedral was disturbed by another kind of sound: boots upon stone, their rhythm neither pious nor hesitant but possessed of that unpleasant assurance which belongs to men who move in any place as though it already belonged to them.

Two figures came striding up the nave.

Holmes's gaze shifted—and then fixed."There," he said quietly.

I followed his line of sight—and felt at once a tightening in my chest.

The man then stood half in shadow among the pillars: bulky, immovable... and unmistakable.

The same brute who had delivered the deed.

Even at this distance, the deformity was plain—the ear, or what remained of it, a jagged ruin against the line of his skull.

He stood there in his Sunday, coat which strained a little at the seams. When he moved, he carried his hat in his fist—not with reverence, but like a man prepared to use it as a weapon.

"Our acquaintance returns," Holmes murmured.

Remington followed his gaze first. "Hell," he muttered. "That's the same ox who brought the paper."

Beside the brute moved a wiry shadow of a man, shorter and less immediately imposing, his gaze nervous and intent—rat-quick, and never still. His hair hung longer than was proper, stringy and unwashed, clinging in damp strands about his temples. A hat sat low upon his head, and the boots he wore were a size too large, as though he sought to borrow height where nature had denied it.

His eyes skittered from face to hand to doorway, measuring, always measuring—like a creature that lived by knowing precisely when—and where—to scurry when the moment turned.

As he shifted, the collar of his coat pulled slightly aside, revealing for an instant the dark curve of a tattoo at the base of his neck—something small and clawed, its form indistinct, but suggestive of vermin rather than ornament.

"A useful sort," Holmes murmured. "The kind that survives by running first—and remembering afterward."

Remington gave a short, humorless laugh.

"Yeah," he said. "Every ox needs a rat. One to break things open... and one to run through them."

He watched the short man for a moment, then added, almost as an afterthought—"Reckon we could draw him out with a bit of cheese."

They were, I knew without being told, not merely servants but enforcers: men in the employ of the Society of the Ancient Gold—whose hand we had already begun to feel tightening its grip upon Pamplona.

As they passed the chapel, the brute made an exaggerated sign of the cross, dragging it across his chest with a careless, almost bored motion.

"Not your church," he said in Spanish, his voice low and thick. "Not your bull either."

His small, porcine eyes flicked toward Santiago and Mateo.

Beside him, the short man's lips twitched.

Then he smiled.

Not broadly—never broadly—but with the thin, private satisfaction of a creature that had tested the air and found it safe to linger.

He stepped half a pace forward—just enough to be seen. Emboldened by the strength of the brute at his side, he moved with that quick, unthinking instinct of a lesser creature—one that does not act, but only reacts, borrowing courage where it finds it.

The smaller man reached out—quick as thought—seized and gave a sharp, tug to Mateo's rosary. The beads clicked, but the rosary held.

Mateo's hand came away just as swiftly. He struck the man's wrist aside, not violently—but with finality.

Then he looked past him—past the smaller man entirely—and fixed his gaze upon the brute.

"Not your decision."

For a moment—no longer than a breath—the chapel held still.

Remington's fists clenched at his sides. I saw the muscles in his jaw jump.

Before he could lunge, Holmes cast him the smallest possible shake of the head—a fractional movement, yet it carried the force of command. The American stopped, every line of his body straining toward violence—but the restraint held.

The smaller man's smile faltered. Not from fear—but from something less certain, as though the air itself had shifted against him.

The brute stepped forward then. Not quickly. Not angrily. Simply forward—placing himself once more between the friar and his shadow.

His gaze settled on Mateo, heavy and without expression.

Then, very slowly, he reached out and closed his hand around the smaller man's shoulder. Not gently.

The small man stilled at once.

"Not here," the brute muttered.

Two words—but they carried the weight of instruction.

He gave a slight push—not enough to stagger, but enough to remind.

The smaller man withdrew half a step. His eyes flickered once more—doorway, pillar, exit—calculating, recalculating.

Then the brute turned.

And this time, the smaller man followed without hesitation.

They left the chapel and took a place in a rear pew of the church, not to pray, but to wait—the kneeler dragged forward and used as a footrest, their posture one of occupation rather than reverence.

Beneath them, the marble bore the marks of their steps: dark flecks of drying mud, ground into the stone where no such stain had any right to be.

"I've met that one before," Remington muttered. "At the del Castillos'. He's the brute who kicked the dog."

Holmes did not answer at once.

He watched.

"The ear," he said quietly at last. "Not torn—crushed."

He paused, then added, "A short blade. Close work. The sort of fight where men do not step back."

A faint narrowing of the eyes.

"He has been rewarded for force," Holmes murmured. "Not thought."

A pause.

"Men like that mistake cruelty for authority.

"And when such a man kicks a dog," he finished softly,

"it is not anger. It is rehearsal."

The Del Castillos Entrance

The organ had begun to sound, and the congregation was rising in that soft rustle of fabric and whispered protest which always precedes the opening hymn, *Pange Lingua Gloriosi*.

They came then: the Del Castillos.

Don Ramiro walked with his chin a shade too high, his dark hair oiled, his moustache trimmed with that care which bespeaks not vanity alone but the need to present oneself as unassailable. At his arm, in a gown of understated but unmistakable expense, glided Doña Ysabel de Arriaga, herself, carrying that knowledge in the composure of her features. There was a refinement in her bones that made even the better-dressed women of the congregation seem slightly provincial by comparison; her eyes, heavy-lidded and cool, swept the Cathedral not with piety but with appraisal.

"Hell of a family portrait," Remington quipped out of the corner of his mouth.

Holmes's gaze remained on Ysabel. "Observe," he said. "She is not praying. She is counting heads."

A pace behind them came von Helldorff.

He wore black—unrelieved, severe—as though colour were a concession he refused to make even to God. His coat was cut impeccably, his gloves immaculate, yet there was something in the way he moved that did not belong to the place: a stiffness at the waist, a slight economy of motion, as if he were careful not to disturb something carried close to the body. He did not look about him. His eyes stayed forward, alert without curiosity, a man present not for worship but for control.

Holmes's attention shifted then, subtly, like a lens refocusing.

"Armed," he stated.

I did not look at him. "Certain?"

"Quite," Holmes replied. "Observe the posture: the rigid spine, the right side favoured when he turns, the hesitation before sitting. A weapon carried under the jacket, likely forward of the hip. He is unused to churches, but very used to readiness.

"And note this—" Holmes inclined his head a fraction. "He chooses a seat with a clear aisle and an unobstructed exit. That is not devotion, Watson. That is anticipation."

Remington's mouth tightened.

"Moriarty with a missal," he muttered.

Holmes did not smile.

"No," he said quietly. "Moriarty would have left the gun at home. This man expects trouble—and intends to survive it."

We stood through the Mass with that peculiar doubleness of attention which comes when one is in a holy place but cannot detach the mind from earthly perils. The Latin rose and fell; incense made its slow climb toward the vaulting; the priest's voice hummed through Gospel and homily. Around us, the devout knelt and crossed themselves, their brows furrowing not with suspicion but with ordinary cares—harvests, illnesses, sons at war or in foreign cities.

Yet beneath it all, there ran another current: the old aristocracy taking measure of its dwindling power; the monks of San Telmo and the Cistercian archivist standing as quiet rebukes; the American and the Englishman in the side aisle, foreign bodies in a fragile organism.

When the final Amen had faded and the congregation began to spill out through the great doors into the hard noon light, that tension, which had been diffused by ritual, gathered itself again in the crush of departures.

In the side aisle, near the chapel of San Fermín, the brutish henchman reappeared, planting himself deliberately in Santiago's path. For a moment the two men stood thus, the friar in his patched brown habit, the enforcer in his ill-fitting finery, and all the unspoken history of Spain—the conflict between those who possess and those who serve—seemed compressed into the space between them.

Holmes's voice sliced through the murmur like a blade.

"I advise you to move," he said, in Spanish so exact and cold that one might have mistaken him for a magistrate rather than a foreigner.

The man hesitated, and in that hesitation I saw something remarkable: the awareness, however fleeting, that he was being measured—physically, morally, intellectually—and found wanting. His eyes darted toward Don Ramiro, who lingered a short distance away; the aristocrat gave the smallest of nods, and only then did the brute step aside, with a grunt that tried to make the retreat a favour rather than a concession.

He Moves Unseen

We emerged into the sunlight.

The square in front of the Cathedral was already alive with post-Mass chatter: women clustering in little knots, children released to run, men lighting cigarettes in the lee of the stone. Somewhere a guitar was sounding a few tentative chords, like the first thoughts of a song not yet fully born.

Holmes had just turned to speak to Santiago when a smaller figure detached itself from the swirl of bodies and sidled toward us with the cautious agility of a stray cat.

He was a slight country boy; a thin, sharp-faced lad of perhaps fifteen, with dark eyes that took everything in and a mop of hair that looked as if it had only ever known the rough comb of his own fingers. He had narrow shoulders and the nimble caution of a creature that had learned to live in the margins.

His clothes, patched in multiple places, had the ragged look of having served several owners before reaching him; they were clean but worn.

His sandalled feet made no more sound than a field mouse crossing a granary floor. People did not see him so much as look past him; servants ignored him, aristocrats never noticed him, and even the monks forgot he was still there once his message was delivered. Yet he heard everything—overheard it, rather—the way a mouse hears the conversations of giants, half-hidden beneath the wainscot.

It was the shepherd boy.

"Señor Holmes," he said, tugging lightly at Holmes's sleeve. "Señor."

Holmes looked down with a faint smile that softened the angles of his face.

"Ah," he said. "Our young Miguelito. You have news, I see."

The boy glanced around, as if to ensure that no one of importance was within earshot, then leaned in closer.

Miguelito shifted from foot to foot, cap in hand, his thin shoulders hunched in that instinctive posture of boys accustomed to being overlooked.

"Well, Señor Holmes... I don't usually sleep indoors," he began, eyes lowered. "Most nights I stay with the flock—out on the grass, up where the wind keeps the wolves quiet. Don Esteban pays me two pesetas a week to watch his sheep, and the sheep don't like being alone."

He gave a shy, apologetic smile, as if embarrassed by the simplicity of his life.

"But last night... the rain came hard. Cold. Nasty."

He mimed a shiver. "Couldn't keep the lambs out in it. So I drove them into the little stone barn. Shut the doors. And I needed a roof myself."

His voice dropped to a whisper, almost conspiratorial.

"The plaza is easy, Señor. Easy for a small boy."

He threaded his hands through an invisible railing. "I slip between the bars. No one sees. No one ever sees me."

Holmes exchanged a brief glance with Santiago; the boy went on.

"I meant only to sleep," Miguelito said. "Up under the eaves where the wind don't bite. But then I heard them. Boots. Chains. Men speaking low like thieves do."

He swallowed hard.

"And El Toro..."

His breath hitched.

"They were dragging him, Señor Holmes. Dragging him like a cart. Pulling at his head with ropes—hard. Too hard. He fought 'em. Oh, he fought 'em. You could hear his hooves scraping on the stone."

I felt a chill run through me.

Miguelito's hands curled into small fists.

"They were angry. Angry that he wouldn't move. One of 'em struck him with the butt of a pole."

The boy's voice trembled. "And the bull... he made a sound I never heard before. Not a roar. Not fear. Something like... like a mountain groaning."

He looked up then, eyes dark with earnest outrage.

"They have him in an old holding corral near Calle Estafeta. Behind the old walls. Behind the shops. A small pen once used for mule stock, years ago," the shepherd said. "Close enough for the run. Hidden."

He swallowed.

"Then they took him down. Into the floor. A hatch—big iron thing. Hidden. They opened it and pushed him down inside. And they kept hurting him, Señor Holmes. I saw it. I swear it."

Holmes crouched slightly, bringing himself level with the boy.

"And you followed them?"

Miguelito nodded quickly.

"Yes, Señor. I kept to the shadows. I went down as far as I dared. Saw the torches. Heard the gates slam. El Toro is there now. In the bunker. Where no one can see him.

"They saw the footprints," the lad said.

"The men of Don Ramiro—they saw your boots in the dust by the first stall.

"They cursed.

"They said the monks have long noses and worse friends.

"So they took the bull away in the night in the rain, with cloth over his eyes, down to the lower place."

Remington glanced back toward the chapel doors and brushed the sweat from his forehead.

"They moved El Toro last night in that storm. No wonder we were greeted so warmly in church."

I frowned. "When they found our tracks by the pen, we forced their hand."

Holmes adjusted his cuffs. "Rain is rarely conducive to serenity, gentlemen—particularly when one is obliged to relocate half a ton of temperament."

Miguelito hesitated, then added with a sudden, embarrassed frankness, "It is not easy to come by shoes, Señor Holmes. Or meat. Or paper for school. I have cousins. Many cousins."

Holmes's hand went into his pocket; he brought out a few folded notes and a silver coin, which, to my surprise, amounted to nearly half a week's wages for a labouring man.

"One does not expect a boy to serve for faith alone," he said, pressing the money into the lad's hand. "You have earned this. And more. Keep your eyes open."

The boy's eyes widened at the sum, then narrowed with a shrewdness beyond his years.

"I can show you," he said quickly. "Tonight. The place where the lower door is. But you must come when the men are at their wine, or they will see."

Holmes nodded. "We shall come," he said. "At the hour when the city is asleep. You will meet us by the pens above the river gate?"

Miguelito let out a breath of relief—the breath of a child used to being unnoticed, suddenly seen.

The boy nodded eagerly. "Sí, señor. I will be there."

He slipped away into the crowd, disappearing with that uncanny speed of the very poor, who have learnt to move like smoke around those who do not see them.

To Liberate El Toro

"Well," Remington breathed, letting out a breath he had not realised he was holding. "They're spooked. That's good. Scared men make mistakes."

"Scared men also hide what they value most in deeper holes," Holmes replied.

"We have lost the advantage of surprise. We must now rely upon precision—and, if our brothers are correct, upon something more."

We withdrew then to a small winter chapel off the sacristy, a side room of stone and worn benches, where the chill seemed to rise from the floor like unspent prayers.

A single statue of the Virgin stood in a niche, her face more sorrowful than triumphant; a few candles guttered before her. Here, away from the bustle, Santiago drew his hood back, revealing worried lines in his face which the Mass had not smoothed away.

"The del Castillos grow bolder," he said. "Falsified relics. Bulls stolen from cloisters. Henchmen make threats in the house of God. I fear what they will do next."

"And yet," Elías added quietly, folding his white sleeves, "their very boldness is a sign of weakness. Strong houses do not need to invent their past."

"We cannot count on their weakness to save the bull," Remington said bluntly.

"Or the monks.

"Or the city.

"You heard the kid—they've shoved him underground now. Next step is a ring, a trumpet, and a sword."

Holmes stood in the centre of the little chapel, his eyes half closed, as though listening to a voice inaudible to the rest of us.

"The shepherd has given us the lay of the land," he said at last.

"The American threat, as Brother Santiago so delicately named it, we have considered and set aside for the moment; the more immediate peril is not what papers in Kansas may print ten years hence, but what trumpets in Pamplona may herald in one day's time. Between now and then, the factions will tighten their hands upon every symbol they have claimed: relics, bulls, processions."

Santiago moved to the small votive stand and lit a candle, his long hands steady even as the flame caught. His voice, when he spoke, was low but carrying.

"If it pleases God, grant us a miracle, grant that this poor creature may not die for the pride of men."

He stood back. The little flame burned with a stubborn clarity.

Holmes did not smile. His gaze rested on the small, stubborn flame, as though measuring its resolve against the shadows gathering in Pamplona.

"Gentlemen," he said at last, his voice low and taut with purpose, "we have invoked our miracle. But even miracles sometimes require precision, courage, and no small measure of planning."

He turned toward the streets beyond the cathedral doors.

"Come. Let us discuss our strategy to liberate El Toro."

Remington lifted his hat. "Amen to that."

CHAPTER XXII

Appeal to a Higher Authority

The Sacristy

It is a strange fact of strategy, that the boldest plans often begin in silence. After Sunday mass, the first phase of our design to free El Toro—and, in a quieter way, to free Pamplona from the shadow cast by *La Sociedad del Oro Antiguo*—The Society of Ancient Gold—began not with shouts, nor with the clash of wills, but with our footsteps whispering along the cool stones of the cathedral's northern transept.

The plan, as we had shaped it through the long hours after Mass, depended upon many things: upon stealth, upon timing, upon Santiago's knowledge of the Church's inner rooms, upon Remington's volatile courage, upon Mateo's bond with the beast, upon Holmes's deductions, and not least, upon the intervention of one man inside the Church who still held truth above fear.

We went to find him.

Santiago walked ahead of us, his sandals soundless on the stones, a man carrying both dread and hope in equal measure.

Holmes followed with his long, quiet stride.

Remington walked last, hands shoved into his pockets, jaw set with the grim resolution of a man preparing for a fight not of his choosing, but of his conscience.

Santiago guided us along a narrow side aisle to a low wooden door half-hidden behind a pillar of carved oak.

A soft knock.

A pause.

Then the door opened a hand's breadth, a thin blade of candlelight cut across the flagstones.

After a moment, the door creaked wider, and a gaunt man in a black cassock stepped into view—his face narrow, ascetic, his eyes bright with the sleepless vigilance of a soul accustomed to guarding holy things.

"Diácono Honesto," Santiago whispered. "We come with a burden we cannot carry alone."

He studied Santiago first, then Holmes.

"What troubles you, hijo mío?" he asked, his voice gentle but edged with concern.

Santiago bowed his head. "Diácono... it is about the relics."

The deacon's brow tightened. "What of them?"

Holmes stepped forward, his expression grave but courteous.

"Sir, we believe," he chose the word with surgical care, "that several of the recent donations appear to be manufactured."

Remington exhaled, flicking a hand as though brushing sawdust off a bar counter. "What he means," he said, "is that those phoney relics are about as real as a Cracker Jack diamond."

"Please, come in," Honesto replied.

He closed the door behind us and only then turned to face us, leaning back against it as though the strength had gone out of him all at once and required the support.

"I too have doubted their authenticity," he said quietly. "The gold too bright. The wood too new."

He rubbed his hands together. "For weeks," he whispered, "my prayers have grown heavy."

His gaze moved to Holmes, steady and unflinching.

Holmes asked, "Tell me plainly, Señor: have you spoken with the priest?"

"When I voiced my doubts to Padre Basilio, he dismissed them outright—and warned that further questions would border on excommunication."

His hands tightened on the edges of his sleeves.

"So I prayed, Señor Holmes. Night after night. I asked for clarity... for a sign. And now you stand here."

Santiago spoke softly, "Can you help us, when the hour comes, to reveal the truth to our brothers in the laity?"

Honesto replied, his voice low but steady, eyes fixed upon the crucifix hung near the ceiling.

"What is not of God... is of the Devil."

He drew a slow, trembling breath.

"I have prayed for a moment to expose them. A deacon is not a bishop, nor a canon—but I am entrusted with the sacristy, the vessels, the relics."

His eyes sharpened. "If God grants me the chance to speak truth before men, I shall take it."

"You understand," Holmes studied him with keen interest, "that such candour may cost your position... livelihood... even the peace of your future years.

"You would be stepping, Deacon, onto the narrow path of the martyrs."

Honesto's expression did not waver. "A shepherd is judged not by the wolves he fears, but by the flock he defends."

His gaze flicked towards the crucifix. "Give me one piece of evidence—one relic whose fraud you can demonstrate with certainty—and I will stand with you."

Santiago crossed himself and whispered a Glory Be.

Santiago exhaled, half relief, half awe.

"Elías will give us the proof," he said quietly. "Now we must wait until the Fiesta of San Fermín to carry this into the light."

Deacon Honesto invoked, quietly and gravely, with spiritual authority:

"Nada hay encubierto que no haya de ser revelado, ni oculto que no haya de saberse."

Matthew 10:26 — For there is nothing concealed that will not be disclosed, nor hidden that will not be made known.

Holmes's voice dropped to a silken thread. "Then, Deacon, we have found our lantern-bearer."

Honesto made the sign of the cross, touching two fingers to the small wooden crucifix at his throat. "No, Señor Holmes. You have found a servant

"The light... is truth itself."

CHAPTER XXIII

Fiesta de San Fermín

At First Light

Night had released its grip, and the bells of Pamplona rang out—lively and vibrant—over the markets, the mule-carts, and the gossiping balconies in those shadowed hours before sunrise.

I remember standing with Holmes in the narrow street that led toward the Plaza Consistorial, where a crowd was already compressed into a breathing, murmuring wall of humanity, and thinking that never in London—no, not even on those fog-drowned nights when the river itself seemed to conspire with crime—had I felt so palpably the air thicken with expectation.

Above us the balconies were laden with figures in white and red, those sharp, almost liturgical colours of San Fermín—white for the soul, red for martyrdom—that made each narrow street resemble a vertical chapel; below, the cobbles shone with the damp sheen of recent washing, for Pamplona, despite its madness, would not send its bulls to run through filth. A faint scent of soap mingled curiously with the darker perfumes of wine, sweat, and stable straw.

Holmes, in an uncharacteristic concession to local custom, had bound a red *pañuelo* about his throat, which lent his gaunt, ascetic features a strange episcopal air, like some lean prelate of reason presiding over the mysteries of chance and blood.

"You observe, Watson," he pointed out, as we pressed ourselves into the shadowed recess of a stone portal, "that even the cobblestones bear witness."

"Cobblestones?" I repeated, somewhat preoccupied with keeping my hat upon my head amid the jostling crowd and the intermittent volleys of laughter and shouted toasts.

Holmes's eyes flashed. "And yet the city cleaners have been ordered to scrub this section no less than three times since midnight. The Oro Antiguo would guide not merely the herd, Watson, but the narrative; they are attempting to dictate the story that Pamplona will tell itself tomorrow. We are here to alter that narrative."

Before I could reply, a familiar, roughened baritone broke in upon us.

"There you are, English," said Remington, shouldering through the throng with the easy brutality of a man born to crowded bars and little patience.

His white shirt was open at the throat, his red sash tied with a casual defiance that seemed to treat the whole festival as a personal duel.

"I was beginning to think you'd gone back to London and left me to dance with the Del Castillos alone."

"I don't dance, Señor Remington," Holmes remarked dryly. "I merely keep time."

Remington laughed. "Well then, keep it well. Soon the first *cohete*, the opening firework, goes up—the city will be watching the sky, and the Oro Antiguo will be watching each other. It's the only window we'll get."

"And Brother Santiago?" I asked.

"*Buenos días*," came a quiet voice behind us.

We turned to find the two monks of *Los Hermanos Custodios* standing in the penumbra of a recessed doorway. Their brown habits blended so completely with the ancient wood and stone that, for an instant, they might have been carved figures suddenly come alive.

Brother Santiago, with his grave, leonine head and green eyes that seemed perpetually fixed upon some higher horizon, inclined his head in greeting.

Brother Mateo, smaller and more nervous, clutched at the rope cincture about his waist as though it were both habit and lifeline.

"The key to the *Cámara Vieja*, the Old Chamber?" Holmes asked.

Santiago drew a small, iron-grey object from within his habit—a key not of the modern sort, but an ancient, heavy thing whose wards were as much symbol as mechanism.

"It was an old Roman cellar, converted into a hermitage food cellar in the Middle Ages, sealed for centuries beneath San Lorenzo. Our monastery guarded this long before bulls ran these streets," he said. "It opened once upon a chapel where relics were kept. Now it opens into a tunnel that will connect to where our bull is held captive."

Santiago's voice darkened. "El Toro was never meant to stand as a chained trophy of the Oro Antiguo."

"Good," Holmes said. "This will admit us to the old passage."

"The city thinks it will see a *corrida*—bull fight—today," Mateo said, a hint of a smile passing and gone.

Remington adjusted his hat. "That depends on who gets there first."

Holmes slipped the key into his pocket, and with a nod that was almost ceremonial, said, "Then let us move swiftly, gentlemen. The hour of reckoning is at hand."

We separated, each man falling into his appointed role in the plan, formed in those sleepless hours—each realizing that there is only a hair's breadth of margin for error between success and catastrophe.

Holmes spoke in that low, precise tone he used when the architecture of a plan depended upon minutes and shadows.

"Watson, we must reach the arena before the crowds press in. Before the gatekeepers begin scrutinizing every face, every hesitation, every man who looks as though he knows where he is going."

Holmes turned to Remington, eyes sharp beneath the brim of his hat.

"Which means, my dear Rem, we shall be relying on you. There is a small park beside the service gate, a tangle of shade and confusion during the fiesta. I have every confidence you will... improvise an appropriate distraction."

The corner of his mouth flickered, the faintest ghost of a smile.

Remington stood at the mouth of the narrow street, rolling his shoulders like a boxer loosening up before stepping into a ring.

"Well, gentlemen," he said, tugging his cap low, "this is where we part ways."

"Remember," Holmes replied, "your assignment is not chaos for chaos's sake—only enough disturbance to thin the watchers at the gates."

Remington gave a crooked grin. "Oh, I'll thin them. One way or another."

I glanced at him. "You're certain you don't need one of us?"

"I've got something to settle first," Remington said, his tone sharpening. "A little business. I'll meet you at the arena when it's done."

Holmes studied him with the faintest arch of curiosity.

"I trust, Mr Remington, you will handle this business without starting a civil war."

"No promises," Remington smiled, and strode off into the tide of revellers.

By the Back Way

There were errands still to be run. Holmes and Brother Santiago departed together beneath the cloisters, their faces already set in the discipline of men who know what must be done.

They descended to the sacristy and spoke there with Deacon Honesto. The design they placed before him was dangerous and delicate, demanding a courage few clergy would dare muster.

What mattered was this: when the bells began, when the procession formed, when the city turned its eyes toward spectacle and prayer, each of us would be exactly where we had been told to stand—and nowhere else. Everything else would depend on timing. And on Remington.

Brother Mateo and I were off to descend into the bowels of Pamplona by way of the hidden door that the Custodios maintained beneath a modest side chapel.

As I followed the monk down a narrow street of shuttered storefronts and shuttered lives, where only a few cats and one or two late drinkers moved like ghosts, the distant murmur of the main square receded, replaced by another kind of silence: the silence of sleeping masonry, of arches that had watched many dawns.

"You are certain there will be no guards stationed at this entrance?" I inquired, for the sympathetic imagination that has ever been both my strength and my weakness had already populated the shadows with bayonets and smirking figures.

"It is not an entrance," Mateo replied. "Not to their minds. It is the door of an old chapel—raised in the days when San Ignacio de Loyola walked these northern roads as a young hidalgo seeking God's voice. This little chapel was a refuge for pilgrims and penitents. They sealed it later, in an age of wars, reforms, and practical men—the brothers when the bishops closed small chapels they deemed unnecessary."

He touched the plaster gently.

"But plaster is more faithful to San Fermín than the men who ordered it laid here."

He knelt before a recessed stone panel half-obscured by ivy. His fingers traced the outline of a carved shell, the sign of the pilgrim, and then pressed inward. The stone gave with a soft reluctance, as though acknowledging a long-forgotten password, and pivoted just enough to reveal the darkness beyond.

"I must commend medieval masonry," I muttered, ducking my head to follow him into the half-light. "It seems to have been designed principally for intrigues."

"Or for prayer," Mateo said. "Sometimes the two are the same."

We made our way along a passageway hewn from the earth itself, the ceiling so low in places that I found myself instinctively stooping, conscious of the tonnage of stone and history that lay above us. The monk's small lantern shed only the thinnest blade of light.

"The underground old chamber lies just ahead," Mateo whispered at last. "Beyond the cellar, there is a larger modern tunnel for livestock that leads above ground. When the moment comes... El Toro will know his own path to freedom. A bull raised in the open hills never forgets the way toward air and light."

I said, worried, "You mean to release him directly into that tunnel? Without halters, without men to guide him? My dear fellow, is that not sheer madness?"

In the dimness his eyes shone with quiet faith. "He has known every indignity at their hands. Yet he was bred for the field, not the chain. Give him a crack of light and the scent of his brethren, and you shall see what path he chooses."

We reached a heavy wooden door banded with rusted iron. Mateo raised the lantern; the keyhole yawned like a small, dark eye.

"Holmes has the key," I reminded him, and my heart sank.

"The key to the chapel door," he replied. "But this—this is ours."

He reached again into his rope belt and produced not a key but a slim metal rod, the end of which had been filed and bent into a variety of delicate angles. For a moment, incongruously, I saw in his movements an echo of Holmes himself, that same peculiar reverence with which a craftsman approaches his chosen instrument.

"The vow of poverty has its usefulness," Mateo smiled, working the improvised pick within the lock. "We learn to make do with what the world discards."

There was a soft click, a sigh of released tension from the ancient mechanism, and the door shuddered inward.

What lay beyond was not a chamber in the ordinary sense but a hollowed womb of stone. For in the centre, tethered by a chain that bit cruelly into the thick muscle of his neck, stood El Toro.

I had seen bulls in Spain before, had watched them from the relative safety of shaded seats, had even tended, in my medical capacity, to the injuries they inflicted; but nothing in those spectacles had prepared me for the almost human gravity of this creature.

His coat, midnight blue, black as a moonless night, seemed to absorb the lantern light; his horns, cruelly tipped with metal for some private ritual of the Ancient Gold Society, swept outward in a curve that might have been drawn by a sculptor rather than nature; his eyes, when they turned upon us, held that unfathomable mixture of terror, fury, and incomprehension which belongs to all beings who sense that they have been dragged into a story not of their own choosing.

Mateo leaned close.

"Eso es. Tranquilo, torito... conmigo, compañero," he said—not softly, not loudly. Just enough.

That's it. Easy now, little bull...with me, my companion.

The words were less a name than the way one speaks to a close friend.

The bull snorted, a hot, explosive breath that sent dust and memory swirling in the lantern-glow. His hoof struck the packed earth once, twice, as though punctuation. He let out a low, repeated, almost singing grunt, lifting his massive head toward Mateo as though recognizing a lost friend.

For a moment, I confess, my medical instincts—those ingrained reflexes of caution and anatomy—bade me retreat. To stand in an enclosed chamber with such an animal, unarmed and with only one agitated monk between myself and those terrible horns, was to gaze very directly into the raw arithmetic of survival.

And yet, as I looked upon the beast, another feeling arose: a curious feeling of pity. For he, too, was a captive in this drama.

As I edged backward, partly to give the bull his breadth, partly to steady my own pulse, my boot struck something brittle half-buried in the straw. I stooped, lantern held low, and felt the unmistakable jolt of recognition that only a physician can know: a splintered glass vial, its label half-torn yet still legible enough to chill the blood. *Chloralum Hydratum*. A second bottle lay nearby, uncorked, reeking faintly of a sweet, chemical stupor, and beside it, a crude metal syringe, the sort used by livestock medics with more zeal than skill.

I lifted the lantern higher, and the light revealed drag-marks in the dust: the scuffed, uneven furrows left by a creature not moving of its own will, but hauled, drugged, half-stumbling, toward the very corner in which we now stood.

"Great Scott!" I exclaimed. "They forced him here. And doped him to do it."

¡Ay, no...! Mateo gently knelt beside the shattered crate, his rough fingers hovering over the vial as though afraid to touch it. A sorrowful, grief-struck exhalation escaped him. "They did this to him," he whispered. "My poor chico... they clouded his mind like a lantern smothered under damp cloth."

His eyes lifted toward El Toro—not with fear, but with a hurt that seemed to crease him inward. "He would never have followed them willingly. Never."

"So they dulled his senses, numbed his courage... stole his strength the only way cowards ever do—from behind, and with poison."

El Toro gave a low, rumbling moan, and Mateo's jaw tightened.

"I raised him from a calf," he murmured. "He took his first steps toward my voice. And now these men—these butchers—seek to turn him into a puppet for their pride."

He placed his palm flat against the bull's brow.

"*Perdónalos, mi amigo*," he said softly in Spanish, "*porque no saben el corazón que hieren*."

Forgive them, my friend, for they do not know the heart they wound.

Then, to Watson, his voice steadied, though grief still trembled beneath it:,"This will pass. The drug cannot dim what is born in him. Help me, Doctor. We must clear his breath... bring him back to himself... before the hour comes."

"No," I replied after a careful look. "Whatever they gave him has long since burned from his blood. His pupils track with intention, his balance holds firm, and his breathing is strong and even. He is roused, alert... very much awake."

Mateo approached slowly, his hands open, his lips moving in a low murmur that I at first took for a prayer but which gradually resolved itself into words of gentle command.

"*Tranquilo, hermano...tranquilo, compañero.*

"No hemos venido a herirte.

Easy, brother...easy, companion.

We have not come to harm you.

"*Hoy es tu día.*"

Today is your day.

He reached the chain and, with a shaking hand, examined the lock. "They do not trust even iron," he muttered. "They have added their own padlock to the old ring. Always mistrusting, these men of 'Ancient Gold'."

From within his habit he produced a small bundle of tools, their metal dulled with years of clandestine use. As he bent to the lock, I watched El Toro, his great flanks rising and falling with each breath that seemed to make the very air tremble.

Somewhere, far above us, a muted roar surged, the voice of the crowd as it reacted to some unseen signal.

Then, sharp and unmistakable even through layers of stone, came the first *cohete*: that long, rising scream followed by an abrupt, percussive blossoming of sound, which every soul in Pamplona that morning interpreted as the proclamation: the bulls have left the corrals.

"*El Encierro* —the Running of the Bulls— has begun," Mateo said grimly. "We are late."

With a final twist, the lock surrendered, and the chain fell away with a clatter that sounded, in that small stone chapel, like an organ crashing from its loft.

El Toro did not bolt. He stood for a moment, swaying slightly, as though struggling to redistribute the weight of his captivity; then he took one deliberate step forward—another—his hooves striking sparks from some hidden fragment of stone.

I stepped back instinctively.

"Doctor," Mateo urged, "stand to the side. Give him the tunnel, and he will take it to the stalls outside."

Then Brother Mateo stepped forward, not boldly, but with the humble assurance of a man returning a lost child to its path. He lifted two fingers to his lips and gave a soft, rolling click of the tongue, the very sound he had used since the bull was a calf learning to follow him through the pastures of San Telmo. It was a strange, tender music—half lullaby, half command—and its effect was immediate.

El Toro's ears twitched.

The great animal exhaled, steadied, and moved forward again.

He answered with a low, resonant rumble, half breath, half memory, then moved, one heavy step after another, toward the hand he trusted above all others.

We pressed ourselves against the rough wall, the lantern held behind us so as not to blind him. For one charged instant the bull hesitated, his nostrils flaring as he sampled the stale air. Then, as if some ancient instinct had stirred—a memory of sun and sand encoded in his very blood — he lowered his head and moved inexorably toward the tunnel beyond.

When he passed us, the proximity of that immense, controlled violence sent a physical shock through me; I felt my ribs vibrate with the echo of his mass, smelled the hot, living rankness of him, saw the faint sheen of perspiration on his hide like dew on black stone. Then he was gone, his heavy steps receding down the tunnel, the sounds blending soon with a more distant reverberation that climbed from below: the thunder of multiple hooves upon confined earth.

The Confrontation at the Gate

Mateo and I followed the bull up the sloping passage, our lantern throwing long, wavering shadows ahead of us. The air grew fresher; the scent of dung and straw thinned into something sharper—dust, sun-warmed stone, the faint metallic tang of distant excitement. Above us, somewhere close, the muffled roar of the festival pulsed like a great, slow tide.

At the top of the incline El Toro paused, lifting his head toward the faint square of daylight.

Mateo making a, “tk, tk, tk” noise.

El Toro then moved and trotted into the open air.

The passage opened at last into a small outer courtyard, a rough-fenced enclosure through which mule stock were once driven toward the pens. A tall wooden gate loomed ahead, its iron latch gleaming dully. Beyond it, I could hear the distant bells, the shouted warnings, the stamping of hooves—all the chaotic dance of the *Encierro*.

Mateo reached for the latch.

He never touched it.

From the shadow beneath the lone plane tree by the fence, a hulking figure surged forward—the brute with the missing ear from the cathedral, the enforcer of the Oro Antiguo.

He had been sitting in the shade of the tree, waiting, his bulk folded like a coiled beast.

Now he rose with a grunt.

Seized a weather-beaten length of timber

An old plank of fencing

And swung it with savage force.

The blow caught Mateo full on the shoulder.

The young monk crumpled without a cry, clutching his left arm, his thin body folding like a reed struck by sudden wind.

I felt something cold and furious ignite in my chest.

My fist clenched of its own accord; I stepped forward, half prepared to strike the giant myself—foolish, perhaps, but instinctive—when the brute lifted the timber a second time.

And then to my astonishment.

El Toro had witnessed the blow to Mateo.

He lowered his head with terrible deliberation.

His hooves scraped the earth in a single, decisive arc.

His breath burst from him in a low, rolling bellow that vibrated in my bones.

Then.

El Toro charged.

The brute had barely time to turn before the impact lifted him off his feet.

He struck the fence, splintering it, and flipped the brute, head first, tumbling out into the narrow street beyond—directly into the path of the oncoming rush of bulls.

What followed lasted mere seconds.

The tide of bulls swept past, hooves hammering the cobbles in thunderous unison. The brute flailed, roared, then vanished beneath that living torrent.

The last I saw of him, he was lifted bodily into the air, carried a dozen feet, then lost entirely in the roiling mass of horns and backs and Pounding legs—a man swallowed by the very spectacle he had sought to control.

Into the Run

El Toro stood at the gate's threshold, sides heaving, head held high, bellowing.

Mateo groaned softly. I knelt beside him at once.

"Mateo, are you hurt badly?"

He winced, clutching his shoulder. "It is... nothing, Doctor. A bruise. A bone that will complain for days." His eyes flicked toward the gate, then back to the bull. "But you see... El Toro knows his own."

Outside, the festival roared on, unaware that a reckoning had just passed through its streets.

And in that enclosed yard, with dust settling around us, I understood that the plan—our mad, precarious plan—had already begun to write itself in the language of Navarra: hooves, courage, and the fierce bond between a boy and the beast he had raised.

El Toro pawed once at the earth, twice, a great, resonant clack of horn against wood as he swung his head toward the barred gate. His breath steamed in the cool morning air, a forge-fire exhalation. The bells of the Ayuntamiento were tolling somewhere up the street; the roar of the *encierro* swelled like a storm tide.

Mateo tried to rise, faltered, and let out a hiss between his teeth.

"Easy, easy," I pleaded, slipping an arm beneath his good shoulder.

"No, Doctor—" his voice was tight with pain but fierce with urgency. "The gate—open it. He must go. He must join the herd, or the men of Oro Antiguo will find him penned again. *Rápido.*"

I helped him to his feet. Dust clung to his robe in pale patches; his left arm hung stiff at his side, trembling. But his eyes, dark and steady, were fixed on the bull as a father might watch a son stepping toward destiny.

"Ahora, torito," Mateo commanded.

"Corre con los otros. No mires atrás."

Now, little bull.

Run with the others. Do not look back.

The great head turned. The bellow dwindled into a deep, vibrating hum, not rage now, but recognition.

I stepped to the iron latch. My hands were shaking more than I care to admit; the weight of that moment, of that beast's freedom, of our entire desperate design, pressed upon the metal like an invisible hand.

"Mateo," I said, "once this is open—"

He nodded sharply.

"He will go with the herd. He was born for the run. And we," he grimaced, clutching his shoulder, "we will follow as best we can."

The hoofbeats were still near.

I drew a breath, felt the cold sweat at my collar.

Mateo leaned close, just once.

"Buen viaje, mi torito grande... que Dios te guíe."

Safe journey, my little big bull. May God guide you.

Then I wrenched the bolt free.

The gate shuddered wide.

El Toro did not hesitate. He surged past us like a dark tide, muscles rippling beneath his hide, horns catching a sliver of sunlight as he leapt into the street.

The herd had already passed.

The calle lay open before him—empty but for drifting dust, scattered hats, and the echo of thunder retreating around the bend. El Toro took it in with a single glance and drove forward, hooves striking stone in a measured, gathering cadence. He was not fleeing. He was following.

A few breaths later, he closed the distance, his stride lengthening, his pace folding into the rhythm of the herd ahead of him, joining by force of will, his bellow harmonising with the collective thunder of Navarra.

Mateo leaned against me, breath ragged.

"He runs," he whispered, awe and pain mingling in his voice. "*Gracias a Dios...* he runs free

CHAPTER XXIV

The Matador

Gathering in the Callejón

We entered with the last wave of runners through the *paso de callejón*—that narrow, protected corridor circling the inside perimeter of the arena like the hollow of a giant bone.

Men stumbled, shouted, laughed, prayed. The smell of sweat, dust, and fear thickened the air.

The gatekeepers, overwhelmed and half-blind with the crush of bodies, could not possibly scrutinise every soul who spilled into that funnel—and certainly not a trio such as ours.

There we found Holmes, dusting a trace of sawdust from his sleeve, standing beside Santiago exactly where he had said they would be.

Holmes looked at us once—only once.

His eyes moved with quiet economy: the blood drying at Remington's temple; Mateo's wounded shoulder; the faint smell of gunpowder on my hand from my service revolver.

He said nothing.

But I knew, then, that nothing had escaped him.

Then he turned to Remington, his gaze briefly, almost imperceptibly, warm.

"Mr. Remington, your contribution was... decisive. The distraction you engineered did precisely what was needed. The guard abandoned his post to spectate, and Santiago and I slipped through the service gate without so much as a raised eyebrow. We took the opportunity for a brief reconnaissance—charting passages, mapping the arena, and waiting for its hour. Thanks to your diversion, the plan may proceed."

Remington gave a grunt of satisfaction, half pride, half bruised irritation.

He adjusted the brim of his hat, listening to the rising tremor of the crowd above us.

Santiago, who had been steady as a pillar beside Holmes until that moment, stepped toward Mateo with sudden concern.

"Brother," he murmured, his voice taut with worry, "what has been done to you? Your shoulder—*¿estás entero?* Are you all right?"

Mateo gave a rough laugh. "*Entero* enough, Padre."

"Mr. Remington," Holmes said evenly, "have you been wounded?"

"Only my pride," he said, flexing one hand, "for not finding the bastard I was looking for."

Mateo blinked. "You mean... the ranch hand with no ear? The brute from the house of the Del Castillos?"

"That's the one." Remington cracked his knuckles. "After the way he kicked that poor dog? I've been hoping to rearrange his jaw since the moment I set foot on their estate."

I exchanged a brief look with Mateo—a solemn, charged one.

"Remington," I said carefully, "there is no need to look for him."

He frowned. "And why's that?"

"Because," I said, "El Toro found him first."

Remington blinked once.

Then twice.

A slow, incredulous smile spread across his face. "You're telling me... that bull sent *el bastardo* flying?"

"Like a child's rag doll in a storm wind," I said. "Straight into the path of the running herd."

Remington blew a long, thin, low whistle, shaking his head side to side.

Then Remington let out a bark of laughter—raw, savage, satisfied.

"God bless that animal," he said. "Smartest damn creature in Navarra."

Mateo, bruised and battered, managed a weary, reverent nod.

"He protects what he loves," the monk murmured.

Santiago muttered a prayer to himself. His fingers brushed the rosary at his belt, not in fear, but in resolve.

Holmes's gaze flicked between the two men, measuring the wound, the resolve, the implications.

The Drugged Bull

"Holmes!" I called over the roar of the crowd.

He turned—sharp, alert, searching my face.

"I've something you must hear at once," I said, leaning close.

"I found vials. Chloral hydrate. Enough to fell a bull twice over."

Holmes's eyes flashed like struck flint.

Mateo drew a sharp breath. *"¡Que Dios nos proteja...!"*

God protect us.

Then Mateo exclaimed. “I knew El Toro would not move for them. *La Sociedad del Oro Antiguo* only understands force.”

He pressed his good hand to his wounded shoulder. “They will answer for that—if not to men, then to God.”

“Sedated,” Holmes said quietly. “*Chloralum hydratum*—administered to ensure compliance.”

He glanced toward the arena sands, where attendants were unbolting the final gate.

“So that,” he added, “is the entire mechanism.”

Santiago nodded grimly. “A lie layered upon a lie. May God grant that Navarra sees the truth today.”

A Wrinkle in Silk and Sequins

“Not so fast,” Remington growled, lowering himself onto a crate with the air of a man who had wrestled the devil himself on his way here.

“Before we stride into any damned ceremony, you ought to hear what I found out there.”

He wiped the blood from his eyebrow with the back of his hand.

Holmes’s eyebrow lifted.

“Oh? Another complication?”

“Call it,” Remington said.

“A wrinkle in silk and sequins.

“After I left you,” he went on, wiping a thin line of blood from his wound, “I cut through Calle Mercaderes. Packed shoulder to shoulder, but with enough air between bodies for a man to notice things if he knows where to look.”

He spat dust from his mouth.

"And I saw him. Full *traje de luces*. Gold heavy enough to catch every eye. Jacket shining."

Remington paused.

He shifted his weight, replaying it.

"The cape wasn't wrong—just too careful."

Remington's lips tightened.

"Then I heard him speak," Remington said.

"French."

He let the word sit there, sour.

"Clean French.

"South of France. Nîmes, Arles—places where men learn to survive bulls but not honour them."

He wiped his thumb against his knuckle.

"In Pamplona," he went on, "men still argue about Belmonte as if he were alive, and Joselito as if he were a saint. The young ones want to be Niño de la Palma. This town doesn't need to import courage."

Remington catching his breath, shook his head once and looked at Holmes,

Holmes's expression did not change, but something behind it sharpened.

"An import," he said softly. "An unknown."

Holmes leaned back slightly.

"This man," he went on, "has been selected."

Remington frowned.

"For skill?"

"For discretion," Holmes replied.

I stared at him.

"A Frenchman... disguised as a matador?"

Holmes considered this for a moment longer than was comfortable.

"A French matador," he said at last.

"Disguised—as we shall see."

When the Mask Slips

"And then?" I asked Remington.

"Oh, it gets better," Remington laughed. He made a short, dismissive sweep of his hand toward the park.

"He sashays across that tiny park by the arena—the one where the vendors hawk rosaries and sausage. The crowd splits for him like he's Belmonte reincarnated.

"And when he ducks toward the service alley behind the cypresses, I follow him."

He paused.

"But when he slipped behind the alley, he stopped performing."

"Performing?" Holmes asked.

Remington nodded once.

"The walk changed. Shoulders settled. The show went out of him."

"Why?" I asked.

Remington looked straight ahead. "Because any man putting on airs can only be headed somewhere dishonest or dangerous."

Moral Collision

"He leads me straight to a little side courtyard behind the arena. Who's waiting for him there?"

Remington jerked a thumb backward. "Your old friends, Holmes—the Del Castillo bruisers. Two of them. Arms crossed. Watching him like he's late with their wages."

Holmes's eyes narrowed. "And the nature of their arrangement?"

"Oh, they weren't rehearsing Sevillanas," Remington grunted. "One of them handed him an envelope. Thick. The sort you give a man for a job you'd never put in writing."

"The Frenchman opened it," Remington said. "Counted nothing. Just felt the weight. Nodded once. And then—in that accent of his—said, *'Oui. Je comprends.'*"

"Curious," I exhaled.

Holmes made a small, thoughtful sound.

"Then the payment precedes the crime," he said. "Which means the outcome has already been agreed upon."

"Exactly." Remington's grin was somber.

Santiago crossed himself, slowly, deliberately.

"A purchased courage," he murmured. "A martyrdom bought in advance."

Holmes turned toward him.

"You object to the bargain?"

Santiago's voice did not rise. "I object to our bull being used this way," he said. "God does not forgive bargains made in blood."

The words hung there—quiet, immovable.

"Then, I was done," Remington said simply. "I'd seen enough. I turned, already beginning to move away."

He paused, touching the split skin at his brow with a knuckle, more thoughtful than pained.

"I took three steps," he went on. "That's when one of them decided I'd seen too much."

Holmes lifted his chin and crossed his arms.

"A hand on my shoulder," Remington said. "Heavy. Familiar. The kind that doesn't ask."

Remington gave a brief, serious smile.

"He leaned in close enough that I could smell the wine on his breath and said, 'You didn't see anything, americano.'"

"And you?" I asked.

Remington shrugged.

"I shrugged him off," he said. "Kept walking."

Remington eyes flicked up, meeting Holmes's for a fraction of a second.

"That was my mistake."

The smile vanished.

"The next thing I knew, the same hand had my collar. Not hard. Not yet. Just enough to remind me they were deciding whether I was a problem."

Remington drew a slow breath. Another followed, rougher than the first. He steadied himself before continuing.

"I told him he'd chosen the wrong man to educate."

Santiago crossed himself.

"He struck first," Remington said. "The thin, short fellow from the church—scar for an eyebrow, crushed fedora—slipped in close like a dockside rat, all elbows and impatience."

Remington glanced toward me again. "You saw it Watson," he said. "You know how he came."

I shifted forward, the memory drawing me into the conversation.

"Certainly, we were walking up the alley then," I replied. "Mateo and I. Not close enough to stop the fight but close enough to see."

Mateo, still holding his shoulder, gave a quick nod.

"He came in fast," Remington continued. "Low. Hurried, aimless punches. Trying to knock me down—trying to make it hurt enough that I'd think better of standing."

"And you didn't," I said.

"No," Remington replied slowly. "I did not."

I nodded my head in agreement.

Remington wiped his brow and drank deeply from the bota Holmes had handed him. The exertion of recollection had left his breathing rough.

"From where we stood, I saw it clearly: the wiry fellow darting in—sharp and mean—swinging short and quick like a man used to hurting people who never hit back. Remington didn't dance. He set his feet, absorbed the rush, and let the man come to him."

"Helldorff stayed back," Remington said. "Watched. Hands clean. Let the other man do his work." He paused, breathed and took another deep drink from the wine bota.

As he drank, I continued.

"Then Remington stepped inside the wiry man's reach—

"No wind-up.

"No flourish.

"Just a clean, short punch.

"Up and across.

"Shoulder and forearm behind it.

"The blow snapped the man's head back as if a cord had been cut.

"The alley rang once with the sound of bone on stone."

"He rushed," Remington said. "Thought speed was the same thing as control."

"The wiry man staggered, heels skidding on the damp stone, then went down hard—back first, arms slack—his head striking the wall with a sound I did not care to hear twice.

"I saw him groan, turn unsteadily onto his side, and crawl away with the miserable persistence of a wounded rat."

"He didn't know when to let go," Remington finished.

The Cross and the Luger

I continued.

"Von Helldorff stepped forward then.

"Smooth.

"Unhurried.

"He reached inside his jacket.

"And produced a Luger P08.

"The motion practised, almost courteous—like a man setting down cutlery. The metal caught what little light the alley offered.

"He did not point it.

"He did not hurry.

"He simply held it there, letting the shape of it finish the conversation.

"Remington stood there a moment, chest rising and falling, one hand braced against the wall as he drew breath. Sweat cut pale tracks through the dust on his face.

"That was when Mateo moved.

"He stepped between them without hesitation, his hand already at his cincture belt.

"'Enough!' he said—not loud, simply spoken.

"'No killing.' He pleaded."

Santiago looked up and gestured the sign of the cross

"At the same instant I had my old service revolver out, the weight of it familiar in my hand.

"'Hold it there,' I said.

"Von Helldorff's eyes flicked to the gun, calculating.

"For the first time, something like irritation crossed his face.

"Mateo did not wait for permission.

"He snapped his cincture rope belt free and swung it hard, the cord whistling once through the narrow air.

"The large wooden cross struck Helldorff's wrist with a sharp crack. The Luger spun from his gloved hand and skidded across the stones.

"Mateo was already moving. He kicked the Luger away, down the alley, as though it were something unclean.

"For a heartbeat, Helldorff stood very still.

"Then he surged forward, shoving Mateo aside with a sharp, angry motion and turning to bolt.

"Remington was ready.

"He stepped wide to avoid Mateo, caught Helldorff's leg as he passed, and sent him stumbling. Helldorff wheeled back, off balance now, and threw a punch—fast but desperate.

"Remington slipped it, ducking cleanly, the way a man does who knows the rhythm of blows.

"He came up inside Helldorff's guard and drove a short, hard punch into him—nothing fancy, just bone and weight and decision behind it.

"Helldorff staggered backward and crashed into the garbage tins. They went over with a clatter, lids skittering down the alley.

"He sat there for a moment amid the refuse, blinking, breath knocked out of him.

"'This,' he muttered thickly, 'is not what I am paid for.'

"As he went back, something slipped free of his coat and skittered across the stones. I saw it before anyone else did—a glass vial and a syringe, rolling apart.

"I bent and picked them up. The label was intact. *Chloral hydrate*. The label bore his name, Dr von Helldorff, neat and clinical.

"I looked at Remington. He understood at once.

"'That won't be touching the bull,' he said.

"I pocketed the vial and syringe. 'Evidence, now.'

"Remington stooped, retrieved the fallen Luger from where it had slid, and tucked it into his coat without ceremony.

"'Let's go,' he said.

"We did."

I took a deep breath and leaned against the railing for a moment's rest.

Remington rose from the crate on which he had been seated and handed me the bota. I took a long drink of the sun-warmed wine.

"What they wanted," Remington finished, "was to make sure I stayed quiet."

He looked down at his hands.

"What they taught me," he said, "was how afraid they are of being remembered."

I winced and set the stopper back into the bota.

Remington was still breathing heavily.

Santiago was muttering prayers as Mateo held his shoulder and said nothing.

Holmes was very still.

For the first time since I had known him, he did not speak at once.

His eyes moved—once—to Remington's bloodied brow, then to my coat pocket, where the vial now rested, and finally to the mouth of the alley beyond.

Holmes inclined his head slightly.

Then Holmes regarded Mateo with a curious intensity.

"That was... nearer than I like," he said quietly.

Theatre in the Ring

"And the Frenchman?" Holmes asked.

Remington's grin widened. "Gone," he said. "Fast."

He exhaled sharply.

Holmes's gaze sharpened as Remington finished.

"I suspected as much," Holmes said quietly, "from the moment I glimpsed the French matador inside the arena."

I blinked. "You saw him?"

"I did. Only for a heartbeat. But it was enough."

Holmes lifted a finger, enumerating each detail like a professor unmasking a forgery. "His montera sat far too high—tilted at a theatrical angle meant to be seen, not worn."

He continued without haste. "His capote was pressed, not broken in. The folds too clean. Too obedient. No man who has ever truly faced horns keeps cloth so pristine."

Remington's mouth twitched.

"And when he pivoted toward the barrier, he did so on his heels, not the balls of his feet—a dancer's turn, not a fighter's. That alone condemned him."

Remington barked a short laugh. "A ballet step. The poor devil probably thinks he's dancing *Swan Lake*—with horns."

I frowned. "But why go to such trouble?"

Holmes's voice tightened just perceptibly as he lowered his head.

"Elementary, my dear Watson: an imported second-rate matador combined with sedative drugs can only ever lead to one thing—a contest whose outcome was never in doubt."

"Chicago, 1919, White Sox, my guess," Remington said darkly.

"To display the bull," Holmes said, his voice tightening, "without risking it."

He let the words hang.

Remington nodded, grim.

"Breed him first.

"Sell the legend.

"Then kill him later when the papers are watching."

Holmes lowered his hand.

"In short," he added, "the spectacle was real. The courage was not."

Remington smiled. "The bull may be the only honest participant in the entire affair."

"Indeed," I added.

Santiago folded his hands, not in prayer but in restraint. "A faith that fears risk," he said, "is already hollow."

Holmes nodded his head.

"Precisely," he said. "And like all such bargains, it requires silence. Which explains the alley—and your experience there, Mr Remington."

"Gentlemen," he said, "the Del Castillos have made their wager."

Remington looked down and shook his head.

"We are about to see whether the bull agrees."

Holmes stilled. "Gentlemen," he said quietly, "listen."

From behind the arena walls came the low, impatient thunder of hooves. The crack of the third *cohete* split the air like a rifle report.

Remington's head snapped toward the arena.

"That's it," he said. "*Tercer cohete*. The herd has entered the plaza!"

CHAPTER XXV

Fireworks

The Arena Transfigured

The arena hummed like a living creature.

The city had surrendered itself to a passion that was half religious ecstasy and half deliberate flirtation with annihilation. The chant—

¡A San Fermín pedimos,

Por ser nuestro patrón,

Nos guíe en el encierro

Dándonos su bendición!

We pray to Saint Fermín,

Our patron,

May he guide us in the running

And bestow his blessing upon us.

had risen and fallen like the response of some vast, drunken litany, and now it fragmented into screams, laughter, prayers shouted to no one in particular, the hoarse exhortations of men who ran from bulls.

Suddenly, from the city beyond the stone wall, came the first ringing of the bells of the Cathedral of Santa María, rolling outward through the streets and into the Plaza like a tide changing—slowly, measured, deep, and deliberate—stating that this was ecclesiastical time, not festival time. For the crowd, this was the first signal: the sacred had entered the arena.

The arena did not go quiet—but it changed key.

There was a brief, uncanny settling of the crowd.

The shouting softened.

Hats came off.

Men who had been drunk ten minutes earlier suddenly stood straight, sobering, almost embarrassed.

Murmured prayers.

Women crossing themselves in the stands.

Silence... then sound.

Then came the *clarines*—high, piercing trumpets. Short, formal calls, ancient and unmistakable. These trumpets were felt physically in the chest, especially in the enclosed bowl of the Plaza. Their authority imposed order upon chaos.

Immediately following, interwoven, came the ceremonial drums.

Slow.

Processional.

Measured like a heartbeat.

This was not entertainment.

This was ritual.

Just after that, the procession entered.

First, the master of ceremonies strode into the arena alone.

He was dressed in black, severe and unadorned, the cut of his coat echoing an older century—narrow through the shoulders, high at the neck, designed to constrain the body as much as command it.

He walked to the exact centre of the ruedo—the ring—and halted.

For a breath, nothing moved.

In his hand he carried the short black staff, dark wood capped with dull silver.

He held it upright, never swung it—raised once, deliberately, to command attention.

Then lowered it with finality, signalling that the arena was now under formal order.

Behind him came the civic authorities.

City officials entered in measured pairs, dark suits and sashes. Medals caught the light and gave it back without warmth. These were men accustomed to balconies and proclamations, to being applauded from a distance; here, under the open sky, they walked stiffly, aware of the thousands of eyes weighing them.

Arena administrators followed—keepers of keys and gates, men who understood timetables, procedures, liabilities. They took their places with practiced economy. Hats were removed. The Plaza settled further, as though a door had closed somewhere deep inside it.

Next came the music of low chant, humming through the arena, the notes carried as if by a multitude of bees.

Then the first ecclesiastical figure entered the ring.

Soon, the formal procession of San Fermín's clergy, bringing the saint's relics into the arena to bless the opening of the festival and its first corrida.

First, the cross-bearer entered without announcement, dressed in plain white, his robe stirred by the breath of the arena.

A single cleric, carrying a processional cross—no flourish, no gesture, just steady forward motion. He held the wooden cross upright and close. No ornament marked him. Only the cross mattered.

This was the Church saying:

Before anything else—Christ.

Next came the incense bearer, robed in white, following shortly after the cross.

The brass censer, suspended on its chains, swung in slow, pendular arcs in rhythm with each step. The scent drifted through the air—frankincense and myrrh—dry and bittersweet, the smell of stone churches and saints, cutting cleanly through dust, animals, and heat.

After the incense came the candles.

Two acolytes entered together, young and solemn, each carrying a tall wax candle held steady at the chest. The flames burned clean and pale despite the open air, sheltered by glass chimneys that caught and softened the light. They walked in measured step, eyes forward, neither hurried nor hesitant, as though the arena itself had narrowed into a nave beneath their feet.

A boys' choir followed, thin voices of piety lifted in an old antiphon—

Christe, lux vera, quae illuminat...

O Christ, true light, who enlightens...

The sacred words were carried on the wind, seeding the arena like a dandelion blown to air. Their voices harmonised into a single line of sound, quieting the heartbeats of the plaza to one shared tempo.

Behind them followed the minor clergy—seminarians and junior clerics in simple white albs, hands folded, heads bowed just enough to signal discipline as well as humility. Their presence carried no authority yet, only promise: the Church in its apprenticeship. They moved as a body, quiet and obedient, their sandals brushed the sand with a sound scarcely louder than breath.

After them came the religious orders.

The Franciscans entered in quiet ranks, their brown habits darkened and frayed by age and travel, rope cinctures hanging loose at the waist. They walked without ornament or banner, hands folded, eyes lowered. Bare sandals scarcely stirring the sand, as though they walked a fraction above it.

Among them I recognized Brother Santiago at once, though nothing in his bearing betrayed it. He walked as any friar would, measured and composed, his gaze fixed ahead.

Beside him moved Mateo. His step lagged by the smallest fraction—no stumble, no break in discipline—but enough, to an eye that knew him, to reveal the bruise beneath his sleeve and the pain he carried without complaint. He neither favoured the shoulder nor turned his head. He endured.

Around them came other brothers from San Telmo, faces weathered, habits dust-worn, the look of men more accustomed to fields and stone corridors than to spectacle. Together they formed a line of humility—heads bowed, hands in prayer.

They did not acknowledge the crowd. The crowd, sensing something ancient and devout, grew very still.

After the Franciscans came the cathedral clergy, rank settling upon rank like the gradual deepening of a chord.

First entered the canons of the chapter, vested in black cassocks edged with violet, rochets falling white and stiff over their shoulders. They walked with practiced gravity, men accustomed to stalls and statutes, guardians of order as much as prayer.

Behind them followed the deacons and subdeacons, their vestments lighter, more angular—dalmatic and tunicle catching the sun in brief flashes of colour—the Book of the Gospels raised in solemn prominence, the others carried close and still, movements precise, the machinery of liturgy advancing step by measured step.

Deacon Honesto emerged then from among the deacons. Nothing in his bearing invited attention—no flourish, no hesitation—only obedience to a ritual he had performed a hundred times before.

This time, however, he was bearing the reliquary of San Fermín's staff. It was massive and gilded, chased with worn saints and curling vines, heavy enough that his arms tightened as he lifted it. He raised it aloft, as custom required, so that the people might see and be blessed.

His steps were slow, even, each footfall placed with conscious precision, the chains of incense still faintly ringing in the air behind him. He did not brandish it. He did not sway it toward the crowd. He carried it forward with deliberate restraint, as one who knows that what is elevated before men must also endure the gaze of God.

Then came the priests, ranks of them, vested in white and gold, murmuring responses only the initiated could hear. With them walked the senior clergy and archpriests, men whose authority had been earned in years rather than conferred by office alone. Their pace was slower, their bearing assured, as though the arena itself must accommodate them.

The Bishop of Pamplona entered last, crozier in hand, his mitre gleaming softly. The crowd rose as one. The Bishop, with a single, unhurried gesture, marked the arena with the sign of the cross—blessing it, claiming it, for this one hour, for God rather than men.

The Church had arrived entire. What followed now would be done before God and half of Navarra.

Staff of San Fermín

In the *palco*, the dignitaries' box, Don Ramiro del Castillo rose. with practiced gravity, his head inclined in a gesture meant to pass for reverence. Yet his eyes never softened, and the faint tightening at the corner of his mouth suggested calculation rather than prayer.

Beside him, Doña Ysabel smiled faintly, the smile of a woman watching a drama whose ending she believed already written. Her eyes never left the reliquary. When the staff caught the light, they gleamed.

Around them, applause began—tentative at first, then swelling—an uneasy fusion of devotion and anticipation. The saint had entered the ring. The crowd had acknowledged him.

Deacon Honesto slowed.

It was not enough to halt the procession—only enough to alter its geometry. His steps angled subtly toward the inner arc of the arena, just beyond the prescribed line of march. To any casual eye, it might have appeared a momentary adjustment: fatigue, weight, the natural correction of a man bearing something heavy. But those who understood ritual felt the shift at once.

The reliquary no longer moved with the procession.

The Franciscans responded without signal. Santiago was first to turn, then Mateo, then the brothers of San Telmo, their brown habits closing in with practiced instinct. They formed a quiet circle around Honesto—not shielding him from the crowd, but enclosing the space itself, as monks might gather around a sick man or a vow being taken. Sand stilled beneath their sandals. The chant thinned, then faltered.

Something ancient was reasserting its claim.

May God Answer

Santiago stepped forward and extended a single candle.

It was already lit.

Holmes leaned toward me and whispered,

"He carries the courage of Saint George today, Watson—and you are about to witness the slaying of a golden dragon."

Holmes continued, "Observe the grain, Watson. Modern lathe work. Not a single wormhole. This *relic* has not weathered a century, let alone thirteen."

A ripple of unease passed through the crowd.

Some gasped.

Some scoffed.

Some crossed themselves without knowing why.

A priest near the stand hissed, white with panic:

"¡Diácono! ¡No! ¿Qué hace usted?"

Deacon—no! What are you doing?

Honesto did not so much as flick an eye toward him.

He bowed his head for the briefest of moments and whispered, just loud enough for those closest to hear:

"Si esto es santo, que Dios me perdone

"Si es engaño, que Dios me ampare."

If this is holy, may God forgive me.

If it is deceit, may God protect me.

He raised the candle high above his head like a sword, looking upward.

A small, stubborn flame burned.

Then, in a voice pitched just loud enough to ride over the stillness that had gathered in the arena, Honesto proclaimed:

"If this staff be truly the relic of San Fermín—oak hardened by sixteen centuries of prayer and pilgrimage, protected by divine sanctification—no flame shall harm it.

"But if it be false—if it be deceit, newly fashioned, pinewood dressed in silver—then it will burn like dry thorn-brush, and let God's truth judge it."

He straightened, lifting the candle so that every eye in the amphitheatre could see its flame.

Holmes leaned toward me again, whispering like a scholar recalling an Old Testament fire:

"A quiet echo of Elijah, Watson—calling down flame to expose falsehood."

The deacon lowered the candle to the staff.

One second.

Two.

WHOOSH.

The staff caught fire in an exploding plume, racing up its length in a single hungry breath, a searing hungry blaze that leapt skyward like a guilty conscience suddenly laid bare.

"Guess it wasn't built for the heat," Remington said.

A murmur rippled outward—gasps, hushed protests,the rustle of scandal drawing its first breath.

The fire raced up the length of the staff in a single ravenous surge.

Silver paint blistered. Cheap wood shrieked as sap burst. Smoke billowed with the acrid reek of resinous pine.

His voice, when it rose, was clear and solemn—not triumphant, but wounded, pastoral:

"Y que Dios perdone a quienes erraron por orgullo...a quienes ofrecieron esta falsa reliquia a Su Iglesia para honrarse a sí mismos.

Que Dios perdone...a la casa del Castillo."

And may God forgive those who erred through pride...those who offered this false relic to His Church for their own honour.

May God forgive...the House of Castillo.

The crowd recoiled—then surged forward, crying out as one:

"*¡FALSO! ¡FALSO! ¡RELICARIO FALSO!*"

Fake! Fake! The reliquary is fake!

Santiago crossed himself quietly.

For a long moment, the Bishop of Pamplona did not move.

He stood with crozier planted, mitre steady, his gaze fixed not on the flames themselves but on what they revealed. Smoke curled upward between him and the crowd, blurring the gilded fraud into something unmistakably human: pride and deceit.

A hush rippled across the stands.

Around him, the other clergy reacted not as one body but as individuals exposed. One priest froze with his hands raised, the blessing unfinished. Another bowed his head sharply, as though struck by a sudden pain. A third stood rigid, lips moving without sound, caught between prayer and flight.

None spoke

None stepped forward

Not from confusion, nor from reverence, but because each, in his own guarded heart, had already entertained the possibility that the relic was false.

Padre Basilio—the priest into whose cathedral the relics had been entrusted—went very still. The colour drained from his face until it matched the white of his alb, and in the wavering firelight he looked less a servant of God than a man caught mid-confession. As the staff blackened and cracked, collapsing in upon itself, his expression seemed to mirror it—something hollowing, something giving way.

"Faith endures heat," Holmes said. "Fraud does not."

Behind them, the boys' choir faltered. The antiphon thinned, then unravelled. A single treble voice wavered and fell silent; another boy stared at the burning staff, mouth parted. Murmurs rippled among them—*falso*, someone whispered, scarcely louder than breath.

A few of the boys glanced instinctively toward the private box where Don Ramiro sat, and one, emboldened by youth or terror, lifted his chin and pointed before being pulled sharply back by his neighbour.

The choirmaster raised his hand at last, too late to salvage the song.

Then the Bishop raised one hand.

Not in alarm. Not in condemnation. But in command.

The uproar faltered. The chant of ¡FALSO! broke apart into uneasy whispers, then into silence, as though the arena itself had remembered where it stood.

The priests nearest the dais froze, eyes wide, hands uncertain upon their stoles. One half-stepped forward, then stopped. Another lowered his gaze, lips moving in a prayer not meant for public hearing. No one spoke.

At last the Bishop inclined his head—once—toward Deacon Honesto.

It was not approval. It was not rebuke. It was acknowledgment.

"This matter," the Bishop said, his voice carrying without effort, "has been placed before God and the faithful."

He turned slowly, letting his gaze sweep the stands, the ring, the blackened remnants still smouldering in the sand.

"And God," he added, "has answered plainly."

The Crowd Turns

A shiver passed through the clergy ranks. One priest crossed himself. Another removed his biretta and held it to his chest, as if steadiness might be found there.

The Bishop lifted his crozier again, its silver head catching the sun, and motioned for the procession to continue out of the arena.

Every eye in the arena looked upward to the dignitary dais.

Don Ramiro del Castillo sat frozen—with the stiffness of one caught mid-lie.

His face blanched to the colour of unbaked clay.

Beside him, Doña Ysabel de Arriaga did not rise.

Her fingers tightened imperceptibly on her fan, the knuckles whitening beneath her silks.

She stared straight ahead, chin high, lips pressed into a line so thin it could have been carved by a jeweller's tool.

And the crowd...

The crowd pivoted like a great living tide, its fury focusing upon the dais with the inexorable force of the encierro itself.

Cries rose sharp and multiplied:

"*¡Engaño!*"

"*¡Vergüenza!*"

"*¡La casa del Castillo nos ha mentido!*"

Deception!

Shame!

The House of Castillo has lied to us.

The priest, Padre Basilio, a man whose principles softened under pressure, looked as though the earth had betrayed him.

His eyes darted from the burning staff to the crowd, to Ramiro, to Honesto, as though searching for the single direction in which to flee. He stumbled backward, crossing himself wildly.

He would not meet Ramiro's gaze. His eyes slid past the procession instead, with the strained reverence of a man pretending not to see a serpent coiled among the pews.

Only when he reached the sheltering shadow of a pillar did he stop—his breath quick and shallow, fingers trembling as they clutched at the edge of his stole, as if cloth might steady what conscience could not.

A woman near the barrier spat on the ground in the old Basque manner meant to ward off evil.

Men pointed.

Children clutched their fathers.

Even the musicians fell silent.

In that suspended second, the House of del Castillo, once proud, once unassailable, looked very much like a great dam that has held back the river for generations, until one fissure appears, and every eye knows the flood is coming.

Haste

Holmes leaned toward me, his voice a mere thread:

"Truth, Watson...moves faster than any bull."

From the the presidential box, the president of the bullfight, had not yet risen.

He sat very still, one hand resting on the rail, the other folded over a neatly pressed handkerchief. His face was composed—too composed—eyes fixed not on the smoking ruin of the false relic, but on the crowd itself, measuring its temperature the way a physician reads a fever.

Below him, confusion swelled.

A cry rose. Then another. A thousand murmurs collided.

The last cries of "¡FALSO! ¡RELICARIO FALSO!" were still crashing against the stone walls of the arena when Don Ramiro lurched to his feet—pale, sweating, the false dignity of his seat among the dignitaries collapsing visibly around him.

Don Ramiro leaned toward the *presidente de la corrida* and spoke a single sentence, low and urgent.

He did not speak loudly. He did not need to.

A few words passed between them. Ramiro's hand made a small, dismissive motion, as though brushing ash from a sleeve. His expression was one of mild regret, the look of a man inconvenienced by disorder rather than implicated in it.

The *presidente* inclined his head.

A moment later, the *presidente's* fingers closed around the white handkerchief.

Holmes, watching from below, felt the shift before it was visible.

The *presidente* rose.

His voice cracked like a whip over the uproar.

"*¡Basta!*"

Enough.

Silence fell—not complete, but cowed.

He lifted the handkerchief high.

Once.

Clean.

Decisive.

"*¡Que comience la corrida—ahora!*"

Let the bullfight begin—now.

The handkerchief dropped.

The trumpet answered at once—sharp, metallic, unmistakable.

The gates below began to move.

And just like that, the crowd turned—from sacrilege to spectacle, from doubt to blood.

Holmes did not look at the gates.

He watched Don Ramiro.

Ramiro had already settled back into his seat.

His hands were folded. His face serene.

As though nothing at all had gone wrong.

Doña Ysabel seized the edge of her fan so tightly the lacquered ribs creaked. Her eyes flicked—first to the smoking ruin of the relic, then to Honesto, and finally back to the stands, already calculating how swiftly scandal might be buried beneath spectacle.

A ripple of unease passed through the crowd.

Voices rose, overlapping.

A question moved through the stands like a chill:

So soon?Already?

¡YA! Now!

Only the sudden understanding that the bull would be loosed at once—raw, unprepared—before the ring had settled, before the ritual had done its quiet work.

It was not command—it was panic wearing the mask of authority.

The crowd knew it.

Holmes leaned toward me, his voice dry as bone:

"Observe, Watson—the first refuge of the guilty is haste."

CHAPTER XXVI

The Bullfight

The Peacock in the Sand

Holmes's eyes narrowed as the toriles gate stirred.

Remington inclined his head toward me, a faint gleam of wicked anticipation in his eye. "Ah. Now comes our dancer."

The matador emerged and did not hurry. He paused beneath the archway, one foot still in shadow, as though allowing the crowd a moment to admire him. He adjusted his sash with deliberate care, tugging it twice, then once more, until it sat exactly as he wished. Only then did he step forward, lifting his chin toward the stands rather than the sand.

He crossed the arena at an angle that favoured the crowd, not the bull's gate, letting the cape trail longer than necessary behind him. He raised it once, testing its fall, then again, higher, the cloth opening wide as if already mid-pass. The gesture earned him a murmur of approval. He acknowledged it with the smallest nod, as though confirmation had been expected.

He did not test the ground.

He posed.

Legs planted apart, chest lifted, chin raised—not in defiance, but display. He shouted to the crowd, the sound sharp and foreign in the vast bowl of the plaza, more announcement than challenge.

Remington did not smile.

"That's not courage," he quipped. "That's choreography."

Remington's eyes tracked the matador's shoes, his feet set flat and final. His weight transferred fully and early. No testing of the sand—just full confidence that the sand would hold as expected. The matador stood with a stillness that belongs to rehearsal, not danger.

Remington muttered, "Feet like that belong to a man who thinks nothing's coming."

Then I said it:

"Holmes—Remington," I said. "I'd wager he believes the bull has already been dosed with chloral hydrate. He is counting on a slow-moving and groggy bull. Sluggish reflexes. Delayed response. A false sense of control."

Holmes did not look away from the man.

"That," he said, "is going to be the shortest education in Spain."

Remington laughed.

"Drugged bull? Hell, he's about to meet El Toro—wide awake, angry, and fresh from tossing Del Castillo's brute. If that French peacock thinks he's getting a docile parade bull, he's about to learn why Navarra breeds legends."

The Frenchman gave a flourish.

Above the ring, the presidente lifted the white handkerchief. Too soon, some thought.

The crowd buzzed—confused and unsettled.

The toriles gate lurched.

A tremor went through the sand.

A hush swallowed the arena.

Remington folded his arms.

"Well," he said quietly, "this should separate silk from spine."

Holmes's eyes did not leave the gate.

"Observe closely, Watson," he murmured. "This is where we shall have the truth—and truth, as it happens, has horns."

Entrance into the Arena

The afternoon light bleached hard and merciless. White shirts rippled in the stands, red scarves flared like wounds against linen, and the crowd—pious an hour ago—had already surrendered itself to appetite.

A roar swept through the stands, first a ripple, then a wave, then a single unified exhalation from ten thousand lungs.

The toriles gates shuddered.

The French matador paused. He adjusted the knot of his sash, smoothed the line of his jacket, then raised the cape into position and held it there—still, formal—before the bull had even entered the ring. Then he struck a pose, his posture radiating the supreme confidence of a man utterly convinced the bull behind the gate was still drugged into passivity.

"He's standing like he's already won," Remington observed.

Suddenly—

CLANG.

GRIND.

BOOM.

The gate lurched upward.

For a heartbeat the arena held its breath.

El Toro

And then he appeared.

Not trotting

Not prancing.

Not stumbling

He arrived.

Not charging blindly as lesser bulls often do, all hormones, raw emotion, and muscle.

El Toro walked from the gate and stood.

Watching.

Reading the arena.

This was the kind of bull matadors feared most: not blind force, but intelligence.

Remington watched the bull and shook his head once.

"Here's the trouble," he said. "A man brings the most powerful weapon he has, intelligence. On the other side the bull brings his most powerful weapon, incredible strength. That's usually a fair match. That's the ancient question of a bullfight. Who wins? But today we have a bull with strength and intelligence. Two qualities. That makes the match-up 1–2. For the bull."

A mountain of obsidian muscle, shoulders rolling like surf, hide gleaming with the pitch-black sheen of midnight rain. He was colossal, larger than any fighting bull I had ever seen—all mass, majesty, and vengeance.

The crowd gasped.

Someone near the front dropped their fan.

A small boy shouted, "*¡MADRE MÍA... ES MÁS GRANDE QUE UN CARRO DE HENO!*"

Mother of mercy... it's bigger than a hay wagon.

Holmes's eyes shone.

"Ah. There he is. Navarra's sovereign."

Suddenly it was clear to all: this was not a usual bullfight. It was a contest of wills.

The matador moved to assert control, attempting to impose form upon stillness, raising his cape deliberately, offering it low and open, as if inviting a charge that had not been agreed to.

When none came, he stepped laterally, closing distance rather than yielding it, attempting to force the encounter.

A seasoned matador would have waited—tested, unsettled, read the animal. This man could not. The bull's stillness denied him affirmation, and he answered it with movement.

It was not recklessness. It was impatience disguised as confidence.

It was haste.

To a bull like this, haste signalled weakness.

Holmes inclined his head a fraction.

"Observe, Watson. The bull waits. That alone gives him command."

Pride Cometh

Still, he strutted on, chin lifted, attempting the practised swagger of a seasoned torero, exuding a melodramatic seriousness characteristic of men who have ventured beyond their depth.

He advanced, measuring his steps as though the sand itself were obliged to accommodate him. He raised the cape with care and held it open, low and inviting, its line precise, its fall rehearsed. There was a stiffness where there should have been suppleness. He lingered in the position a moment too long, waiting for a response.

None came.

He shifted his feet and reset them—flat, final—then adjusted his stance again, widening it slightly, as if certainty could be achieved by geometry.

The cape moved once more, higher this time; the cloth snapped lightly to stir the air. A second pass followed, broader, more emphatic, meant to wake the bull, which he assumed had been dulled with a sedative.

El Toro did not move.

He did not paw the sand.

He watched.

He stood.

He breathed, the great barrel of his chest rising and falling, his head angled just enough to keep the man within his sight and enough to deny him the dignity of being in command.

In his stillness there was no stupor, no fog, no drugged confusion—only a calm rooted in strength.

At last, the matador, unable to bear a silence that did not applaud, shifted his stance with a sharp little scrape—an impatient torero's sidestep—and flicked sand toward the bull's nostrils, as though to wake him, to move him.

Then there was a brief, unnatural stillness, the kind that follows insult. The crowd felt it before it understood it.

One forehoof shifted—not backward, not forward, but setting. The weight redistributed. The great line of the shoulders tightened.

It was not motion toward the matador; it was preparation.

The bull turned his head fully now, bringing both eyes to bear. The matador was no longer part of the arena. He was the arena. The bull was done reading.

The slow breathing stopped.

Not replaced by panting but by holding.

That held breath was the last warning.

The matador interpreted this as success. He believed the sand had "woken" the bull. He lifted the cape again, stepped once more, sealing his error.

Suddenly, El Toro lowered his massive head, shaking it side to side, dragging his muzzle through the sand with a long, rumbling scrape.

Not a clumsy gesture, a deliberate one.

He gathered up the dust, rolled it across his face and horns, covering his face with dust like war paint, preparing for a charge.

When El Toro lifted his head again, his eyes burned through the curtain of dust.

He let out a loud groan, a deep bass note howl, a cavernous, bone-deep bellow.

"murrraaaahhhh!"

The sound he made shook the timbers of the plaza.

A hush swept the arena.

He repeated this moan several times, shaking his head, sending a warning.

His tail snapped side to side, slicing the air like a whip.

The matador froze.

El Toro answered with another cavernous, bone-deep roar:

"MMMUURRRAAAAHHHHHH!"

A sound so low it seemed to vibrate through the sand, up the barrier, and straight into the impostor's spine.

Then, El Toro lowered his head.

The great neck settled, the massive skull angling down as the horns came level. He did not shake them. He did not paw the sand. He did not rush.

He aimed.

The matador felt it before he understood it. The cape, lifted again in habit, hesitated in his hands. His weight shifted back a fraction, unbidden. For the first time since the gates had opened, he did not move first.

The matador did not move at all.

A hesitation.

So slight the crowd did not see it.

At that moment, he truly looked at the bull.

Something in the animal had changed.

Formidable.

Fierce.

The matador's breath caught.

This was no dulled creature, no softened charge blunted by the chemist's hand. No stupor. No fog.

Suddenly—Clarity.

Then—Fear.

The matador realised the bull before him was entirely sober—not drugged into passivity. A drugged bull would have blundered forward.

El Toro targeted.

The bull did not follow the cloth.

The pink capote circled uselessly in the air, unanswered.

El Toro's gaze never left the man.

Eyes locked together, one in fear, the other in force.

The matador stopped breathing,

Stopped moving,

Stopped pretending.

Remington exhaled once.

"That's it," he said. "He's done."

The bull began pawing the sand, tail whipping faster now.

The matador started to step backwards.

The bull pawed the earth once.

Twice.

A third time.

The crowd leaned forward as one.

In a flash,

El Toro charged.

The matador took a step back, then another, waving his capote to his side as though it might still distract the bull.

It did not.

El Toro came on, all muscle and ferocity, lightning-fast, directly towards the matador

The matador next did the unforgivable as far as corridas are concerned.

He turned and ran.

He took three steps.

The horn caught him high in the left thigh and lifted him as easily as a rag. He fell face-first into the sand, the capote crumpling beneath him as the plaza erupted.

Remington gave a low whistle, the kind he might give when a trout snaps a line.

Remington pointed. "Look at him, Watson—a face like a man who's just realised the piano he's been playing is actually a bear."

Holmes observed in that icy whisper he reserves for catastrophe: "The charade is over."

Chaos in the Arena

A gasp knifed through the arena.

The crowd erupted, half laughter, half contempt, wholly merciless. Someone shouted:

"*¡MATADOR DE MANTEQUILLA!*"

BUTTER MATADOR!

The peones burst from the barrier at once, capotes flaring red and gold, their shouts sharp and urgent. They ran toward the danger, not away from it, snapping the cloth low and wide to draw El Toro's attention while hands reached for the fallen matador. He was dragged backward across the sand, shoes scraping, blood darkening the white beneath him as the capotes formed a moving wall between him and the bull.

Above the ring, the presidente waved the white handkerchief again—once, sharply.

A signal of intervention.

The picadors entered.

They came mounted on heavy, blindfolded draft horses, massive and patient beasts bred for steadiness rather than speed, their padded flanks armoured thickly beneath layers of protection. One of them advanced, lance lowered, trying to claim the space and restore order.

El Toro did not slow.

He came at the horse straight on, undeterred by the height, the bulk, the unfamiliar shape. The lance glanced, skidding uselessly along muscle and horn. The horse reared in panic, its hooves churning the sand, and the picador was pitched hard to the ground.

The bull wheeled and came again.

The horse, eyes wild behind the blindfold, bolted—not forward, but sideways—leaping the barrier in a clumsy, desperate bound that sent the crowd recoiling. The picador lay stunned in the sand as peones scattered, capotes snapping frantically, trying to pull El Toro's focus from one moving target to another.

One peón was too slow.

El Toro turned on him without hesitation. A single, brutal sweep of the horns caught the man at the hip and flung him clear of the charge, his body skidding across the sand as the capote fell from his hands.

The bull did not pursue him.

It was no use.

The ring had lost its rhythm.

The sequence had broken.

El Toro was no longer answering signals.

He charged again—at movement, at mass, at anything that dared to stand—driving men back toward the barriers, capotes tangling, horses screaming, the crowd rising as one in alarm.

This was no longer a bullfight proceeding by rule.

The arena belonged to the bull now.

No man moved to challenge him.

The bull was wild with fury.

CHAPTER XXVII

Thunder and Silence

Into the Ring

No one noticed the limping man at first.

There was too much motion: men scrambling for the barriers, capotes flaring, voices cracking in panic and outrage.

The crowd shouted now—not in unison, but in fragments—curses and prayers colliding as El Toro stood amid the wreckage of order, flanks dark with sweat, tail cutting the air.

Only I saw him.

The brown habit marked him as a Franciscan.

Mateo slipped through the gate like one more shadow in the confusion, favouring his right side and keeping his left arm close. His habit was torn, darkened with blood and dust. He held one shoulder slightly too high and stiffly. As he walked, his right leg led—faster than a wounded man should manage.

His head was up.

His hood was down.

His gaze was fixed straight ahead on the bull.

El Toro ran the ring in a fury, bellowing low and raw.

Rage had taken him fully now.

Blind.

Directionless, absolute.

Without warning he wheeled and drove his horns into the wooden barrier, striking it with such force that the timbers shuddered. The entire north section lurched under the blow as he surged forward again, tearing a jagged breach through the boards.

He tore the timber free without slowing.

Splintered boards dragged from one horn. Sand churned like water behind him.

When he wrenched his horns free, the wood bore their deep impression—and with them, the silver tips the Del Castillos had cruelly fastened upon him.

Nothing built by men seemed made to withstand him.

He no longer ran at men—he ran at the world.

The Power

Power ran in the ring and no man could master it. Even the picadors backed their mounts away. No cape held him. The shouting fractured into screams.

Laughter was gone.

Then—through the noise—something moved steadily. Only one man moved forward.

The brown habit looked very slight in the widening ring. The ring seemed suddenly enormous.

He walked toward the bull.

He walked toward a force greater than flesh and horn—toward chaos—and did not hesitate.

El Toro circled wide, testing the air, and Mateo tracked him instinctively, adjusting his course to keep distance without retreat. A bruise darkened his cheekbone. He did not touch it. His shoulder throbbed. He did not slow. Whatever had been done to him remained behind him.

This was where he belonged.

He stepped into the open sand with the quiet authority of a man entering a chapel.

El Toro wheeled, breath roaring in his chest—a tornado of strength and sand.

Mateo walked toward the center of the ring, closer to the bull, bearing nothing but

A limp.

His robe

His faith.

El Toro thundered to the barrera, snorting, flanks heaving, horns carving furious arcs. He turned once more, the sand tearing beneath his hooves, his charge still unbroken.

He sensed Mateo.

Then he saw Mateo.

The arena held its breath.

Then—

the bull charged.

The crowd screamed.

Men scattered

Someone fell.

The crowd broke into a single ragged cry that seemed to tear itself from the stone.

Mateo did not move.

He stood in the open sand, small against the mass of the charging animal.

The bull came on—a storm of muscle and dust.

Mateo's torn habit stirred faintly about his legs. He looked toward heaven and prayed.

"Señor, hazme un instrumento de tu paz."

Lord, make me an instrument of your peace.

Then—almost absently—he raised his hand.

Not as a challenge.

Not as spectacle.

Simply as a priest might, greeting the suffering.

He raised his hand, palm outward, and traced the cross slowly in the air before the charging animal—not as one commanding a beast, but as one blessing a fellow creature beneath the same Creator.

Simply natural.

As if Mateo's body knew the motion before his mind did.

Simply as reflex.

A Franciscan reflex.

The bull thundered forward.

Ten yards,

Five,

The earth trembling beneath its weight.

And then.

It faltered.

The bull slowed.

Stopped.

Breath thundering.

It Bellowed.

And pawed the earth.

Dust rising.

Not tamed.

Not gentle.

But suspended.

Checked, as though an invisible boundary lay beneath its hooves.

The arena full of able-bodied men retreating, gasping.

El Toro's great head lifted.

For the first time since entering the ring, El Toro seemed to look—not at movement, not at color—but at the still figure before him.

Mateo's lips moved.

Whether in prayer or breath, I could not tell.

In the sudden pocket of silence that gathered around them, he made a small sound.

"Tk... tk... tk..."

Soft.

Patient.

The way one might coax a frightened animal from a hedge.

The dust curled around his sandals.

Mateo lifted two fingers to his lips and made a soft clicking sound again—hardly louder than a pebble tapping glass.

"Tk... tk-tk..."

It was almost nothing. And yet—everything.

Suddenly the crowd became still.

A hush travelled across the arena like a great sheet drawn over a lantern.

"¡Un fraile!" someone shouted.

Friar!

"What's he doing—?" Came from the stands.

Alarmed, I said quickly, "Holmes... he'll be killed. We must do something."

Beside me, Holmes said quietly, "Steady now...he has help we cannot give."

Remington said nothing. He stood transfixed—as though afraid even movement might break whatever held the bull at bay.

El Toro snorted, shook dust from his horns, and snorted again.

The massive head lifted.

The tail stilled and lowered.

The ears relaxed—then came forward.

Dust drifted from his muzzle like incense.

Silence fell.

Twenty thousand hearts forgot to beat.

A murmur ran through the stands—disbelief and awe.

The bull pawed—slowly now, no longer in rage.

Mateo made the sound again, gentle this time—and spoke, not loudly, not for the crowd.

"Tranquilo, torito, mi torito grande...

conmigo, compañero."

Easy, little bull, my little big bull...

come with me, friend.

The bull turned his head. Not sharply. Not in challenge. He looked at Mateo.

"Tranquilo, amigo mío. Tranquilo."

The tail slowed. The great shoulders eased. El Toro lowered his head, in recognition—and began to turn, slow and deliberate, toward the monk.

Mateo did not move.

He uttered one word, in a slow, drawn-out chant.

"T r a n q u i l o ."

His voice carried cleanly across the ring—unforced, pastoral, the sound of a man calling livestock at dawn.

El Toro's ears twitched.

The bull took one step toward him. Then another.

No one breathed.

Then, with a low rumble deep in his chest—not anger, not warning—he trotted toward Mateo, stopping just before him, head bowed, the dust of the arena rising in a faint halo around them both.

A collective gasp pulsed through the amphitheatre.

Women clutched their fans to their mouths. Men leaned forward gripping the railing. A picador crossed himself twice, forgetting which hand to use.

Remington sat down hard, shook his head, and let out a low whistle—but said nothing.

He caught his breath as though he had been the one in the ring.

"Upon my word, extraordinary," I said.

Remington slipped his hat off and looked at the ground once before speaking.

"That's how it's done," he said quietly. "I've seen men face raging bulls, but I've never seen..." He stopped, searching for the word, then gave it up.

Holmes watched intently. "We may be witnessing the miracle Santiago dared to expect."

For a heartbeat, the plaza seemed to forget itself.

In that instant—the monk still and small, the bull towering yet gentle—the whole of Pamplona fell silent as stone.

When El Toro reached the monk, the great bull lowered his head until one horn brushed the brown wool of Mateo's habit.

Mateo extended one hand and laid it upon the bull's broad forehead. The touch was steady. Familiar. As though this were not the first such meeting. This was a bond between a boy of Navarra and the beast he had raised by hand.

A collective exhale moved through the amphitheatre —a single breath from twenty thousand souls.

Then the crowd erupted.

"¡Olé!"

"¡Olé!"

"¡Olé!"

It was impossible not to feel the ring had made its choice.

Remington let out a long breath beside me.

"Well," he said quietly, "there's your real matador."

CHAPTER XXVIII

Holmes Steps into the Ring

Before the Commissioner

From the dignitary box, Ramiro lurched to his feet, voice cracking as he bellowed:

"Stop that mad monk! Security! Do you not see? He's absconding with my champion bull! My investment! Do you hear me? Thievery! Arrest him at once!"

Don Ramiro had no brutish henchmen left to step in and physically stop Mateo.

A ring-attendant, realising what was happening, vaulted the rail and sprinted toward Mateo.

"*¡Fuera! ¡Salga, fraile!*"

Out! Get out, friar! You cannot—!

Mateo did not flinch.

Holmes, Remington and I descended from the stands into the arena's inner passageway, the roar of the crowd shifting into a hollow thunder around us. Dust clung to our boots; the air shimmered with heat and confusion.

Toward the arena sands, where Mateo stood beside El Toro, serene as a shepherd with his charge, stood The Commissioner of Pamplona—broad-shouldered, stern, his insignia gleaming against his dark uniform. He had come running at the sight of Mateo in the ring, the bull at his heels, for no lesser authority in Navarra would dare intervene in such a moment.

Holmes stepped forward, the dust of the arena swirling about his boots, and addressed the commissioner.

"Commissioner," he said, lifting his hat with calm precision, "my name is Holmes. Sherlock Holmes."

Recognition sparked at once in the man's eyes.

"Sí, señor Holmes," he replied, lowering his voice. "I know you by reputation—a man of the law, of Scotland Yard, called upon when matters turn... unusual."

Ramiro, still red-faced and sputtering in the dignitaries' gallery, bellowed: "*¡Mi toro!* Arrest that monk! Arrest them all! They are stealing my prize bull!"

"Your bull?" Holmes repeated softly, almost politely.

Holmes did not look up at him. Instead, he reached inside his coat and produced the folded parchment.

Then Holmes looked squarely at the chief of police.

"Then you will understand the gravity of this," he said quietly. "Señor Ibarra, this is the deed Don Ramiro claims as proof of ownership. I advise you to examine the signature.

You will note—"He unfolded it with surgical precision, exposing the signature, "that it is forged. Poorly. Brother Elías, the diocesan archivist, confirmed as much."

The police commissioner took it, his brow knitting as his thumb traced the ink.

Holmes continued: "You will observe several inconsistencies.

"First: the ink is recent. It has not had time to settle into the fibres of the parchment, as genuine age would require.

"Second: the parchment itself has been artificially aged—treated, no doubt, to produce the appearance of time without its passage.

"Third: the bishop's seal is a forgery—crude, though effective at a distance.

"Fourth: the ribbon is of a type not manufactured until two years after the date inscribed."

He paused, then pointed with one slender finger.

"And finally—the signature purporting to be that of Bishop Arguedas is misspelled. A detail unlikely to escape the bishop, but entirely consistent with a man working from memory... rather than truth.

"—and, if you consult your own records, you will find that Bishop Arguedas has been dead these twelve years."

El Comisario Ibarra looked from the deed to Ramiro, whose mouth opened and shut in silent outrage.

Holmes's voice sharpened, not loud but honed like steel. "If there has been a theft today, Sheriff, it is not Mateo's. It is not the monk who walks unarmed beside the bull he raised."

He turned his gaze toward the dignitaries' box, where Don Ramiro paled beneath his silks.

"The true theft is the one committed by Don Ramiro del Castillo, the unlawful seizure of this animal, the fraud of this false deed, and the deception of Navarra under his name."

Holmes placed the document into the sheriff's hands. "There, sir, is your criminal."

The sheriff straightened slowly—very slowly—as though feeling the weight of Navarra's eyes gathering upon him.

He folded the deed with sober deliberation, tucked it into his breast pocket, and rested a hand on the baton at his belt.

Holmes's voice hardened.

"If a crime has been committed this day, it is not the liberation of an animal from unlawful captivity. It is the attempted theft of that animal by Don Ramiro del Castillo—through fraud, coercion, drugging, and deceit."

He folded his hands behind his back.

"The bull belongs to Navarra, Sheriff. Not to that man."

Ramiro's protest cracked into a shriek.

"Mentiras! Lies! Arrest him! Arrest the monk! Arrest..."

Holmes finally looked up. "Sheriff," he said with quiet finality, "arrest whomever the evidence compels you to arrest."

Mateo rested a gentle hand on El Toro's flank.

El Comisario took one long, damning look at the deed, the scorched remains of the false relic still smoking at the edge of the ring, and the panicked faces of Don Ramiro and Doña Ysabel seated above the barrera.

He straightened to his full authority.

"Don Ramiro del Castillo... Doña Ysabel de Arriaga..."

His voice carried across the entire arena like a bell summoning judgment.

"You will accompany my officers at once. You are to be held on charges of fraud, forgery of ecclesiastical property, and the unlawful seizure of livestock belonging to another house. This day's spectacle has revealed enough to shame a province."

A collective gasp rolled through the crowd.

Ysabel's fan slipped from her fingers. Ramiro sagged as if the spine had gone out of him entirely.

Holmes stepped forward, hands loosely clasped behind his back, gaze cool and unhurried.

"Comisario, you will find additional corroboration in the statements of Brother Elías," he said.

"And I need hardly remind you that the burning relic alone renders their innocence mathematically impossible. Navarra has been duped, but not for a moment longer."

Remington grinned like a man who had just watched justice land a clean uppercut.

"Well," he drawled,

"That's one—a forged deed.

"Two—an imitation relic.

"Three—a farce of a bullfight.

"Commissioner... where I come from...three strikes. You're out."

He crossed his arms, bruised knuckles resting against his ribs, and eyed Ramiro.

One of Holmes's eyebrows twitched upward.

I tried not to smile.

In the hush that followed, Mateo placed both palms gently against El Toro's great muzzle.

"Vamos, viejo amigo," he whispered.

Santiago, face soft with reverence, stepped to the bull's flank, murmuring prayers older than the streets of Pamplona.

Together, a humble monk, a friar, and the great bull passed calmly side by side through the open gate.

CHAPTER XXIX

Franciscan Feast

The Note at El Pasiano

The bar of Hotel El Pasiano was uncommonly subdued that evening, perhaps out of collective exhaustion after the chaos at the Plaza de Toros. The lamps glowed low and amber, reflecting in half-emptied glasses; a gramophone in the corner crooned a melancholy jota.

Remington sat with his boots up on a second chair, a cold compress pressed rakishly to his cheek and nursed a glass of Rioja, still feeling dust in his lungs. Holmes approached us with that unmistakable swiftness of step that meant something had just occurred.

He carried an envelope.

A simple one—rough paper, sealed with a thumbprint of wax, and addressed in a careful monastic hand:

A Don Sherlock Holmes,

Hospedaje El Pasiano,

El Pasiano Guesthouse.

Holmes tapped the envelope once, thoughtfully, before breaking the seal.

"From San Telmo," he said.

Remington lowered the compress. "News about the bull?"

"About many things, I suspect."

Holmes unfolded the letter. The script was spare but steady—unmistakably Friar Santiago's.

He read aloud:

♦ ♦ ♦

Estimado Señor Holmes,

The brothers of San Telmo offer you, Doctor Watson, and Señor Remington our deepest gratitude.

The good creature El Toro is returned safely to our care and rests now in the lower pasture.

His wounds are minor; his spirit, unchanged.

Though our table is humble, we ask that you honour us with your presence tomorrow at the hour of vespers.

We wish to give thanks.

In friendship,

Fray Santiago

Holmes folded the letter and gave one of his rare, quiet smiles—the sort of expression I had learned signalled both affection and approval.

"Well then, Watson," he said. "It would appear the monks of San Telmo wish to honour their unlikely champions."

Remington, still smelling faintly of dust, Rioja, and victory, sat with his sleeves rolled up and his grin unapologetically wide.

"A feast?" Remington said, eyebrows rising. "From Franciscans? I thought their idea of a banquet was a boiled root and a prayer."

Holmes poured himself a fresh measure of Rioja.

He did not drink it at once.

"Even a humble table," Holmes replied, "becomes a banquet when gratitude is its host."

The Banquet

The monastery of San Telmo greeted us with celebration.

As we stepped through the low stone archway, the oak door creaked open to a chorus of bells and cooking smells—herbs crisping over coals, onions sweetening in a pan, bread breaking somewhere out of sight.

The courtyard was alive with motion. Barefoot monks bustled like kindly sparrows, darting from table to table with armfuls of earthenware bowls, pitchers of watered wine, baskets of garden greens still glittering with dew.

Mateo was already waiting for us, leaning on his good shoulder beside the enormous, contented bulk of El Toro, who grazed peacefully near the well as though he had never known an arena.

The beast flicked an ear at Remington, who gave him a respectful nod; at Holmes, who raised an eyebrow in greeting; and at me—upon which he let out a soft, satisfied snort that set the dust dancing.

Long rustic wooden tables had been carried into the courtyard, their uneven planks freshly scrubbed. Several monks were laying sprigs of wildflowers along the centre—simple blossoms from the hillsides, arranged with the quiet pride of men unaccustomed to ornament.

Holmes, Remington, and I paused at the threshold, momentarily disarmed by the sincerity of the scene.

"Not quite the Diogenes Club," I murmured, adjusting my cuff, "but I could get used to this."

Friar Santiago's Blessing

Santiago spoke standing at the head of the long wooden table, hands folded in his sleeves, the firelight of the roasting pit flickering behind him.

"Friends... *hermanos*... honoured guests of San Telmo," Brother Santiago began, his voice soft but carrying, as all good monastic voices do. "The Lord has delivered us many blessings in these days, some in the guise of trials, some in the guise of strangers who arrived as wanderers and now sit as family."

He inclined his head toward Holmes, myself, and Remington in turn.

"In the Scriptures it is written that the truth shall set you free. Today, truth set free not only our beloved El Toro, but all that had been falsely elevated—and falsely staged—before the eyes of Navarra."

A gentle ripple of agreement murmured along the table.

"Saint Francis taught that it is in giving that we receive. You three men—by wit, by courage, and by a generosity of spirit rare in this world—have recovered the innocent and restored peace to a humble monastery. And so tonight, in the small ways we can..."

He gestured to the roasted lamb, the bowls of herbed potatoes, the fresh loaves steaming beneath linen cloths, and the short clay cups of rough monastery wine.

"...we give back."

He smiled, a shy, unpolished thing.

"I prepared many words earlier... but Brother Mateo reminded me that God is more pleased with simple thanks than with clever speeches."

Mateo, already blushing behind a basket of bread, drew a soft chuckle from the monks.

"So I will say only this:

"May the peace of Christ go with you. May the courage of San Fermín guide your steps. May the truth you defended here echo longer than lies ever could. And may you always find a welcome at the table of San Telmo."

He lifted his cup.

"*A los amigos que Dios envió,* to the friends God has sent."

The monks raised theirs, a soft clatter of clay, a warm sigh of gratitude, and the feast truly began.

Courage, Faith, and a Rope

Remington rolled his shoulder once and winced.

"I've been in bars where courage was cheaper than wine," he said. "But I don't think I've ever seen a man step in front of a gun with nothing but rope and prayer."

Mateo shrugged, embarrassed. "I only—"

Remington winked. "King David's got nothing on your aim."

Santiago allowed himself the smallest of smiles. "David had stones. Mateo had a cross."

Mateo shook his head. "It was not my aim." He looked up and quickly crossed himself. "And besides, the Doctor"—he nodded toward me—"kept the giant distracted."

I gave a small shrug. "It's been with me since Afghanistan," I said. "I hoped never to draw it again. But some habits are harder to retire than others."

Holmes allowed himself the faintest smile. "I have not seen that particular restraint since *A Study in Scarlet*," he said. "It remains effective."

Saint Francis

Remington set his wine glass down and looked around the table.

"All right," he said. "What do Franciscans actually do all day?"

Santiago adjusted his chair and smiled. "Oh, the usual," he said. "Feed who we can, mend what we can... and trust God with the rest."

Santiago chuckled softly and leaned back.

"Saint Francis used to say, 'Start by doing what is necessary, then what is possible, and suddenly you are doing the impossible.'"

Remington studied him. "Tell me more about Saint Francis—and what drew you to this life."

Santiago considered the question longer than it required.

"Francis did not begin as a saint," he said at last. "He began life as a wealthy young man with many friends. You could say he was a merry sinner."

Remington held Santiago's gaze. "Seems to me... he knew what mattered."

"It came to him," Santiago continued. "Francis set out as a soldier to the south of Italy, hoping for military glory—to become a famous knight."

Remington pushed his plate away, listening intently.

"Soon after his departure, he heard a voice from above that rebuked him for following vanity and the will of men. He understood then that he was not called to be a soldier for men, but a soldier of our Lord."

Santiago crossed himself.

Remington leaned forward. "That saint of yours—was he always that calm... or did he learn it?"

Mateo spoke quietly. "He was a changed man from that point onward. Many of his friends and family thought him mad. When Francis resolved to give all for God, he gave his fine clothes to beggars, sold his father's wares, and offered all the money to the Church."

"Was he ever afraid?" Remington asked.

Mateo looked upward. "One day Francis came upon a leper. Yes—he was afraid. His instinct was to turn away. But he listened to the words of our Lord, who told him to love all men. He chose not to let fear rule him. Instead, he let God work through him—and he embraced the leper."

Remington nodded, saying nothing.

"Tell me something," he said. "That saint of yours... Francis. Was he truly the sort of man who walked toward danger?"

"He walked toward what frightened other men," Mateo said.

Remington turned the stem of his glass but did not drink.

"I saw you in the ring," he said. "You never hurried."

Mateo smiled faintly. "I assure you, it was not calm. It was the limp."

Remington studied him for a moment. "Most men with two good legs wouldn't have walked in there."

Holmes gave the faintest inclination of his head, as if the matter required no further comment.

For a moment, no one spoke.

Remington set his glass down. “Is it true he walked into a village that feared a wolf?”

“Yes,” Santiago said.

“And he went alone?”

“At Gubbio, the villagers were terrified by a fierce wolf that had killed livestock and men. Francis walked into the woods alone, unarmed, to seek it. When the wolf rushed at him, he made the sign of the cross...and the wolf lay down at his feet, meek as a lamb.”

No one ate, spoke, or drank for a moment.

Remington clasped his hands beneath his chin.

“That’s a different kind of brave—he didn’t try to beat it.”

He paused.

“Just faced it.”

Holmes inclined his head slightly.

“Physical courage is common enough,” he said. “Moral courage is far rarer—and often the stronger of the two.”

After a moment Remington said, almost to himself,

“Seems to me... a man could spend his whole life learning how to walk that way.”

Santiago smiled at that but did not contradict him. “Francis discovered that courage does not always mean advancing,” he said. “Sometimes it means turning the other cheek.”

I leaned forward. “That sounds harder.”

At that moment, the birds started chirping, and one landed on the statue of Saint Francis.

Miguelito, the shepherd boy, who had just finished pouring wine for the table, took some breadcrumbs from his plate and tossed them towards the birds.

No one told him to do it.

Remington observed him. "Courage is quiet. When it grows loud, it is often only bravado."

They drank.

There was silence for a moment.

The birds serenaded the banquet.

The Deacon and the Bishop

Remington lifted his glass but did not drink.

"Composure... that's what I saw," he said.

He considered it for a moment.

He paused.

"No—more than that. A kind of grace... grace in the face of danger."

He glanced toward Mateo. "A strength from within."

Mateo shook his head gently.

"Not from within," he said. "From above."

A murmur of agreement moved around the table.

Remington's eyes lingered on him a moment longer than courtesy required. Then, at last, he took a slow drink.

Then he spoke. "The only man who matched it was Deacon Honesto."

He turned.

"So—how did the matter of the relics conclude, Deacon? I trust they will not be inclined toward a Joan of Arc solution."

The table laughed.

It faded quickly.

Honesto did not answer at once. He reached for his glass, then stopped.

"Sometimes," he said at last, "it is necessary to be right in the eyes of God, whatever follows."

"And the Bishop?" I asked.

Honesto smiled faintly. "He thanked me. Privately."

Santiago inclined his head. "Privately, gratitude. Publicly, caution. Rome requires both."

Mateo shrugged. "A bishop sometimes wears two faces. One for God. One for Rome."

Honesto nodded. "God does not always reward loudly."

Remington brushed the recent scar above his eyebrow with the back of his hand. "And when there is no reward?"

Mateo glanced down at his rope, then back up. "Sometimes it comes in the form of forgiveness, sometimes as mercy—and sometimes," he smiled, "it arrives with two horns, four legs, and a tail."

Remington smiled. "Sometimes the reward is truth—however bloody it chooses to reveal itself."

Remington studied the table for a moment.

Honesto nodded. "Yes...and truth is the light on God's path."

Mateo looked up, suddenly earnest.

"Saint Francis would say,

"'All the darkness in the world cannot extinguish the light of a single candle.'"

Santiago inclined his head.

Remington observed the the candle that stood between the bottles. For a moment he watched the flame move. Then Remington reached into his pocket, drew out a small notebook, and wrote something quickly before closing it again.

El Toro's Future

Remington looked around the table. He leaned an elbow on the wood.

At last, he spoke.

"Tell me something... What of El Toro? What happens to him now? The Del Castillos are finished, and Von Helldorf has left Pamplona — but Old Gold remains. There will be other attempts to take the bull."

Santiago folded his hands before speaking.

"Señor Remington," he said, "the answer is simple."

A smile touched the corners of his mouth—tired, gentle, but steadied by purpose.

"My son," he said, "we do not intend sorrow for him... but future."

He paused, letting the words settle.

"Our cows are gone. Our bulls, once a dozen, are now but one."

He inclined his head slightly.

"El Toro returns to the hermitage—because there is nowhere else left on God's earth for him to go."

Brother Elías, who had been waiting for his moment, spoke. "Los Toros del Silencio," he said quietly. "And now, because of you three, there is still one left to graze our fields."

"It is true," he began, "that the great disasters nearly ended the Pyrenean line. But the lineage is not extinct. Not yet."

He lifted a finger. "In the high valleys of the Baztán and Roncal, beyond the old beech forests, where the roads thin and the mountains rise like grey cathedrals, there remain small, hidden herds. Daughters of the same ancient blood. Cows of Los Toros del Silencio, tended by Basque families who keep traditions older than maps."

Remington's brow rose. "So there are cows left."

"Sí," Santiago said, with a spark of hope. "A few. Brave creatures. Hardy as stone. But without a bull... without him..." He nodded towards the courtyard, where El Toro was grazing under the monastery fig tree. "Their line cannot continue."

Holmes steepled his fingers.

"And thus," he said softly, "the problem becomes a solution. You have the last bull... and somewhere in the mountains, the last cows."

Elías nodded vigorously. "Exactly so."

I asked, "What then is your plan?"

Santiago answered, voice deepening with quiet resolve:"We shall take him home."

Remington blinked. "Home?"

"A journey," Elías explained, "to the Hermitage of Saint Mary Magdalene—the *Ermita de Santa María Magdalena*—perched upon the high ridge of the Occitan Pyrenees, on the slopes the shepherds call *La Ciudadela del Cielo*, the Citadel of the Sky. Built in devotion to the Magdalene's own mountain refuge in the south by hermits drawn to the same solitude that calls men there still, it has long been a place of penitence and protection.

There, the Custodians of the high valleys have promised to gather every remaining cow of the Pyrenean line."

Holmes inclined his head, eyes narrowing with that particular gleam he reserved for deductions already half-made. "Ah," he said quietly.

"The oil painting of the Magdalene in your entry hall. I wondered at the intensity of San Telmo's devotion to her."

Santiago continued: "We will travel with El Toro across Navarra, first by train, as far as the lines will bear us... then by lorry or cart when the tracks end... and lastly on foot, up the mountain paths where only shepherds and angels have walked."

I raised my glass. "And once they reach the hermitage?"

Elías smiled. "Then we leave nature to her work. Two seasons in the high pastures, among the daughters of his own bloodline, and..."

He spread his hands.

"Next spring—calves. Many, God willing. Enough to begin anew."

Remington let out a low whistle.

"So the old fellow gets the happiest ending of all," he grinned. "A holiday in the mountains with a whole herd of lady friends."

Laughter rippled among the monks.

Santiago bowed his head, hands resting lightly on his corded rope belt.

"If Providence allows it, señor Remington... El Toro will not be the last. He will be the father of a beginning."

Outside, as if in answer, El Toro lifted his head towards the hills and gave a low, resonant bellow—a sound that rolled through the courtyard like a promise.

I cleared my throat.

"What of the Bonheur bronze, Brother Santiago? You promised we might yet see it returned."

A faint, guilty colour rose in Santiago's cheeks. Mateo shifted beside him, equally sheepish, as though both monks had been caught with jam on their fingers.

Holmes leaned forward, steepling his fingers.

"I take it," he said mildly, "that your order does not habitually engage in international art theft."

Santiago winced.

"*Señor Holmes...* we are not *ladrones*—thieves. We could never steal. It would be a mortal sin."

He cast a glance at Mateo, who nodded with vigorous sincerity.

"So," Santiago continued, "we did not steal the statue."

Holmes's eyebrow arched with the slow, deliberate elegance of a man who has just been presented with a paradox he already suspects he will enjoy unravelling.

"Indeed?" he said softly. "Then what precisely did you do, Brother Santiago?"

The Franciscan lifted both hands in a gesture of penitence and mild embarrassment.

"We... *misplaced* it, Señor Holmes."

Remington choked on a mouthful of wine.

I sputtered, "Misplaced?! A bronze weighing nearly ten kilos?"

Santiago nodded earnestly.

"Sí. Misplaced. Quite intentionally. Theft would be a sin. But a temporary misplacement for the sake of righteousness... that is merely an inconvenience."

Mateo grinned into his cup.

Elías sighed.

Santiago pressed on:

"My brother in Paris—asked three of our cousins—who work in the quarter as restorers. Good, pious men. Helpful men. And very strong."

He cleared his throat.

"They removed the wooden support board beneath the statue's pedestal. They slipped the Bonheur bronze inside. It sits now exactly where it once stood—only hidden."

Holmes blinked once.

"Hidden," he repeated, "inside its own plinth."

"Sí, Señor Holmes," Santiago said proudly. "Perfectly safe. Perfectly undamaged. And your Mademoiselle Aubry will find it restored to its rightful place at the very moment she seeks to open the pedestal for cleaning."

"And the drawing?" I asked.

"Inside as well," Santiago replied.

"And..."—Santiago turned to Remington with a shy, knowing smile—"your full manuscript, Señor Remington."

Remington stared at him without blinking.

Then he barked a laugh that startled three sparrows from the monastery rafters.

"Well I'll be," he said. "You holy men run a tighter operation than half the newspapermen I know."

Holmes steepled his fingers, studying Santiago with an expression that mixed admiration, astonishment, and the faintest glimmer of mischief.

"Brother Santiago," he said at last, "you have accomplished what no thief could: a perfect restoration disguised as a disappearance.

"A theft that is not a theft."

The friar beamed.

Remington lowered his cup just enough to squint at Santiago.

"But hold on," Remington said. "I thought you told me my manuscript was burned."

A faint movement passed among the monks of San Telmo—not guilt, but something closer to shared unease. Santiago lowered his eyes, his hands folding together, not in defence, but as a man gathering courage.

"Yes," he said quietly. "That is what I believed."

He drew a breath.

"I asked my brother—Tomás—to remove it from your possession. He works at a café where the American writers gather. I feared men were watching. I told him only this: take the pages and place them where they could not be reached—with the statue."

Remington stiffened.

"Tomás took the manuscript in his satchel," Santiago continued. "He left it in the café kitchen, with his other belongings. That night, there was a fire."

The word hung between us.

"When he returned to Pamplona," Santiago said, "he told me the bag was gone. He believed it was burned. I believed him."

Holmes said nothing. He was watching Santiago's face with that quiet, merciless attention that allowed no refuge but honesty.

"What none of us knew," Santiago went on, his voice tightening, "was that before the fire, three men—Spanish craftsmen—had already taken the satchel, as planned. They did what I asked. They placed the manuscript where I had intended it to be all along."

He lifted his eyes then, and there was no cleverness in them—only relief tempered by shame.

"I learned the truth yesterday," he said. "On the eve of the feast."

Remington was silent for a long moment. Then he exhaled.

"So the manuscript's intact?" he said slowly.

Santiago nodded once. "Yes."

Remington slapped the table, hard enough to make the cups jump.

"Well, hell," he said. "if that isn't something."

Hc glanced around the table.

"Excuse me, friar."

He smiled.

Holmes inclined his head and allowed the smallest nod, as though a long equation had at last resolved itself and the world had, at last, agreed to behave logically.

"Elementary," Holmes said. "Misplaced, mislaid, and misburned—three errors, one conclusion. The manuscript survived not by miracle, but by miscommunication."

As the monks cleared the platters and the bells of Compline drifted faintly from the chapel, the candles upon the long rustic table burnt low, each flame bowing to the night breeze. The last of the Rioja glimmered ruby in our cups; laughter had thinned to contented murmurs; the stars danced and flickered against the deep blue heavens like wandering constellations far above the courtyard stones.

Mateo fed El Toro a final armful of hay, the bull's great head bending with a serenity one would not have believed possible only a day before. Santiago clasped Holmes's hand with quiet gratitude. Elías tucked a bundle of folded linens beneath his arm like a father settling a child to sleep. Even Remington, usually restless, leaned back with a sigh that hinted, just faintly, at peace.

Farewells in Starlight and Silence

At length we rose. The brothers saw us to the ancient oak gate, offering blessings in low voices. Our boots found the narrow road leading down the hill toward Pamplona; the dust glowed pale beneath the drifting lantern-light.

For a while we walked in a silent conversation. Of one mind, the meaning, the laughter, and the replies were all there—only language itself was absent.

After a long hush, Holmes spoke.

"Watson," he murmured, "notice how the world insists on parading its excesses before us—fraud, ambition, cruelty—yet here, in a small, unknown monastery, what endures is neither deception nor spectacle, but fidelity."

Remington glanced toward the courtyard, where El Toro stood serene beneath the stars.

"And in the end...it is fidelity, not force, that outlives us all."

Holmes, hands folded behind him, regarded the starlit countryside with that peculiar, almost prayerful stillness he reserved for moments when the world felt balanced upon a thin and perfect edge.

The quiet of the night was not without its music. Our footsteps against the packed earth provided a rhythm. Crickets sounded like a chorus in unison, steady and insistent. The dry whisper of wheat waved to and fro in the night air, and the occasional sheep's bell in the distance rang gentle, unpredictable, and never in a hurry.

We listened and walked on without speaking, knowing that the most important things cannot be said.

CHAPTER XXX

The Curious Correspondence

Letters and Tea Among the Bees

Late August had settled over Sussex like a down quilt, golden, drowsing, faintly humming with the last industry of summer.

Holmes's small estate near the South Downs lay wrapped in a tranquillity so complete that it seemed a deliberate rebuttal to the chaos of Spain: rolling meadows browned at the edges by the sun, apple trees bending under the weight of ripening fruit, and, most constant of all, the murmuring republic of Holmes's beloved bees.

It was this humming kingdom, he insisted, that restored a man's sense of proportion after the crowded passions of human affairs.

I had come to stay a fortnight under the pretence of "recuperative rest," though Holmes, with his usual accuracy, had remarked on my arrival:

"My dear Watson, men who require rest generally cease moving. You, on the other hand, have been pacing the platform since the train stopped."

To which I replied, truthfully enough, that I felt "I must leave the London heat before I melt into a medical puddle."

But the deeper reason was simpler: after the feverish intrigues of Navarra, my old friend's quiet company felt very much like medicine.

Now, as we walked the narrow flagstone path toward the apiary, Holmes carried his smoker under one arm and a linen veil folded neatly under the other. The air was warm, thick with the perfume of clover and late roses. Bees drifted around us like living flecks of amber.

I broke the silence first.

"You know, Holmes," I said, "one forgets how peaceful your home can be. It is difficult to reconcile this serenity with the image of you leaping barricades, outwitting forgers, and confronting maniacal cattle barons."

Holmes gave a thin smile without looking up.

"The world, Watson, is divided into two equal parts: that which roars, and that which hums. Spain roars. Sussex hums. A man must find equilibrium between the two."

He paused by the nearest hive and set down the smoker.

"And besides," he added, "I find in bees a far more honest society than in most governments. They are industrious, orderly, and seldom attempt forgery."

"True," I admitted. "Though I doubt they would appreciate your comparison."

Holmes raised a brow. "On the contrary. Bees possess no vanity, one of the few creatures, I may add, for which that can be said."

A breeze rustled the heather. The hives thrummed with life. For a moment neither of us spoke.

Then Holmes straightened, brushed a speck of pollen from his sleeve, and said with that unmistakable note of anticipation:

"Come, Watson. There is something inside awaiting us—a letter which arrived this morning, posted from abroad. I confess... I have a suspicion as to the sender."

He glanced toward the house, where Mrs. Hudson's silhouette passed briefly behind a curtain.

"And if I am correct, our quiet Sussex afternoon is about to be enlivened by a most curious piece of correspondence indeed."

LETTER I

From Mademoiselle Evelynne Aubry

The letter was written on thick cream stationery, faintly scented with French perfume and the dry sweetness of old paper. The hand was precise, elegant—unmistakably Parisian. It bore the address of Galerie Aubry, Rue du Faubourg Saint-Honoré, and was dated one week prior.

To Monsieur Sherlock Holmes

& Docteur John H. Watson

Sussex Downs, England

Mes très chers Messieurs,

I scarcely know where to begin.

There are debts of gratitude so profound that language, even in my mother tongue, proves a poor vessel. And yet I will attempt, with all sincerity, to convey what your actions have restored, not merely to my gallery, but to my family's heart.

The morning I received your telegram, "The Bonheur is safe; prepare for its return," I confess I sat down at once, unable to stand beneath the sudden lifting of a weight I had carried for months. My father's sculpture, the pride of his collection and his dearest acquisition, was restored to its rightful home not by chance nor by the laws of men, but by your perseverance, your honesty, and, dare I say, your friendship.

The Bonheur bronze, long thought lost to greed and misfortune, stands once more upon its pedestal in Galerie Aubry. I found it exactly as you said I would—hidden within its own plinth, like a treasure returned to its chest. When I lifted the wooden panel and saw the sculpture resting there, whole and unharmed, my breath quite deserted me. How you contrived such a recovery, I shall not ask. Knowing you, the answer would only bewilder me further. I will call it a small miracle—and be content to let it remain one.

My father would have praised your cunning as loudly as I now praise your goodness.

The Bonheur sculpture shall not be returned to the catalogue of sales. It shall not be sold. It shall remain where it is—in Galerie Aubry, as the centrepiece.

And though you sought no payment, I cannot allow such heroism to pass without a token of gratitude worthy of your names. Please accept, then, my gratitude in its imperfect form, though I fear no letter could fully express the relief and joy that now inhabit our quiet rooms.

Enclosed with this letter is a modest token: the framed charcoal drawing recovered with the bronze—the charcoal study of *Toro Noble* by Bonheur. The drawing you found missing from my father's old studio. I had it cleaned, mounted, and framed. It is my gift to you, Monsieur Holmes, but I ask that you accept it in the spirit with which it is meant.

You will, I hope, find it a suitable adornment for your Sussex study.

I beg you to accept it as a sign of my esteem.

Holmes, the gift is addressed to your household, yet you will permit me—I hope—to add this:

Should Dr. Watson ever find himself in Paris again, my doors, and my gratitude, remain open.

There are matters of art and memory I would gladly discuss with him further...over tea, or perhaps a stroll along the Seine, where the afternoon light suits conversation better than ink.

With sincere affection and all gratitude,

Mademoiselle Evelynne Aubry

Directrice, Galerie Aubry

Paris

Holmes read the letter through twice, the corners of his mouth lifting by the smallest, driest increment—the Holmesian equivalent of a broad grin. He tapped the paper once against his knee, as though confirming its material reality.

"Well, Watson," he said at last, "I believe Mademoiselle Aubry has managed the rare feat of expressing gratitude without once lapsing into sentimentality. A French achievement worthy of record."

"Come now, Holmes—there is warmth in it. And generosity. Sending the framed sketch, no less. A princely gesture."

Holmes glanced toward the mantel, where he had set the parcel, still wrapped in brown paper and string, awaiting its ceremonial untying.

"I intend to hang it in the study," he said. "A reminder that not every case ends with Scotland Yard blundering through the evidence."

He folded the letter neatly and slipped it back into its envelope.

"And as for her postscript..." His eyes flicked toward me with unmistakable mischief. "...I suspect the good Mademoiselle Aubry believes you the more gallant of our partnership."

I felt heat rise in my cheeks despite myself. "Nonsense. She merely meant—"

"That you are invited," Holmes interrupted smoothly, "with an emphasis sufficiently clear that even Lestrade would detect it."

"Holmes!"

He waved a hand dismissively, though amusement danced in his gaze.

He poured himself a small measure of honey-sweetened tea.

Holmes settled back into his chair, the Sussex sunlight laying warm upon the Persian rug, the bees humming faintly beyond the open window.

Holmes set the letter from Paris aside, the faintest curl of a smile lingering at the corner of his mouth.

For a moment, neither of us spoke.

Outside, one of his hives gave a contented hum—the measured industry of creatures who never wasted a motion nor faltered in purpose. It seemed, oddly, to mirror the quiet satisfaction in Holmes's manner.

At last he said, "Curious, Watson. Paris sends gratitude, charm, and an invitation you would do well not to disregard."

"Holmes," I protested again, though far less convincingly.

He ignored me entirely and reached for the small stack of unopened envelopes beside the tea tray.

"Let us see," he said, "whether the mountains have been equally industrious."

He broke the next seal with a thoughtful tap of his finger.

The hand upon this envelope was rougher, the wax darker, the script unmistakably monastic.

Holmes's expression softened—not with amusement this time, but with something closer to respect.

"Ah," he said quietly. "From Santiago and Mateo. And posted from high country."

He handed it to me.

"Go on, Watson. You will read this one aloud."

I unfolded the letter, the faint scent of pine and cold mountain air seeming to rise from the parchment.

LETTER II

From Friar Santiago and Brother Mateo

Ermita de Santa María Magdalena

Hermitage of Saint Mary Magdalene

Laderas de Montségur

Pirineos Occitanos

Occitan Pyrenees

Estimados Señores Holmes, Watson y Remington,

We write to you from the high pastures of the Pyrenees, where the wind carries the scent of beech and wild thyme, and where El Toro now walks with the dignity of a king returned to his kingdom.

We are most pleased to tell Señor Remington that El Toro is happily mixing with the ladies of Los Toros del Silencio. On our second evening here, he discovered the herd grazing near the ridge-line meadow. You would have smiled to see him—rubbing his massive head in the grass, throwing up great clods of earth as though to announce his arrival with trumpet and drum.

The cows noticed.

Ay—how they noticed.

Within minutes they all circled him, watching him very intently. One brave little cow approached and touched noses with him. Brother Mateo insists she "kissed" him; Brother Elías says it was merely bovine courtesy. I will let you decide which seems more likely.

In any case, the signs are auspicious. We believe—God willing—that many calves will be born next season.

But, my friends, something else occurred. Something we did not expect. Something we have come to believe was a miracle.

As we neared the Hermitage of Santa María Magdalena, the custodian brothers led us to a small mountain cave kept as a place of devotion in her honor—not her dwelling, but one long held in local tradition to have been touched by her presence.

We entered with reverence. The air was cool and faintly mineral, touched with the scent of candles kept burning by shepherds for generations.

Brother Mateo—whose shoulder had never properly healed after the blow he suffered on 7 July—could not kneel for long, yet he remained beside me, chanting the psalms despite the pain. We prayed there through the night. Held a vigil.

Sometime before dawn, we must have fallen asleep while praying.

When the morning light reached the mouth of the cave, Mateo woke with a cry—not of pain, but of astonishment.

His shoulder... was whole.

Not merely mended—whole.

Healed. Strength returned. Movement restored.

The ache gone as though swept away by a gentle hand.

We do not rush to label miracles.

But we know gratitude when it burns in the heart. And we know mercy when we meet it.

We thank you again, dear friends, for guiding El Toro safely home, for protecting our monastery, and for helping preserve a lineage older than Rome. We have finished our part of the labour. Now the rest belongs to the mountains, the cattle... and to the birds and the bees, as you say in your lands.

May the peace of Christ guard you always.

Que Dios esté con vosotros.

Fray Santiago and Hermano Mateo

Holmes listened without interruption as I read the final lines—the blessing, the signatures, the small cross drawn in Mateo's hand. When I looked up, he had removed his spectacles and was staring out through the open window toward the hives, their gold bodies drifting in gentle circuit above the lavender.

"Well, Watson," he said at last, very softly, "it seems our old companion has found a new kingdom."

"El Toro?" I ventured.

Holmes inclined his head. "A sovereign among mountains... and now among his own kind."

A pause, thoughtful, almost reverent. "I confess, Watson, it is not often that a case concludes with progeny instead of peril."

I smiled. "And Mateo's shoulder—healed."

Holmes folded his hands. "Faith, rest, or miracle... I make no attempt to classify it. Some truths require no dissecting."

For a moment, neither of us spoke. The Sussex breeze slipped through the open sash, stirring the pages of Santiago's letter and carrying with it the fragrance of clover from Holmes's meadow. It was a peaceful sound, the kind a man rarely hears except after storms that have ended well.

Holmes cleared his throat, the spell broken only gently.

"Two letters read," he said, "and at least one more calling for its moment."

He gestured to the last unopened envelope by the tea tray: heavier paper, battered by travel, its stamp a familiar Parisian blue.

Holmes's expression shifted: amusement returned, edged with curiosity.

"Ah," he murmured, "the handwriting of a man who prefers fists to ink, yet writes with both." He pushed the envelope toward me. "Remington. And judging by the state of this envelope, the postman suffered for it."

I reached for it.

Holmes settled back in his chair, eyes half-closed.

"Go on, Watson," he said with a sigh of near-contentment. "We have heard from Paris in gratitude, and from the mountains in hope. Let us hear now from the Gentleman Boxer of the Rue Cardinal Lemoine—for he is capable of both."

I broke the seal.

LETTER III

From Albert Remington

74 Rue Cardinal Lemoine

20 August 1924

Dear Holmes & Watson—

Found your note waiting under the cracked blue vase by the stairwell when I came back from Closerie tonight. Thought it was the landlord again. Instead it was Santiago's little cousin, barefoot as a bird, who delivered the parcel earlier in the day. Inside was the manuscript, my manuscript, folded neat as hospital linen, smelling of wood polish.

Aubry wrote too. Said she found the whole bundle in the pedestal "right where it must have always belonged," which is gallant of her, considering the truth. She says the Bonheur is restored and no longer for sale. Sensible. Some things aren't meant to be traded.

Anyway I read the damned thing again, my big Paris book, my Great Effort, capital G, capital E. I read it straight through while Haddey slept and the mill downstairs shook the floor. And do you know what happened?

Nothing.

Not a thing in it rang true. The words marched but they never lived. All polish, no pulse. Like handling a stuffed trout.

So I took it downstairs, set it in the furnace, and burned it. Page by page. Didn't feel tragic. Felt clean.

Pamplona did that for me.

Cleaned house.

Later that day, after the chaos, when the bullring had emptied, drained of all activity, I lingered awhile and found myself studying the arena.

Without the noise, it changed.

The once strong barrier showed itself plainly—splintered in places, its paint flaking, more like the fragile frontage of a theatre set than anything built to face what had entered the ring.

Programs lay scattered in the sand, their bright inks paling under the heat of the Spanish sun, illusion printed cheap and already fading. A strip of crimson cloth stirred against the barrier, no more impressive now than a forgotten rag.

I left something of myself out there—and knew, as I walked away, that it was better left behind.

I did not look back.

I carried one thing away from that ring.

It was not the bull—though he was the truest creature I've seen since the war—but the way Mateo walked toward him.

No show in it. No noise. Just a man who had decided what mattered and stepped forward.

Courage isn't talk. It isn't posture. It's what a man does when there's nowhere left to hide.

That monk knew it.

The bull too.

Made the rest of it look false.

The war's still in me. Don't think it leaves. But the bull put it in order. Put it in a corner where it doesn't grab your throat every time you sit down to write.

And so I'm writing again. Something new. Something stripped to the bone. No faking. People who can't love right. People who can't forget. People who can't go home even when they get there. Spain in it, yes. But not the Spain the tourists clap for. The real one. The one we saw. The one that bruises you and then buys you a drink afterward.

I owe you two more than you think. If I ever get this book done and it sells enough for a bottle decent enough for the occasion, you're both invited to help me drink it.

Holmes—

You see beyond what is there, and you see through what men pretend. Walls don't stop you. I won't call it a miracle, but I know it isn't ordinary. I suppose for you it's just the day's work.

Watson—

You write clean and fight clean. A rare combination.

If either of you come to Paris, you'll find a place at our table, even if the table is borrowed and the wine thin.

Give my regards to the monks. And to the bull—he earned them.

Keep well.

—Rem.

P.S. Paris is ugly as sin today; it rains and rains, but the oysters and wine are good. You can't have everything. Pamplona taught me something: the sun does not rise because the world deserves it, but because it refuses not to.

V

Holmes let the final page of Remington's letter fall against his knee, the paper softly crackling in the mild Sussex breeze. For a long moment he said nothing, only gazed toward the apple orchard beyond his apiaries, where the afternoon light pooled in thick golden bands.

"Well," I said at last, "Remington seems... changed."

Holmes folded the letter once before setting it on the table.

"Changed," he said. "There are moments that divide a life. A man walks into them one person and walks out another."

I watched the firelight settle across the paper.

"It seemed to me," I said at last, "the bull in the ring released the bull within him."

Holmes inclined his head.

"Paris sculpts men, refining what was already there," he said, "but Navarra forges them into something true."

"In adversis constans," Holmes murmured.

"Pardon me—I didn't quite catch what you said," I asked.

"Steadfast in adversity," Holmes replied.

"The Romans admired what they called *virtus*—not bluster, but endurance without complaint; truth lived with integrity, even when no one is watching. The kind found in bulls, monks... and occasionally, writers."

There was the faintest sparkle in his eye.

"He burns one manuscript," Holmes continued, "to write another—which I suspect will trouble the world far more than any theft, conspiracy, or counterfeit spectacle ever managed."

He tapped the letter with a slim forefinger.

"Experience has etched itself upon him. He writes now not of invention, but of consequence."

I leaned back in my chair, letting the quiet settle.

A hive murmured nearby.

A pigeon cooed.

From the eaves; the August sun warmed the stone path where Holmes's bees made lazy circuits.

"It seems," I said, "we have all come home altered."

Holmes did not deny it.

He set the letter upon the small stack beside his chair—Aubry's graceful femininity, Santiago's mountain steadiness, Remington's hard-won honesty, a triptych of lives touched by the same brief, bright adventure.

"The bull is restored," Holmes said softly. "The monks are at peace. Navarra has shed a pretence or two. And a few lingering shadows in Remington's spirit have given way to something sturdier."

He looked over at me with that rare, fond glance—the one reserved for only the most private moments.

"And you, Watson? What remains for the chronicler of bulls, relics, and counterfeit corrida?"

I hesitated—though not for long. My fingers drifted unconsciously toward the edge of Mademoiselle Aubry's letter, still resting atop the tray.

"I think," I said slowly, "I think perhaps I will pay Mademoiselle Aubry a visit."

Holmes's smile, small, knowing, and entirely satisfied, was the final word.

FINIS

www.ingramcontent.com/pod-product-compliance
Lightning Source LLC
LaVergne TN
LVHW090551110826
845146LV00001B/98

* 9 7 9 8 9 9 5 5 4 4 1 0 4 *